Eden's Children

V.C. Andrews® Books

The Dollanganger Family
Flowers in the Attic
Petals on the Wind
If There Be Thorns
Seeds of Yesterday
Garden of Shadows
Christopher's Diary: Secrets of Foxworth
Christopher's Diary: Echoes of Dollanganger
Secret Brother
Beneath the Attic
Out of the Attic
Shadows of Foxworth

The Audrina Series
My Sweet Audrina
Whitefern

The Casteel Family
Heaven
Dark Angel
Fallen Hearts
Gates of Paradise
Web of Dreams

The Cutler Family
Dawn
Secrets of the Morning
Twilight's Child
Midnight Whispers
Darkest Hour

The Landry Family
Ruby
Pearl in the Mist
All That Glitters
Hidden Jewel
Tarnished Gold

The Logan Family
Melody
Heart Song
Unfinished Symphony
Music in the Night
Olivia

The Orphans Series
Butterfly
Crystal
Brooke
Raven
Runaways

The Wildflowers Series
Misty
Star
Jade
Cat
Into the Garden

The Hudson Family
Rain
Lightning Strikes
Eye of the Storm
The End of the Rainbow

The Shooting Stars
Cinnamon
Ice
Rose
Honey
Falling Stars

The De Beers Family
"Dark Seed"
Willow
Wicked Forest
Twisted Roots
Into the Woods
Hidden Leaves

The Broken Wings Series
Broken Wings
Midnight Flight

The Gemini Series
Celeste
Black Cat
Child of Darkness

The Shadows Series
April Shadows
Girl in the Shadows

The Early Spring Series
Broken Flower
Scattered Leaves

The Secrets Series
Secrets in the Attic
Secrets in the Shadows

The Delia Series
Delia's Crossing
Delia's Heart
Delia's Gift

The Heavenstone Series
The Heavenstone Secrets
Secret Whispers

The March Family
Family Storms
Cloudburst

The Kindred Series
Daughter of Darkness
Daughter of Light

The Forbidden Series
The Forbidden Sister
"The Forbidden Heart"
Roxy's Story

The Mirror Sisters
The Mirror Sisters
Broken Glass
Shattered Memories

The House of Secrets Series
House of Secrets
Echoes in the Walls

The Umbrella Series
The Umbrella Lady
Out of the Rain

The Girls of Spindrift
Bittersweet Dreams
"Corliss"
"Donna"
"Mayfair"
"Spindrift"

Stand-alone Novels
Gods of Green Mountain
Into the Darkness
Capturing Angels
The Unwelcomed Child
Sage's Eyes
The Silhouette Girl
Whispering Hearts
Becoming My Sister

Eden's Children

V.C. ANDREWS®

G

Gallery Books

New York London Toronto Sydney New Delhi

G

Gallery Books
An Imprint of Simon & Schuster, Inc.
1230 Avenue of the Americas
New York, NY 10020

Following the death of Virginia Andrews, the Andrews family worked with a carefully selected writer to organize and complete Virginia Andrews's stories and to create additional novels, of which this is one, inspired by her storytelling genius.

This book is a work of fiction. Any references to historical events, real people, or real places are used fictitiously. Other names, characters, places, and events are products of the author's imagination, and any resemblance to actual events or places or persons, living or dead, is entirely coincidental.

First Gallery Books trade paperback edition October 2022

Interior design by Erika R. Genova

Manufactured in the United States of America

10 9 8 7 6 5 4 3 2 1

Library of Congress Cataloging-in-Publication Data

Names: Andrews, V. C. (Virginia C.), author.
Title: Eden's children / V.C. Andrews.
Description: First Gallery Books trade paperback edition. | New York : Gallery Books, 2022.
Identifiers: LCCN 2021035749 (print) | LCCN 2021035750 (ebook) | ISBN 9781982156367 (trade paperback) | ISBN 9781982156374 (hardcover) | ISBN 9781982156398 (ebook)
Subjects: LCGFT: Novels.
Classification: LCC PS3551.N454 E34 2022 (print) | LCC PS3551.N454 (ebook) | DDC 813/.54—dc23
LC record available at https://lccn.loc.gov/2021035749
LC ebook record available at https://lccn.loc.gov/2021035750

ISBN 978-1-9821-5637-4
ISBN 978-1-9821-5636-7 (pbk)
ISBN 978-1-9821-5639-8 (ebook)

Eden's Children

Prologue

In my dream Trevor and I were running in opposite directions, but not deliberately. Panic had sent us fleeing, flying off like pieces of the earth thrust into outer space and not drawn toward anything specific. The shadows and whispers that were always there, but easily forgotten or ignored, had grown darker and louder all around us, even before I confronted the ugly truths. Whether I had imagined it or not, the shadows followed us; they were there when we awoke in the morning, and they leaked in under our closed doors and windows when we went to sleep. We were haunted, but pressed our eyes closed tightly and willed them not to be real. Eventually, in my dream, we found ourselves curled up in corners of the old house, hovering, alone.

But for me there was never any sanctuary in the old shadows that had been there for decades. They couldn't be ignored. "No one ever thinks," Mama once said, "that the shadows in a house are as much a part of it as the furniture. The sun and the moon cast them through the windows the same way, always."

These shadows were thin and weak and sometimes looked like they were shimmering, as if the house itself was trembling. As Mama wished, I had come to believe this house was alive.

It spoke to us in so many ways. It had tried not to give up a tragic secret. I knew that it eventually would be telling me how sorry it was. Never once during its construction, its birth from rich, fresh, natural-smelling lumber, did it dream of becoming a shelter for something so ugly. Like someone despondent and depressed, it would have welcomed an all-consuming fire, suicide. But perhaps even that wouldn't be satisfactory. Its ashes would still reek of sin.

To be sure, long before all this, both Trevor and I had nightmares, just like anyone else our age who had gone through what we had gone through, listening to the cries of other children, smaller and bigger, younger and older, haunted by the same fear of not being loved, I imagine. Maybe Trevor had more of them than I did. He really never willingly admitted to them. I suspected he had them because when we were little, I heard his whimpering, even his crying out for his mother. He remembered his far more than I remembered mine. For years, the bad dreams were mostly born from our pasts. Trevor was obviously left alone a lot. He hated that, even at the foster home. Eventually, my childhood nightmares and most of his were easily smothered and forgotten after the morning sun had burned them away. However, when its time had come, one particular nightmare began in Mama's house. It began as what I first thought was an illusion, the mysterious cries. I could call it a hallucination, even though I could touch it and remember the feel of it on my fingertips.

I think I was always expecting it or something very much like it. As I was growing up, I tried to hide my suspicions from Trevor, but eventually, like water quickly freezing into a shape, it became too real to deny. I had no choice. I finally confronted it. Trevor admitted that he had done the same, long before me. Mama had wanted that.

But what she hadn't wanted was how that nightmare came in crashing waves that quickly overtook us all. The longer I had stood there and looked, the deeper I had sunk into the pool of darkness that had for so many years kept it sacrosanct. Even after it was gone and we had both avoided drowning in it, I knew that didn't mean it was over; it would never be over.

Trevor and I had been living with so much beautiful music and love, making it easier for me to ignore any trembling and fear that would come and go, the cold breezes that nudged me out of sleep or quickened my heartbeat when we were just reading and studying. I'd stop and listen harder, waiting in dreaded anticipation of the whispers.

Early on, I sensed that Trevor was more accustomed to the whispers and the darkness. But I always had believed that he had secrets that were uglier than mine, secrets so deep that I understood why he would rather leave them undisturbed like snakes coiled up in a corner, better ignored. Sometimes, however, when we were younger, Trevor might take my hand unexpectedly without looking at me, and then, as quickly as he had tightened his fingers around mine, he would realize what he had done, loosen his grip, and pretend it had never happened. It would do no good to ask him what had happened or why. He wouldn't remember doing it, and my forcing him to remember would be cruel.

I instinctively knew not to question him or remind him of it, especially when we grew older. Dark childhood memories could be forced down by sweet nursery rhymes and happy tunes, presents and birthday cakes, and of course, layers and layers of prayers. But all this was only temporary. The memories would always rear their heads from time to time. Even as a child, I could sense the rage floating just below the surface of Trevor. Unlike him, I didn't have such daunting recollections from the time before we were here. He had lived in his darker time long enough for those troubled times to start shaping who he was before I had set eyes on him. However, when Mama came, saw us, and chose us, we both thought we had been rescued, maybe he more than I.

I will confess that the smiles that shone upon us in our new home were always reassuring for me. As long as we were all together, I believed we were safe and protected. Rain, as it was for flowers and grass and trees, was full of promise. When it was cold, we were kept warm. And on hot summer days, there was relief at twilight. Tomorrow always meant something better, something good, was coming. It took more to convince me of this than it did him perhaps, but eventually I permitted myself to believe it, stepping into hope like someone easing herself into a warm, reassuring bath. I really believed that we had been successfully planted in a new garden. When you finally accept something and put your faith in it, you become helpless, vulnerable, and naked in the worst way.

"Have no hope," Mama might say, "and you'll have no disappointment. Don't hope—plot, have a strategy. That's how I found you. I had planned for it to happen. I knew I would take you away from them."

Neither of us had ever felt any emotional connection to Fred or Shirley Wexler, who ran our group foster care home along with a nurse we called Nanny Too. We named her that probably because we were old enough to comprehend who she was and what she did at the home. She had told us she was a nurse and now she was our nanny, too. We eventually learned that she was the Wexlers' real daughter, Joanna Birch Wexler, and when Mama Eden thought we were old enough to understand, she told us Nanny Too had been a nun for nearly ten years and had worked in a Catholic health clinic in El Salvador. "But she had to leave because she had broken some of the rules," Mama said. "She was unmarried, of course, and you probably remember she looked like a female Ichabod Crane.

"Ooh," she said, smiling and shaking herself the way you might shake off water after a downpour. "She's gone, gone."

We smiled at that. We wanted to shake off the visions and the sounds and vacuum up every recollection like dust just the way Mama was teaching us to do.

Both Trevor and I had been brought to the Wexlers when we were infants, Trevor older. Why neither of us had been adopted before Mama Eden found us was a mystery until Mama told us the Wexlers made money housing foster children. "They received a subsidy from the state, but they gave you the minimum of anything and everything. Their old tourist house that Fred Wexler had inherited enabled them to have as many as twelve children at one time. They were scroungers squeezing every penny out of the state the way you might squeeze an orange until it was nothing but pulp and skin.

"When someone came to consider adopting one of you, they often managed to discourage them, telling them untruths about you, your behavior and health, and the older you became, the more money they received to keep you. They're closed down now, and who knows where your Nanny Too has ended up. Probably tormenting the elderly in some adult residence."

We had little reason not to believe her then.

With the Wexlers taking so little personal interest in us, and our mysterious backgrounds, and their never mentioning anyone in our families, we had to adopt Mama's and Big John's folks as our own. Mama especially assured us we would digest every story she told about her family, inhale every memento, absorb every keepsake and souvenir, and make it part of who we were. We believed it because we needed it and wanted it so much, no doubt Trevor more than I. As Mama said, "Even a leaf remembers a branch; even a branch remembers a tree, and a tree remembers the seed that gave birth to it. Now you will have my seeds to remember and, most important, claim as your own."

We took comfort in the family fairy tales she could express as easily as she breathed. Her words wove themselves around us into an impenetrable coat, an armor standing between us and the vultures of evil that floated around us, jealous birds with bloody eyes that Mama swore were always out there. Our home, our house, was our fortress, our refuge. Everything and anything around us in it had a family to recall and, in recalling, gave itself meaning and identity. As she had told us many times, where would we be—what would we be—without one? Of course, we who had been adopted had to now be the ones who adopted, adopted a family.

As we grew up, our house became a big classroom, a family museum. Practically everything in it had some historical meaning, a chronology that provided structure and significance, especially for

Mama since it was her house. Sometimes her memories would seep into her smile. Almost anything old in the house could bring it out. She'd pick up a glass from the shelf above the kitchen counter and say, "This Waterford crystal glass is the glass my grandmother used to keep her dentures within reach when she went to sleep or just wanted to rest her gums. Don't ever drink from it. The taste of her false teeth is in the glass itself."

She so wanted us to envision her father sitting in his easy chair when she handed us his meerschaum pipe. Both of us gently pressed our fingers around it, smelled it, and looked at each other, anticipating the other to say something, do something that would convince Mama we did indeed see him.

If she wasn't satisfied, she'd say, "It takes time. Don't worry. It will happen."

Neither of us was quite sure what exactly would happen, but I knew we had to believe that something significant would, and soon, or Mama might stop loving us. I think Trevor feared that more than I did. Although he never came out and said it, I was sure that he believed she might even think she had made a mistake and take us back to the Wexlers', or another place like it.

Big John wasn't as intent on or as willing to talk about his past. When we finally heard some of it, we understood why, but he never disagreed with Mama about what we needed in order to have meaning for ourselves. He often said he wished he had as much family as Mama's family, the Petersens, did.

At night, very late, when it was quiet in the house, Trevor and I would wake and listen as hard as we could, hoping to hear the whispers and laughter Mama said we would. We couldn't lie to each other; we couldn't pretend we had, even though we were each afraid the other *would* and Mama's love would abandon the one who hadn't. Trevor was so much more afraid of that than I was. I never told him I knew that was so, and I never tried to find out why—why was Mama's love so much more important to him than it was to me?

Once or twice, I thought I did hear someone sobbing. It sounded muffled, just the way it would be if it was stuck in a wall. Was that what Mama meant? I looked at Trevor. He had his eyes open, but he hadn't turned to indicate he had heard anything. When it stopped, I was afraid to say I had heard it. He might think just what I feared: one of us would lie to get Mama to love that one more.

But Mama always seemed confident that we wouldn't lie to her when it came to our family and ourselves especially. Ironically, she felt sorry for us because of that.

"The world is so much more difficult for people who cannot lie," she had once said, more to herself than to us.

"Why?" I asked. Nanny Too had taught us it was terrible to lie, a sin for which you would burn in hell.

Mama Eden looked at me, clearly surprised I had heard her, but now she was forced to explain. Trevor looked at her expectantly, too. Her explanation didn't help us then. We were both too young. I wasn't sure it helped us even now.

"I hate logic and truth because there's no escape from them, like there is from something you believe."

We were both staring at her. These words were like clouds too high to touch and too quickly thinning and becoming air. She saw our confusion, but she just smiled, stroked our hair, petted us like our two cats, and, with the promise that we would understand it all one day, sent us off to play and forget our questions and our doubts.

For the longest time, for most of our younger years, forgetting frightening, confusing, and unpleasant things became easier to do, especially for me. I think Mama knew that it wasn't as simple for Trevor. She knew things about him that I was afraid to know. To this day I think that was the real reason that Mama had the Cemetery for Unhappiness.

If something precious broke, she would take it out, bringing us along, and dig a grave. Then she would have one of us bury it, most often Trevor. She did this even with things you couldn't see, like a nasty word or idea that either I, Big John, or, rarely, Trevor uttered. "We'll bury that," she'd declare. We would have to stop everything we were doing and dig a hole in her Cemetery for Unhappiness. We were to concentrate to see the nasty words smothered. Looking down, she'd repeat them and then cry, "Be gone!"

Maybe it was a good idea back then. Maybe it helped Trevor more than it helped me, but I know we both felt better and safer when we returned to the house with her. Big John never came with us when he was home. Only once or twice did he ever say anything critical about the cemetery, and when he did, Mama slapped her hands together like anyone would to kill a mosquito and then turned around and went back to the cemetery to bury what he had just said. So after a while, he knew to keep his thoughts as hidden as he could.

"Oh, Paula," he might start to say, only to smile and quickly add, "Whatever makes you happier."

Contented, she would forget that he even once had suggested she not have funerals in front of us for the unpleasant things, the ugly and fearful things, claiming it would give us terrible nightmares. Neither of us had breathed after Big John said that, so dramatically questioning what she was doing for us, until she nodded and led us out to the cemetery again to bury his very words. Her sigh of relief seemed to echo off the house. We both looked around to see if trees would shake or leaves would fall.

More often than not, we reacted that way, mirroring her mood. We smiled when she smiled, became angry when something made her angry, and felt sad when she became maudlin and stared at nothing. Trevor and I circled her moods like satellites with eyes watching the earth. Big John said we looked like we were attached. Mama liked that. Precious and loving words had to be cherished. When she told him so, he thought a moment and then said, "Maybe you should have a Garden of Happiness, then."

She smiled; she liked that, too.

"Maybe I will," she said.

There was so much to smile about, and there was so much laughter and music back then, that we were sure the garden would be greater than the cemetery. But Mama had her warnings about it.

"Happiness is like a beautiful flower, dazzling and wonderful for a while and then, unfortunately, fading. There should be only one season: spring. If I could keep you young forever, you would be safe. I'll do my best."

But, of course, she couldn't keep us from growing and maturing. Despite how much magic and fantasy there was for us as children, we wanted to grow older. Maybe I wanted it more than Trevor did. I wanted to step out and into the world whizzing by us, a world we could only glance at or see through the window of television. Trevor was never as ambitious. Sometimes I envied him for being so contented, and sometimes I hated him for it.

But the tragedy that befell us didn't come from stepping out. It came from stepping in, stepping deeper into ourselves and who we had become.

Eventually, the house had worked its magic. We didn't have to lie; we could hear the whispers and the laughter and the crying. When we ran our fingers over his meerschaum pipe, we could see Grandfather. We sank deeper and deeper into Mama's world.

And contrary to what she had hoped and we had expected, we desperately tried to flee from it, knowing in our hearts that there was really no escape.

In the end, when all truth came out of the shadows, I knew that we would take it with us wherever we went, whether we were still together or not.

one

Mama Eden was whispering in the darkness with the low hall light smothered in the shadows behind her. Streaming through our bedroom windows, the moonlight turned her face into a silvery mask. Her eyes seemed like emerald-green marbles. Her lips were the shade of faded roses.

I could see her airy words turn into bubbles and float over us. There was always something magical about her. Her words often became wondrous things when she spoke. If she was angry, they'd become darts or rocks, and if she was happy, they were drops of honey.

The wind slithered through the cobweb-thin cracks in our window frames, as if Nature was whispering back to her tonight.

I knew she thought I was asleep because Trevor was, and she was used to us doing the same things at the same time. Just that morning, Big John had said it was uncanny, "cryin', laughin', hungry, thirsty, one wantin' to do what the other does all the time. Uncanny. You'd think they really were brother and sister—or even Siamese twins."

We didn't look alike, so I wasn't sure why Big John said we were like twins. I had to look up the word *uncanny* and then think about it, because Mama Eden said she was *not* surprised and there was nothing uncanny about it. She even chastised him for choosing that word, stressing how normal we were.

"You don't have to be a brother or sister to be tuned in to someone identical."

He laughed. "You sure they gave you the right papers, Paula? Maybe I should look at them to check." He laughed again, his big shoulders trembling.

There were always those seconds of silence during which Big John and I wondered if Mama would go along with his joke or turn angry. Trevor didn't worry about it like I did. He always seemed more unafraid, almost indifferent to what went on between Mama and Big John, his mind elsewhere. But I held my breath.

"Stop that, John. I know they're not blood related," Mama Eden said, fortunately without anger. "Don't you remember how much time I spent with the adoption agency? There wasn't anything about them that I didn't know. And I certainly wouldn't listen to a word those Wexlers said, or their ugly daughter."

She had looked at us, her face softer, her eyes calmer. "It's only natural that they think and feel alike about most everything. Their souls came from the same fountain."

"Fountain?" Big John rose and shook his head. "I'm not even

going to ask," he said, holding up his big hands, smiling, and walking away.

But the two of us looked at Mama expectantly, Trevor now as interested as I was. *Fountain*?

"Well, you should," she shouted after him, and then, like a spring, collapsed back in her kitchenette chair. "You should want to know everything about them. Everything," she whispered.

"What fountain, Mama?" I asked. *I* certainly wanted to know everything about us.

She scowled at her husband as he walked on to his den. I didn't think she was going to answer my question, but she suddenly leaped to her feet and took Trevor and me by the hand to march us to the living room. She told us to sit on the sofa.

"Now, you two pay strict attention to every word I say," she said. Then she hoisted her thin shoulders back so that she looked taller than five foot five and crossed her arms under her breasts.

Sometimes Mama looked like a wind could come along and carry her off. Big John could lift her over his head with one arm. She weighed barely one-oh-five. All her features were small, child-like, her hands barely bigger than mine. But sometimes, more often lately, she looked as solid as the old oak at the west corner of our property, her feet planted like thick tree roots when she spoke.

Whenever she hugged us both to her slim but surprisingly firm body, I felt her strength. Despite her being less than four or five inches taller than we were, she had to do so much more around the house when Big John was on the road. Her muscles might be small, but they were hard. She could split wood, carry heavy pots of soup or stew across the kitchen or into the dining room, vacuum upstairs and downstairs for hours, polish furniture until it rivaled bright jewelry, and tear beds apart to wash the sheets and blankets herself. Eventually, we were big enough to help with it all, but even then, she rarely took a moment extra to rest.

"My children," she said when we did help, hugging us to her and then kissing us both on the forehead. "My family."

She never said one without the other, but I always had the sense that she hugged Trevor just a little bit harder and longer than she hugged me. Maybe that was because he didn't ask as many questions of her as I did. He did once tell me that I was more thoughtful than he was. "I'm more in a daze, Faith," he admitted. Big John often told him that. Lately, I sensed he was annoyed by Trevor's lackadaisical way of doing something he had told him to do or by having to repeat things to him.

"You can't ignore me, and you can't be lazy in this house," he warned Trevor the last time he was home.

Mama came right to Trevor's defense, embracing him and pulling him back against her, her arms around him.

"Trevor is not lazy," she said. "You're not here long enough to witness how much he does for us. He never disobeys me, and he rushes ahead to do a chore even before I think of it or tell him."

Big John didn't argue. He rarely argued with Mama now. She could push him and snap at him just like Nanny Too used to snap at us, but he was like an elephant that knew it had to be gentle. He was six foot four and probably weighed close to two hundred and forty pounds, with his broad shoulders and very muscular chest. I used to imagine the earth trembling beneath his feet when he walked.

Mama said Big John was close to ten pounds when he was born. She said his hands, thumb to thumb, could wrap around my waist almost twice when I was first brought here. I knew that was an exaggeration, but when I was very small, I'd sit on his lap and he'd bounce me up and down as if I was on a trampoline, his hands on my waist. Sometimes my feet would go as high as the top of his head. Mama would scream at him to stop. He had a deep voice, and when he laughed it seemed to echo in his chest.

He was far from ugly, but even though Mama said he was as handsome as Adonis, I would not say he was movie- or television-star good-looking. He had facial features to match his size, his nose prominent and a little crooked, his lips thick, and his black eyes startling like bright ebony, with bushy dark brown eyebrows, eyebrows Mama always had to trim. When I was little and sat on his lap, I was intrigued by the rough ridges in his skin and, unless Mama was after him to pay attention to his appearance, the stiff hairs in his nostrils and the curly ones in his ears. There were always a few growing on his earlobes, too. He was usually in need of a close shave and trimming whenever he returned from a two- or three-week truck journey. He admitted sleeping in his truck cab some nights merely because he was too lazy to find a good motel.

"It smells like it," Mama would tell him, and he would growl like the bear he resembled with his powerful-looking forearms and shoulders.

In the early days, I remembered how he would rush out of the truck when he arrived to scoop Mama Eden up and cover her mouth with his, looking like he might suck her in. She laughed about it then. Now, with us older, she refused to let him do that, at least when he first arrived. "The children are watching," she would say as soon as he made a move toward her.

We knew he kissed her like that in their bedroom upstairs. We could hear her small, kitten-like cries and Big John's grunts. Mama

Eden once said a strange thing about it, maybe more to herself than to us. "It is like holding your hands up to stop the rain when he comes at you. A waste of time and effort. Not that I mind it," she added. "You can't put a cover or a leash on passion."

The last time Big John left for one of his delivery trips, we stood beside her when he drove off. Mama continued to stand there looking after him for a few more moments and said, "You'd think such a big man would have no problem making a healthy child inside me. No matter what was wrong with me, what had happened to me."

Trevor looked at me, but neither of us said anything. What was wrong with her? What had happened to her? She went back inside that day without explaining, and neither Trevor nor I mentioned it to each other. Surely, whatever had happened had been buried in the Cemetery for Unhappiness.

Maybe, I thought when she had brought us into the living room to explain the fountain of the soul, she would tell us what it was now. My heart was thumping in anticipation.

She stared at us for a moment longer before she spoke, and then she did that odd thing I had been noticing more and more lately: she nodded as if someone had whispered in her ear.

"While you're being born," she began, "you're dipped into the spiritual flow, and your soul is washed into you. That's the fountain I mean. You're soaked through and through with what is divine, what comes directly from God. I can look into your eyes and see your souls, pure and good. I know that as soon as you were born, you awoke with more surprise than you will ever have in your life. It's like God struck a match and then, *whoosh*, magic, you're born. Of course, you cried."

"Why did we cry, Mama?" I asked.

"You were afraid."

"Why were we afraid?"

Trevor squinted and sat back as if he was terrified of the answer, especially about us. Was she going to say something different about him? He did look like he was hoping Mama would not say any more. Despite how alike Big John said we were, I was really the one who asked most of the questions. Sometimes it seemed as if they were floating in the air around us, and I could just pluck one like one of the wild apples behind the house and cast it at Mama. Often she would glare at me first, as if she was checking to be sure whether it was really me asking or some devil speaking through me. She told us that could happen.

"I mean, how do you know we were afraid when we were born?" I asked, using basic logic to convince her it was I who was asking and not some evil spirit. "You weren't there, right?"

She squinted. Sometimes I thought Mama didn't want me to be so smart.

"I don't have to be at every birth to know that. Everyone's afraid to come out of the dark and into the light, Faith. Even Big John and I were when we were born. It's only natural. I didn't have to be there to know what is always true. There's nothing different about you," she snapped at me, even though that wasn't what I meant. She brought her right forefinger inches from my face. "Don't ever, ever think that. And never, never tell Trevor such a thing, no matter what your father says."

She didn't often refer to Big John as our father. It seemed she'd do that when she wanted us to fear something or be happy we were a family. She didn't need him to discipline us. There was never a "wait until your father comes home." By then it was too late, anyway.

Trevor's eyes widened with surprise, and so did mine. What had Big John said about him? Whatever it was, clearly she didn't want an iota of discussion about it.

Her green eyes looked like they would explode when she "fanned her anger," as Big John would say. It was as if wrath was always smoldering inside her like the embers of firewood hours after the fire had gone out. You could blow on them and bring back a blaze.

"We're like a sponge," Trevor blurted with confidence, which surprised me. He said it as though Mama had told him this story about sponges without me, perhaps to help him feel better about himself.

She nodded. It wasn't the first time I had this feeling, this terrible feeling that she might like him more than she liked me and told him secret things she would never tell me.

"Trevor's right. You're soaked like a sponge with your soul, and when you die, God squeezes you, and your soul pours out and into his hand. If you're good, he puts you with those you loved and who loved you. If you're bad, he drops you into the fire. Very good, Trevor. That was very smart. It's good to be quiet until you know you have something wise to say." She told him this but was looking at me.

I turned to Trevor. He had a soft, tight, contented smile on his lips. His light blue eyes were glazed with satisfaction as he looked up at her. She spread a compliment over him as she would spread icing on a cake, elaborating on it and building it into something greater with each stroke of his hair or pat on his hand.

"Okay," she said, and then, as she often did, she added, "that's that." It was like slamming a door shut. "Now, go out and bury your father's words in the Cemetery of Stupidity."

We watched her walk off. There was no Cemetery of Stupidity, but I knew what she meant. Our world was filled with things that fell into either *forget this* or *remember that.* And it was practically a sin to forget which was which.

Afterward, when we were outside, I asked Trevor how he knew to say we were like sponges. "You never said that before."

He shrugged, and, like most of the answers he gave me, it was no answer.

"How did you know?" I insisted this time, hovering over him.

"I just knew it," he said, and returned to making arrows out of branches and bird feathers, just the way Big John had taught him. I stood there steaming like a bowl of hot soup, my arms crossed exactly how Mama Eden crossed hers. Trevor never looked up at me. The warm late-spring breeze helped raise my temperature. I felt like the tepid air was swirling only around me. It was even harder to breathe for a few moments. After my pout, I went to help him find bird feathers and never asked him to explain it again. That was how it was with mysteries in our house. They often just evaporated. As Mama often said, "Sometimes forgetting is a blessing." Usually, she was looking at Trevor when she said that, but she always brought her scowl back to me, as if I was more influential and could get him to do or say something wrong.

That entire day had faded into the pages of one of Mama's very old books that smelled like old clothes hanging in the attic.

Right now, I closed my eyes quickly when Mama came farther into our room, until she was practically standing right beside our bed. She was wearing her robin's-egg-blue nightgown, a recent gift Big John had brought home from a trip south. I could smell the scent of her lilac soap. It seemed to rain down from her neck, the back of which had a line of peach fuzz that I knew Big John loved to brush his lips over. She had her shoulder-length light brown hair tied behind her head, just the way she would tie mine, which was close to the same color. Trevor's was more like Big John's, a reddish brown. Mama cut and trimmed all our hair, even Big John's.

When she had first come into our room, she paused just inside the doorway. Her breathing was deep and heavy like it would be if she had run up the stairs to our bedroom. She probably had. Her shoulders rose and fell. She could be like that, impulsive, what Big John called "a hair trigger." She'd be sitting somewhere in the house and suddenly get an idea that she just had to tell us immediately. She would jump up and walk quickly, gazing behind her every few seconds as if she thought there was something or someone behind her, chasing her. She'd even come after us in the woods and say something like, "I want to trim Trevor's hair and trim your fingernails tonight, Faith. I'll do it before you go to bed."

Trevor would say, "Okay," and go back to whatever he had been doing, but I would look at her and wait to see if there was something else. Why did she have to tell us this at that moment and with so much excitement? There was plenty of time before dinner. Were we going somewhere important tomorrow? More than Trevor did, I longed to go to a real school and be with other children our age. That hope lingered like the promise of Christmas. *Be good, and it will come.*

But usually she would say nothing else to suggest why what she had come to tell us was so urgent. She would turn and hurry back to whatever she was doing. I was anticipating something like that when she walked into our bedroom this night, expecting her to nudge us awake to tell us something we had to know before morning. It was more like she had to get it out of her system because it was gnawing at her inside, what Big John would describe as "like a beaver stripping tree bark."

Sometimes I thought the panic came from her fear of forgetting something important but fragile. Tell it now, or it would shatter in her memory and be forgotten. She also believed that you did what you had to do now and never put it off.

"I'm no Scarlett O'Hara," she would say, often to Big John when he would tell her, "Relax, tomorrow is another day." It was something I didn't understand until she let us watch the movie of *Gone with the Wind*, and we heard Scarlett O'Hara say, "Tara. Home. I'll go home, and I'll think of some way to get him back. After all, tomorrow is another day."

The book was in our library, her library, but it wasn't on our reading schedule yet. Because Mama had been a teacher, she kept her library just the way a library was kept in a public school, with fiction distinctly shelved away from nonfiction, every book in alphabetical order by the author's name.

Seconds went by before she began her whispering again, standing above us now.

From the day we were brought here, Trevor and I slept in the same bed, a king-size with a dark maple half-moon headboard designed with embossed quarter-moons. We had oversize pillows that felt like they were swallowing up our heads. We had a beige comforter that always smelled fresh, as pungent as newly cut grass.

Big John Eden wanted us to have our own beds, even our own rooms, even though that meant we'd lose our classroom or have one of us be in the Forbidden Room. We heard them argue about it often, but Mama Eden was insistent that we stay together.

They had just had that same argument two days ago again in the kitchen. Big John was having a cup of coffee. He was going on another trip at the end of the week, and whenever he was leaving, he talked about things he wouldn't talk about much when he was home. She told him that was like leaving a ticking time bomb and running off. Questions were left dangling.

Mama Eden was putting dishes back in the cabinet. I lingered in the hallway to watch them through the door. Sometimes when they talked about us, it was as if they were talking about someone else, two other children. Neither mentioned our names when they had arguments like this. We were either "them" or "the kids."

"I want them never to feel like they are strangers to each other, ever," she told him.

"But how could they, considering where they are and how they came here together?"

"Everyone changes when they get older. Children like that, coming from where they've come from, the horrible Wexler foster home, are expected to have nightmares about being alone, lost in this world, and who better to make the other feel okay than they themselves? Faith is a good companion for Trevor especially. You know how much more important that is for him, and I can't do everything to make them feel happy and secure myself. The important thing is we've got to make them stronger so that they can take care of themselves," Mama told him.

"How's that make them stronger, sleeping in the same bed?"

"Well, just like us, John, it makes us feel closer, doesn't it? You know what it's like to wake up feeling all alone, especially until they truly feel they are waking up in their own home."

"Yeah, but it's really not just like us. It's—"

"And that's just part of it, John. We're here now, but we won't always be, and then they'll have only each other, just like it was for me and for you, only it will be more difficult for them. It's best they know that now. I don't want them running to us with every little thing, especially as they get older. Fear will make them stronger because they'll conquer it themselves with each other's help," she insisted.

"You, of all people, should know that, John Eden. You were an only child of an unwed mother who wasn't there for you most of the time. You had to share your nightmares with imaginary friends. Well, they don't need imaginary friends. They have us, but most important, they have each other. What a difference it would have made to either of us if I had a sister or you had a brother."

He grimaced with the sour and painful memories. I knew that much about him, knew that his father had deserted him and his mother, and I knew it hurt him to hear it. His mother had died before we were brought here, and he had no uncles or aunts. It was why he was willing to accept Mama's family as practically his own.

I pressed myself against the wall, thinking he was looking at me overhearing them. I was wearing a bright blue dress that often made me feel like a lit candle. Mama paused and pursed her lips. Despite what she had said so convincingly, she, like me, could see his skepticism.

"That doesn't necessarily make you stronger about feeling alone. That wasn't what happened with me," Big John said, sounding more self-pitying. It was as if he returned to being a little boy for a few moments. "I never let myself feel orphaned or deserted, and when my mother was gone—"

"That's my point. I want them to have your strength. They're not alone, but they'll always have more responsibilities than others their age, John," she said, sounding more intense. "They might as well understand that as soon as they can. Their childhood won't last as long as it does for the spoiled brats out there, just like it didn't last for you with a mother like that."

"I don't know," he said. "Why will they have more responsibilities than any others their age? It's not like they're going to have to take care of us soon or something. And we're providing well for them."

"They just will have to grow up faster. Didn't you?"

"But—"

"I know what I'm talking about," she snapped back at him. Her words lingered in the air like a sharp slap.

He shrugged, shaking his head. "It don't feel right somehow. Since they got here, they've been sprouting like mushrooms in the grass. Fourteen- and an almost sixteen-year-old sleeping together. Why, when I was only twelve, I'd wake up and discover—"

She slapped her hands over her ears.

"*Stop!* I don't want to hear it. You say whatever you think. Mushrooms? That's what you call them? You leave it up to me to decide what feels right," Mama said. "They're more my responsibility than yours. You're away more than half the time."

She paused and turned fully on him. "You want to stay at home and I go back to work? You want to teach them? Feed them, clothe them? Well? Do you?"

He was silent, and then he stood, picked up a magazine he had been reading, and started out of the kitchen. I hurried into the living room, where Trevor had begun a one-thousand-piece puzzle of the human body, a female. Mama had sent away for it. She had insisted that studying ourselves was as important as, if not more important than, studying anything else.

"There are many ways to know who you are," Mama had said during our science hour, "and knowing every part of yourself and what it does is one way."

Trevor looked up when I entered. I had the feeling he had heard Mama and Big John arguing, but he didn't mention it, and I didn't tell him any of it, especially because of the way both Mama and Big John talked about him.

Most of the time, Big John would end an argument with a loud grunt. When he was still angry or unconvinced, his grunt would last longer. Mama Eden would say, "You make my heart thump with those noises." And she would clutch her breast as if it was going to fall apart at her feet. Sometimes she'd even gasp.

"All right, all right," he might say then. "You're right, you're right."

All Mama had to do was tell him he was making her sick, and he'd shrink. And he'd never choose what she had suggested, of course; he never told her he would gladly stay home and not work. He was more than happy to leave the caring for us to her. I always felt that, to him, Trevor and I were more like toys he could play with and then put in a closet.

One thing he never did was come into our room to say good night to us or make sure we were all right. In fact, the only time I remembered him in our room was to fix something, like replace an electric socket or get a window to stop sticking when we had tried to open it.

It was certainly not that he didn't want us or like us. He especially loved to tickle me and pretend to be a monster, chasing me through the house until Mama made him stop. And he loved grabbing Trevor by the ankles and swinging him around upside down. Trevor screamed, but he never cried. It was his funfair roller-coaster ride. Even Mama would laugh sometimes. And both of us, when we were smaller, would love crawling over him and trying to tickle him whenever he sprawled on the living-room floor. Mama said it was like Gulliver in the land of Lilliput, but we'd have to read *Gulliver's Travels* to understand. She promised that we would.

Maybe for Big John, spending time with us in our room brought back some of his unhappy childhood memories. I easily could imagine how alone he had been, how often there had been silence because his mother had gone to work. Mama was right. If anyone had to have grown up faster than others his age, it was Big John. But I knew there were other reasons to keep out of our room: odors.

We had to admit that our room smelled different from the rest of the house, because Mama Eden cleaned it so often with disinfectants that sometimes made the insides of our noses tingle, and we'd want the windows open, even in the fall and for a few moments at least in the winter. Big John said she'd scrub the paint off the walls and thin out the plumbing because she was at it so often and so vigorously. He was always claiming that it left a bad taste in his mouth whenever he had been in and out of our room.

"I don't know how those kids take it," he'd say.

"You'd live in squalor if it wasn't for me," she'd tell him. "Why, that truck cab of yours must have diseases fighting each other by now. If you took care of that half as well as you take care of what it looks like . . ."

When he was home, he did spend hours polishing out stains and dents and touching up the red-painted cab. Even the tires were clean and shiny before he set out again. Any chrome looked brand-new. Windows glistened. But Mama was right; he didn't do much more than gather up the wrappers and bags he had tossed in the cab. Once in a while, she would go out and spray some scent in it, claiming the odor crawled right up to the house and under the door.

Eventually, he'd laugh and agree and promise to do more. But he never did. Trevor liked to go into his truck as soon as he was home and sit behind the steering wheel. He'd pretend to turn it, even though he could barely see over the wheel. It was a late-model semi-tractor-trailer truck with eighteen wheels. Big John owned it and had his own company because he liked his independence. Big block letters on both sides read *EDEN TRUCKING*. The cab was so high up that Big John had to lift Trevor to get him into the seat.

Trevor said he liked the odors of cigar and Quik Stop sandwiches, candy, beer, and soda. It made him feel like he had been on one of Big John's trips, something he longed to do. He was always the one with the most questions about Big John's latest ride. Big John was good at describing his journeys, filling the story with descriptions of different people, cars, and the scenery he passed, including tunnels and bridges.

And he had what Trevor would think were adventures, too. He had seen terrible road accidents, fights, even the police chasing and capturing someone on the road ahead, guns drawn just like in a movie. He'd add gestures and action, performing what he had seen. For Trevor, more than for me, it was as good as watching television, not that we were allowed to watch all that much until Big John was home and we had to do what every family did, watch television together, though only what Mama approved. Otherwise, we had too many chores and lots of homework.

Either I or Trevor would fall asleep soon after dinner, especially in the winter when night came so early. We'd have to read for an hour. I was always worried we were getting sick, especially when one of us sneezed or coughed. Mama Eden wasn't fond of doctors and medicine. She didn't believe in vaccinations. When Big John suggested she should take us to get one for something or other, she would tell him that since we were not exposed, we had natural immunities. "I'm keeping them healthy," she said indignantly. "They get all the vitamins they need and good food, and I keep them clean. Whatever they had before is enough."

"No one said you weren't," Big John said. "I'm just saying they're kids and—"

"They are not neglected children like most of them out there. Who knows better than I do, having been in a classroom with dozens of them sneezing and coughing on each other? Most were very susceptible to catching colds or whatever the others brought with them from home. Why, I remember—"

"Okay, okay." He put his big hands up in surrender. He knew she could go on for hours describing how terrible her teaching experience was. She blamed something called peer pressure for all the children's dirty and nasty ways. "Rotten apples do spoil the barrel," she never stopped reminding him.

She didn't have to do that much to convince him. Big John didn't like school. He had never gone to college. He had been driving trucks and working ever since he was eighteen. When it came to how Mama said things were in schools, especially now, he'd usually say, "I'll take your word for it."

However, I couldn't help feeling that lately, Mama Eden seemed more concerned about us than usual. Maybe she was having second thoughts about our sleeping in the same bed for reasons other than Big John's. If one of us caught something, the other surely would. She was in our bedroom in the evening more often, standing over us just as she was now. If I didn't look like I was asleep, she would stop whispering, turn, and leave, and I wanted to hear her whispers.

Most of the time now, when she did speak softly in the shadows of my and Trevor's bedroom, she sounded like she was praying for us to do something in the future to make her happy. I couldn't understand what exactly she wanted us to do to please her. She was weaving her favorite two words, *love* and *family*, into sentences about light and darkness, hope and promises, but I didn't hear anything specifically different from what we were already doing.

As I listened to her tonight, I tried to peek at her. Now that she was so close, I could see she wasn't looking at us; she was looking up, maybe at God. When she lowered her head, I closed my eyes tightly. I felt her hand on my hair. She was touching me so softly it was like a breeze, and then, after she had touched Trevor, she started out.

The moon was behind a cloud now. Our room was darker. I looked out at the stars, which had become a little more visible. There were no streetlights near us, and the lights outside our house weren't strong enough to wash out the sky. Our real oak-wood blinds were pulled way up so that the morning sunlight would urge us to wake. Mama Eden liked for us to be up early. "Wasting time is wasting life," she chanted often. Sometimes she added, "And I don't want a moment of yours lost. You can never find it again."

Trevor had looked confused, even a little frightened, when we were younger and she would say that, but I explained it to him. She didn't mean we'd die soon or too early. She had said what she had said about wasting time because she loved us and wanted us to be happy forever and ever.

"How do you know how many moments you have to live?" he asked me. He had found a dead bird on the side of the house, and when he had told Big John, Big John had said, "It just ran out of gas, like a truck."

"You don't know. That's why she's telling us not to waste one."

"But how do you know which have been wasted?"

I don't think my answers satisfied him, especially after what Big John had said, but I wasn't going to ask Mama to explain it again, in more detail. She might frighten him more, and besides, she didn't like explaining what she thought was as clear as day. She'd accuse us of being like the children she taught in public school, lost in a daze and not paying proper attention.

I looked over at Trevor now, deep in sleep. His lips twitched. I wondered if he was dreaming of something to eat or drink or remembering something unpleasant that had occurred when he was an infant. Strands of his hair lay over his forehead. His eyebrows were light, so light that sometimes in the sunshine, he looked like he didn't have any. Mama was always talking about how creamy his complexion was. She even said he was "perfect, clearly shaped by God."

She said nice things about me from time to time, too, but it was more like she had just remembered to say them. When she talked about Trevor, it was as if she was telling someone, even though there was no one there but us. I could hear the pride in her voice and see how deep her smile would go inside her. Maybe she believed Trevor needed the compliments more than I did. She did know everything about us, things she wouldn't ever tell us, no matter how old we were.

"You don't need to know," she would say if I asked a question about myself or Trevor before we were at the Wexlers' foster home. "I've buried all that for you both in the Cemetery for Unhappiness before I brought you here."

Which mound was ours? Now, however, I was even more curious.

My eyes were still wide open when I lay back against my pillow again. I felt warm and protected, especially when we went to bed, and I was sure Trevor felt the same way. Almost from the first day we were brought here, we felt safe enough to close our eyes as soon as we were in bed. That wasn't always true while living at the Wexlers' foster home.

But suddenly, for reasons I could not understand or explain, lately I began to fear closing my eyes. There was something about our life and our home that wasn't safe. I had no idea what it was and not an inkling of an idea how to explain my feelings to Trevor.

Ironically, I felt confident that in time I would be able to do that, explain it to him.

Or worse . . . I wouldn't have to.

He would know already.

He would have known long before I did.

He would simply have never wanted to tell me, never wanted me to know.

I like to believe that was simply because he wanted to protect me and keep me believing we really lived in the Garden of Happiness.

two

Neither of us feared that anything terrible would actually happen to us. Both of us believed we would never have anyone who would love us as much as Mama Eden loved us. The foster home hadn't been a real home, because a real home had to have a family in it, a family we could feel was ours. Neither of us had any family until Mama Eden and Big John Eden signed the papers to take us into their home and then, when they were legally able to do so, adopt us.

Before we came to live with Mama Eden, I felt as if we were part of a herd, moved along like sheep with Nanny Too often standing over us with her X-ray eyes searching for a sign of the devil, some selfish or mean thing that she had to stamp out the way someone would stamp out creepy-crawly things that found their way into our sleeping quarters, bedrooms that smelled like someone had rubbed motor oil into the walls.

Many of the other children would scream at the sight of mice and insects, and then Nanny Too would yell at them, telling them to trust in God. No one said it to anyone else, but if one of us had been bitten and cried because of the itching, we were told it was God's wish. None of us dared ask her, but I thought about it. *What did he or she do to make God so angry as to let a bug bite him or her? Can God ever be mean and do something spiteful just because he is God and can?*

Were orphans more inclined to become evil? Was that why there was so much discipline and so little, if any, affection? There were so many rules. One of Nanny Too's favorites, it seemed, was never ever touch yourself between your legs. If someone, even a three-year-old, was seen doing it, she would smack his or her hands with a hard, black rubber ruler. *Obedience* might as well have been written above our beds.

Whether we liked what they fed us or not, we had to eat all of it. Children were crying because they were forced to sit at the table until they cleared their plates. If Nanny Too finally gave up on someone, she wouldn't let him or her have dinner or breakfast the next day. Neither Trevor nor I was ever in the "bad" seat and forced to watch everyone else eat, but both of us hated and feared Nanny Too.

Ever since I was five years old, when Mama blessed and prayed for us, I felt safer and more protected than I did at the Wexlers', where Nanny Too uttered prayers, hoping we would be good and healthy so we could find ways to serve God. Never did I hear her mention our future families, praying for us to be adopted and find new real mothers and fathers and find love.

I couldn't remember having been brought to the Wexlers' group home, of course. I was too young. I believed that Trevor still had vivid memories of his mother, even though he never made the slightest mention of her. Of course, I knew we both had a mother and a father out there somewhere, and we didn't have to be foster children. I had no idea of the reason mine gave me away. I didn't know why Trevor was brought to the Wexlers, either, but it was clear that neither of our parents wanted us, just like no parents wanted any of the other children at the foster home. The only other reason for their being there was that both their parents had died and no one in their families wanted them. Trevor said that was the same thing, but I said no, "If your mother or your father doesn't want you, that's worse than if your uncle or aunt doesn't."

For some reason, he never liked to hear me say that, even though I was sure he knew I was right. He would just grunt like Big John and stop talking about it.

Eventually, Trevor and I learned little things about ourselves through Mama, who had gone through our files at the adoption agency. She finally told us that Trevor's mother was unwed and simply turned him over to the adoption agency that placed him at the Wexlers'. He came with his first name, and since he was used to it, neither the Wexlers nor Nanny Too tried to change it. His mother or some woman doing her a favor brought him and left him at the adoption agency, which passed him on quickly to th Wexlers.

"They were in cahoots," Mama Eden said. "Paybac under the table," she explained. "We are not the or world where children are bought and sold like some commodity, something on department-store shelves, but it still makes us terrible."

Just imagining ourselves like some commodity gave me new nightmares. Would everyone who knew about us think of us the same way? If so, who would want us to be his or her friends? Would we always be alone, have no one but ourselves? Trevor didn't seem as frightened. When Mama Eden went on a rampage about how we and other orphans were treated, she would even describe us as having tags on our clothes or around our necks listing the price.

Big John calmly warned her it would give us bad dreams about ourselves if she went on about it like that, but she snapped back, "Good. Helps them understand how good things are for them now." He didn't argue.

Mama told me my name had been changed to Faith. She wasn't upset about it, because she said my given name was silly. She never revealed what it had been. Anything buried in the Cemetery for Unhappiness was never resurrected. My real mother giving me away and the question of my original name being discarded like something meaningless upset me, but I'd never been quite sure of what Trevor thought and believed about his mother. When we were very young, I suspected Mama wasn't telling him the whole truth about himself.

If he ever did think she was lying to make him happier, he never said it, and he never looked at me and gave me any hint that he was thinking it. Big John often said that Trevor would make a good spy, because most of the time you couldn't look at him and tell what he was thinking: "He keeps his feelings tightly packed. Maybe his parents were good poker players. He surely will be
e."

"Over my dead body," Mama Eden said. "My children won't be wasting their time and money like some people I know." She practically stung him with her eyes. "And don't call them his parents. We're his *parents*," she emphasized. "For both of them! Forever and ever."

Her angry words were like nails being pounded into walls this time. Even Big John winced.

Once, when I was just eight and Trevor was already nine, Mama Eden sat Trevor and me down on the light blue marshmallow sofa in the living room and then pulled up Big John Eden's cherry-wood foot stool to sit on. His feet were so big that he needed a large one, one she could comfortably sit on. She took our hands, brought them into her lap, and described how our mothers and fathers, who were responsible for us being brought to the Wexlers, were dangling on a string over the mouth of hell. It was practically the only time she ever mentioned them.

She told us that the hot breath coming out of hell's mouth was cooking them alive the way she cooked a potato in the oven. After she had told us all that, she took us to the kitchen to look through the small window of the oven to see it begin to soften and brown the potatoes.

"Think of the potatoes as them," she said, standing behind us with her hands on our shoulders. Then she turned us both around and knelt so she was looking directly into our eyes.

"The heat they feel," she said, with her dark brown eyes widened, "is just enough to keep them very, very hot, but not quite burn them up, not yet. They have to suffer and suffer and suffer. Someday you will hear them. You will hear their screams, and when you close your eyes, if you've been a good boy and a good girl, you will see a curtain open and be able to see them squirming like worms on the sidewalk. They will be in so much pain that they can do nothing else but scream, even though they want so much to cry and beg for forgiveness."

She stood up and stared down at us for a moment. I know my heart was thumping as the images flashed across my mind. Maybe I looked more sad than frightened. I couldn't imagine the faces of my parents, but I knew I had to look like them. All I could see was myself over the mouth of hell, squirming. Mama Eden could tell. She really could look into us through our eyes and see everything, even our thoughts.

Trevor didn't look as frightened. He looked like Mama probably wanted him to look, angry. That made me wonder even more about him. Did he hate his real mother? Did he remember her enough to hate her? Did she tell him something else, something that wouldn't make this tale as horrid?

"Don't feel sorry for them," she said, mainly to me because I was the one looking like I did. "When you hurt family, you stab God in the heart—and there is no forgiveness for that." Her eyes were smaller now, and her lips pressed so hard against each other that there were small white patches in the corners. Her very light freckles seemed to fade or sink beneath her skin. It seemed to me that her face grew thinner as we grew older, too, her cheekbones more prominent.

I looked at Trevor after she had said all this, but he wouldn't look at me. He'd stared at Mama as if he was afraid to look to the right or left. He wanted to show her he had been listening to every word and he believed her. Trevor was more obedient than I was, even at the Wexlers'. Mama never said so, and I didn't tell him he was too trusting and too satisfied. I didn't think he ever had the bad thoughts I had about our life with Mama Eden and

Big John, thoughts about disobedience and thoughts about running away, not because I didn't like our home with Mama and Big John. It was just that I wanted to see more and meet more children our age. I longed for it.

Why didn't he?

When Mama had us kneel to pray, I didn't always pray, but I could see Trevor always did. His lips were moving to the words Mama had dictated. I knew them by heart, too, but I didn't always say them. I just kept my eyes closed and thought about the cookies or the ice cream she had promised us as soon as our prayers were completed. Was that a sin? Would I eventually dangle over the mouth of hell? Nanny Too would say I would. I did worry, but I didn't stop thinking about the ice cream and cookies.

Tonight I felt a little different, however. It wasn't only the whispering that had woken me. My stomach was bubbling as if someone was between my legs and blowing up my delivery system, which is what Mama called my vagina when she gave us a lesson in biology. We were being homeschooled in the ten-room house that Mama had inherited from her parents close to Lake Wallenpaupack, the second-largest lake in Pennsylvania, measuring fifty-two miles of shoreline, thirteen miles in length, and sixty feet deep at points. Since it was close to home, that was one of the first things we had learned in our geography lesson.

"You have to know where you are," Mama Eden said. "You have to know what home means and plant it forever in your hearts. It's like the poet Robert Frost said, 'Home is the place where, when you have to go there, they have to take you in.' We'll always take you in. There will always be a place for you in our hearts as well as our home."

Although it might have been as old, our house was far prettier than the Wexlers' dilapidated, sprawling tourist house with patchy grass and poorly trimmed bushes. Mama and Big John's house was a two-story Queen Anne with a full-width, slightly wraparound porch in front with faded blue and cream spandrels and brackets. The side entrance of the house had gray weathered wooden steps a little longer than the cement stone steps in the front because of the way the land dropped. And there was a back door you'd reach by going through the kitchen and the pantry.

The house had natural cedar-shake siding. All the metal, including all the door handles, was solid brass and looked antique. Mama claimed her father had found some handles at estate sales and replaced those his father had put on the doors. There was a detached garage big enough for two cars and a toolshed where the lawn mower and snow blower were kept.

We had a basement, too. Big John had worked on it whenever he could, putting up panel walls and a slate floor with new lighting. He closed off the storage area where we had our water heaters, boxed it in with a door. He did all this before we came, but shortly afterward, he put a pool table down there. He and his best friend, another truck driver, Nick Damien, played whenever they were both home. Nick also drove a tractor-trailer, but unlike Big John, he didn't own it. He worked for a company that often hired Big John, too. Unlike Big John, he was unmarried and lived with his younger, unmarried sister Gabby in a much smaller house.

Her real name was Gabrielle. Sometimes she came over with him. She was a buxom woman with raspberry-red hair, only an inch or so taller than Mama. She was a secretary at an insurance company. I used to think it was because she had so many freckles even at thirty that she had never gotten married and had short-lived romances. Men thought there was something childish about her, perhaps. But I liked her. She had a smile that reminded me of a full-blown dandelion, one that caught and held the sun.

Years later, oddly, our house seemed smaller when I thought about having grown up in it. I imagined it shrank with age. Mama had added very little furniture to what had been her parents' and never changed a wall fixture, a painting, or a framed picture. She told us, "Your house is your first set of clothes. You can't help feeling a little naked every time you leave it. Always take good care of it. It knows when you don't."

Our bedroom was upstairs toward the front of the house, and Mama's and Big John's was toward the rear, with their own en suite bathroom. Trevor and I had separate dressers for our clothes and shared the closet, his things on the right and mine on the left. Our bathroom was right across the hall. There was another bathroom downstairs.

There was a dining room with a teardrop chandelier over the long, dark oak table parallel to the three windows that looked over the lawn to the thick woods. Our living room was at the front of the house. The large picture windows faced the main highway and the rough gravel road to the left, which went around and back through the forest to the main road farther west.

Although we had never been down the side road, we knew there were three other houses on it, summerhouses. Since there were so few houses on the side road, the government had never bothered to pave it. The road had ruts and dips. Mama said that was fine with her. "There's less traffic. No one except those tourists and us would have reason to drive on it."

The tourists would wave to us when they went by, but Mama had warned us from the start when we could go outside by ourselves not to encourage them by waving back. "Don't even smile at them," she said, "and never look at them first."

Neither Trevor nor I was sure why she was so concerned about it, but we didn't disobey her, even when children who looked close to our age gaped out at us from the rear seats. Their summer homes were far enough away for their parents to forbid them from walking to our house. At least, that's what Trevor and I believed, and of course, we could never walk to them.

Our driveway off this side road widened in a circle as big as our house, making it easy for Big John to pull his semi-tractor-trailer truck in and turn so that when he was ready to leave, he could just drive out. We knew exactly when he had come home, because his truck made so much noise on the gravel, sounding like it was crushing and grinding the small stones into dirt. Sometimes he'd sound his horn to announce his arrival, and we'd scream. Of course, Mama Eden bawled him out for it.

"You're terrifying the animals," she'd say, or even, "You're waking the dead."

Trevor would look at me. I could read his question in his wide eyes. *Where are the dead? Are they in our Cemetery for Unhappiness . . . could all that come back to life?*

Big John would laugh and hop out of the red cab, his arms usually full of presents for us all. He was better than Santa Claus, because we didn't have to wait for Christmas or either of our birthdays. Mama would moan and groan about it, accusing him of spoiling us and her, but I could also see her small smile under her criticism and complaints.

"You have to cherish the peace and quiet around here," she'd tell us, especially in his presence. "It makes our house valuable, even though it's a much older house than any of those around here.

"Older houses have character," she continued when she was into this lecture. "They have the memories of family sunk into their walls. Sometimes," she said with that faraway look she could have, "I can hear the house breathe, or I can hear my grandparents talking or laughing. Even crying. Someday, as I promised you"—she snapped out of her far-off look—"you two will hear it all."

Trevor was always excited about that possibility, because he thought maybe he'd hear secrets.

"What secrets?" I asked him. There it was again, this feeling that he knew a lot more than I did about Mama and the house.

"Everyone's family has secrets," he said. "Secrets you have to keep locked up in your heart and guard."

Even though he was reciting Mama's warning, I remember also wondering if he meant himself, his own secrets.

Except for some area rugs, the floors of all the rooms, even the kitchen, were a pale yellow slate wood. The curtains on the kitchen windows were handmade snow-white cotton. Big John had replaced most of the curtains on the windows elsewhere with real wood blinds, especially in the living room. He was also very good with electric problems and new installations of wires and plugs as well as our plumbing, constantly bringing things up to date. Mama Eden always had something for him to do on the house when he came home. She posted the list on the door of the refrigerator, so when he came in late at night sometimes and opened it to get one of his cold beers, it was the first thing that stared him in the face, because she wrote her directions in big, black block letters.

Just beyond the kitchen and toward the rear of the house, there was a den that Big John used for his private television set and where he would go to smoke a cigar. She wouldn't permit him to smoke in the basement because it would be a "clear fire hazard." Mama wouldn't let him smoke near us, even when we were all outside; and when he was gone on a trip, she would throw open the windows, even on the coldest winter day, and air out his room. Sometimes it was so cold that tiny icicles would form on the beige-colored drywall inside. Only then would she close the windows.

Besides a basement, we had an attic nearly the width of the house, with two small rectangular windows that faced the west side. In the summer, it was too hot up there, and in the winter, we had to wear our coats to go up there. Mouse and rat traps had to be cleaned out frequently. Trevor wasn't afraid to do it. We found a dead bat once, too. It wasn't our favorite place, even though there were many old things to explore and discover. We were never permitted to take anything from it and bring it to our room. Mama called it all "retired memories."

The windows in the attic enabled us to look out over the woods in some places where the trees weren't so high and especially in the fall and winter when the leaves were gone. We could see other people's houses, sometimes only the tops of their roofs and chimneys. I loved imagining who lived in those houses. Surely, kids our age lived in one or two. Perhaps they had gone up to their attics and seen the top of our house and wondered about us, wondered why they had never seen us in school.

There were two guest bedrooms, one that wasn't used and was kept locked since we were brought to the house, the Forbidden Room, which had its own bathroom. Mama never went in there during the day and, I think, only rarely during the night to keep it clean. We hadn't even looked through the doorway. When I asked her about it, she said the floor wasn't safe in too many spots. Only she and Big John knew how to walk around the very dangerous weak places, so they kept the door locked.

"Years ago, there was a terrible roof leak over it and the floorboards rotted terribly in certain places. My father didn't care to fix it quickly, because no one would use it. He locked it, and we've kept it that way. Your father claims he will fix it someday, but I'm not holding my breath. It would, I admit, be a great deal of new construction, beams, ceiling, repainting. I make sure there are no rodents in there and keep it as clean as I can."

The other guest room had been changed and lightly furnished with a sofa, a rocking chair, and now our blackboard and two school desks and a few chairs. Mama added our computers for research. Our workbooks and textbooks, pens and pencils were neatly placed on the wall shelf to the right on entering. Still left there were the crayons we used when we were much younger.

When Mama was proud of something we had done, especially a test, she would pin it on the bulletin board on the hall wall just outside the door until we did something new. She told us that besides Big John, the ghosts of her ancestors would see it and they would be proud of us, proud we were becoming part of their family.

Originally, this room was the one Mama Eden's father, who had been an architect, had used. His desk and materials were up in the attic along with other retired memories, maybe because Mama Eden couldn't look at them particularly without crying. But that didn't mean she'd forget them.

"Memories stick to what your loved ones touched," she told us. "Memories are the way people live on, and when you forget those memories or there's no one left to think of them, that's when the lid closes on their coffins.

"That's another reason why I love living here, living in the arms of my family memories, which"—she smiled—"as I have told you many times, are gradually going to become yours."

Not all the memories were good ones, however. Mama's parents were killed in a truck accident when they were coming down a narrow road in the Pocono Mountains. Grandpa Eden was going too fast, Mama said, and forgot about a sharp turn. His Ford F-150 SuperCab (a framed picture of it was also in the attic) went right through the guardrail, and they toppled down the side of the mountain, "Probably singing 'Nearer My God to Thee' until they died. Your grandmother, my mother, had two places to go, the church and the grocery store; one fed your soul, and the other fed your body."

Mama was already in her second year as an English teacher in the middle school when her parents were killed. She said she hated working in the public school after the first week, because the children were so spoiled and their parents much too into themselves to give their children the attention they deserved and needed. She was grateful her parents had left her enough money for her not to have to work and a house that had been paid for years ago.

Back then, in her early teaching days, she slept in the room Trevor and I now shared. She had already begun dating Big John Eden, who drove a tractor-trailer truck then, too, and who was sometimes gone for over two weeks, even three or four when he went cross country. She said she had ridden with him only a few miles before she had gotten too nauseous to continue and never rode with him again. Of course, he was disappointed, but it didn't stop him from wanting to see her, and she didn't mind the weeks he was away.

"Absence makes the heart grow fonder," she recited when

Trevor and I were younger and she would tell us about her "days of courting," as she put it. We sensed it was a happier time for her and for Big John because they were younger and more carefree.

Every once in a while, she would tell us more about that time, and even if she was repeating something, we would sit and listen as if it was the first time she was telling us.

"He'd carry me around on his back just so I wouldn't get the soles of my shoes dirty. He could run with me on his back. I'd bounce and scream and hold on to him so tightly that his skin was red, even scratched sometimes.

"Our meeting each other was meant to be," she told us. "Some people call it serendipity, our fate to be together. His truck broke down right in front of this house. It was a rainy Saturday. I saw him standing in the downpour and looking at his engine. I felt sorry for him, so I brought him a thermos of hot ginger tea and honey and then invited him to wait in the house. Whoever he had called to help him took hours, but I was glad of that, because we got to know each other quickly. Even though he's so big, he's quite the handsome man. I thought he was like Hercules or Adonis, and I could see he was very gentle. Big hands don't make you mean.

"When he took mine in his, I felt like a little girl, but he was so tender I had no trouble imagining him holding a just-born baby. He returned to see me, and we went on dates to nice restaurants and sometimes a picnic on the lake. He had a friend with a boat who let him use it, too, but that friend moved away and sold his boat before you two were brought here."

She paused and smiled, and then, as if a wind had come in and blown away the happy memories, she stopped smiling. I knew what made her sad. She had told us many times how she had cried month after month about not giving birth to that baby she often imagined practically swimming in Big John's hands and arms.

"It got so sad," she said once, lowering her voice to a whisper, "that the house itself cried for me, all our ancestors. I'd wake your daddy and ask him if he heard it."

"What did he say?" I asked, holding my breath.

"Of course, he heard it. He would put his big arm around me and draw me close to him. My tears made his nightshirt damp, but he didn't complain. He kissed me on the forehead and helped me go back to sleep."

"Do you still hear those cries, Mama?" I asked. After all, she never had that baby.

Trevor smirked as if I had asked something anyone would know.

"Oh, no," Mama said. "They stopped the day you two came."

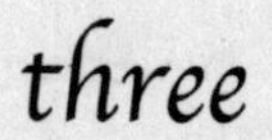

three

Big John and Mama were married six months after her parents died and after she had left her elementary-school teacher's job. She had told us that they had gone four years and eight months without being able to have a baby.

"I told your father we were going to adopt and make a family, that I wasn't going to sit alone in this big house by myself while he was off burning tires on the nation's highways. So I shopped for children and found the two of you, the two of you only a little more than a year apart, with Trevor the older, which was perfect."

Mama told us all of this the way some mothers might tell their children a bedtime story. When we were both old enough to understand it all, she gave us more and more detail each time she told it. She would come into our bedroom after we had washed, brushed our teeth, and gotten into our pajamas. And then she would sit between us on the bed and begin. She made us sound like magical characters.

"Once upon a time, I woke up and realized how lonely I was. The house was so quiet, as it always is, because we have no close neighbors and we're off on this side road. We were never friendly with any of the tourists who had those three summer homes, so there is hardly ever traffic in the spring, winter, and fall, unless someone makes a wrong turn without thinking or looking where they are going.

"As you know, we have bears and squirrels, lots of birds during the year, deer and bobcat, among other God's creatures, but none of them can hold a good conversation or need me to get along in their lives. I might feed the hummingbirds, but believe me, if I didn't, they'd still be humming along. Independent creatures hold no temptation for me.

"Big John always wanted a dog, so we had Critter, our golden retriever, for two good years before a bear swiped him and broke him in half. He'd bark all night sometimes, and I'm sure another dog would have done the same, so I told your father that since he was gone so often on his trucking trips, I'd be the one left with caring for the animal and keeping it from running into the woods to die at the claws of a bear. Critter wasn't willing to be on a leash and just didn't listen. Your father buried him somewhere in the woods. I never wanted to know where. Big John's never even suggested we get another dog, although I know he thinks dogs are as necessary as bathrooms out here.

"Cats like Moses and Becky are fine because they keep mice

out of the first and second floors of the house, and when I let them, they go into the attic and catch something. Those cats come and go as they please, but I know there'll be a day when they won't come back because they've become too deaf or stupid to survive out there. They wouldn't like being house cats. If I keep them in, they just sit by the window and wait for me to open the door so they can rush past me and out. Just the way Critter did that day he died, painfully.

"So . . . where was I . . . oh, yes. 'No,' I told Big John. 'I am not waiting for a miracle any longer. Sometimes God is very plain with his meaning. Children aren't standing in line inside you to grow in me,' I went on. 'We need to get children who need me, really need me, and would make us a real family.' He agreed, as long as he didn't have to go along searching for the right one. He hated shopping of any kind, even for things he needed himself. He still does.

"It was no matter. I didn't have to search long. There you were at the Wexlers' foster home, already playing together and getting along so well. You were there a few years before Trevor arrived, but once he did, you looked like you belonged together forever! Some people might be satisfied calling that luck, just a happy coincidence, but not me.

"Now, you might not believe it. I know Big John doesn't, even though he nods and doesn't laugh or smile when I tell him again and again, but there was a light around both your heads when I looked at you. It was as if God has this searchlight, so powerful that it can be seen in the middle of the day, and it was aimed directly at you two to tell me, 'These are the ones. These are the two who will make your family, Faith and Trevor.'

"Big John was quite surprised that I wanted two children right away. Most only want one at a time. But I wasn't going to separate you. I could see how close you were to each other by then and what a heartbreak it would have been to break you up.

"You both are different from every other child in the world. You are now part of me, my family.

"And so here you are, living safe and happy with me and Big John. We don't need anyone else. Our love for each other is like the love ten people have for each other."

Mama tucked us both in and kissed our foreheads. Then she stood there looking down at us after she had told us all this.

"I can still see that light on you from time to time. God is reassuring me I made the right choice, not that I ever need to be reassured.

"Be sure you pray before you fall asleep and thank God you are with us, and be sure you work hard at loving each other, for real love is a daily task. You must never assume it's there always. Right now, it's in your hearts where it should be, but if you're not careful, you can lose it, and your hearts will be empty and you won't live happily ever after."

She continued to stand there looking down at us and smiling. She had told us this bedtime story many times. It rarely had a word left out, but sometimes she'd take more time describing us, what we were wearing, our faces and our hair, and how she couldn't leave us with the Wexlers one day longer than was necessary. The first times she had told it to us, however, she had always added a promise.

"I'm not going to let anyone steal your love away from me or from each other. That's why I'm homeschooling you. I am a former teacher, so no one would ever challenge me. Until you're older, much older, and smarter and aware of the demons that live in other people, I will keep you safe, and we will be a special family."

Our education wasn't simply math, reading, writing, science, and history. We had to sit and listen to classical music and opera and get so we could identify different composers. There was always a "show night," when Big John came home for a while. We would all gather in the living room so we could perform our new knowledge. Big John would sit in the light brown easy chair with his feet up on the stool. He was quite impressed with us, not that he would know any of the music or could even solve the math problems we solved. He didn't know the Constitution well, either, but he was more impressed with Mama being able to teach us such "highfalutin" stuff at our young ages.

Afterward, we would have a celebration dinner. Mama would bake our favorite cake, chocolate with vanilla icing, and Big John would then tell us some of his road stories while we sat on the floor in the living room and listened to his description of interesting places he had been and people he had met. He went through deserts and over mountains, through small towns and big cities, past lakes and rivers.

Trevor was always asking to go along with him. Just sitting in the truck still excited him, but Mama said he wasn't ready yet. Going too soon into the world was "like looking at a bright light before your eyes were completely formed. You could blind yourself for life," she said. I could see Big John didn't agree and wanted to take him, but he'd have to rip him out of Mama's arms to do so.

The most traveling we could do was go outside and walk the property. We were told never to leave the grounds. It wasn't difficult for us to know where the boundaries were, because we had a fieldstone wall on the north side, and after we crossed the gravel side road that led to the summer homes, there was a fieldstone wall that was supposedly built by Mama's grandfather, who had piled on rock after rock with hands that had palms as rough as tree bark. The wall ran from the main road parallel to our house and a little farther than a half-mile behind it. He had stopped a half-foot from someone else's property.

We didn't know very much about the man who owned the property on the south side of ours, but we did know from little things Mama muttered from time to time that he was a widower, Mr. Longstreet. She said his children rarely visited him. He had been living in his home when her parents were living in ours, and her father liked him. Her parents had him over for dinner from time to time, and that was how she had learned about his children. She felt sorry for him.

"That's the modern family," she muttered. "Everyone for him- or herself. *Family* is like a foreign word these days, especially with all these divorces. But that will never be true for us." She smiled and nodded as if someone else had said it and she was agreeing. She walked away still talking about it, even though we could no longer hear her.

Actually, Mama talked to herself quite often lately, especially when we were upstairs doing our studies. Trevor would look up from his textbook, and then I would stop reading and listen, too. Sometimes we would walk very quietly to the top of the stairway and listen, because it sounded like she was talking to someone else. We both wondered if someone had come in and we hadn't noticed, but after a while, she would be quiet and we heard no one else. Usually, as soon as we knew there was no one else there,

Trevor would want us to go back to our studies. I knew he was afraid Mama would be angry about us listening to her speak her thoughts.

"She'll tell us whatever she wants us to know or thinks we should know when the time comes, Faith. Eavesdropping on someone's personal thoughts is a sin, remember? Besides, maybe she's talking to one of her ancestors," he added, with those eyes of his lit like the Fourth of July sparklers Big John always brought back from one of his spring or early-summer trips.

I stood looking down the stairway. My face was probably awash in worry. Maybe Mama was alone too much. When I suggested that to Trevor, he became as angry as I had seen him about anything.

"We talk to ourselves, don't we? Stop acting like it's anything terrible," he snapped, sounding just like Mama Eden when she lost her temper or grew impatient.

Anyone listening would think he really was her son. Once I even imagined that she had given birth to him, had changed her mind, and had given him to the adoption agency and that years later, she came back to the Wexler foster home for him and decided to take me, too. I told Trevor my fantasy. It made him even angrier, because he could never believe Mama would have done something like give away her child.

"She always tells us how important having a child was to her. You think she would give hers away?"

"It's just an idea, maybe a dream I had," I said.

"It's stupid," he said. "If Mama heard you say such a thing . . . she'd lock you in the woodshed. Maybe I will if you say it again."

He walked off, and I followed, wondering if it really was

stupid. The possibility was as scary to me as I imagined it was to Trevor, which was probably why he became so angry. I wanted him to give me better reassurance, not rage. Better to forget it, I eventually thought, forget I had ever dreamed it. Just as Mama once told us: "Sometimes forgetting is a blessing."

Of course, I wasn't surprised that what frightened him frightened me. His feelings were always very important to me, because if he grew sad, I grew sad, until I cried and he would say, "It's all right, Faith. It's all right."

But if I didn't cheer up quickly, he would get angry.

Usually, what angered him also angered me, even though I really didn't know why, which sometimes ended in his laughing at how quickly and dramatically I followed his lead. I always laughed at things he laughed at, even though I wasn't quite sure why he was laughing. Big John was right about us when he said we were "uncanny."

"I watch them, you know," he said. "Sometimes they even breathe together and take deep breaths at the same time."

"Stop your foolish talk, John," Mama told him.

But even though she didn't want to hear him say such things, I sensed that Mama was secretly pleased. As Big John would say, she, too, believed that we were "plugged into the same outlet."

Trevor and I resembled a real brother and sister from the first time we were brought together at the Wexlers'. I heard Nanny Too talking to her parents about us once, how unusually close we were. She even said, "They share a shadow."

That was practically true. From the day he had arrived, we had always played together, ignoring everyone else. I can't say why exactly, but we always sat together when we ate, and we were permitted to sleep in beds beside each other's. We followed each other everywhere about the house and grounds, and what he liked I liked, and vice versa. That even included what we were given to eat, although we really weren't permitted to dislike anything we were given at the Wexlers' house. I often thought of the way Mama had described us when she first had set eyes on us. Sometimes, especially now, when Trevor didn't realize it, I saw a glow around his head, the glow Mama claimed she saw on each of us.

We are special, I thought. Mama said we were, and who would know more than she did? I believed her when she said we were very different from other kids our age. I was convinced that because she had been a teacher, she would know. From the way she spoke about her pupils from time to time, they sounded almost like another species. But despite that, I would often stop what I was doing and stare out the front window at the main highway that ran by the front of our house, hoping I would see someone close to my age.

Often, if I concentrated very hard, I would see a young boy or girl who looked about our age in a car going by. Even though it was really just a glimpse, it was exciting for me. My imagination could go wild thinking about who they might be and what they would be like. I longed to hear their opinions, see what clothes they had and what interested them the most. Also, I enjoyed imagining things we might do together.

What I really longed to know was how different were we, really? Occasionally, someone would be looking out the car window at our house. I wondered, especially if it was a girl about my age, had she seen me sometime when Trevor and I were outside? Did she wonder who I was? Did she see me and think, *There's someone I could be friends with*?

Recently, Trevor saw me sitting there and staring out the window.

He stepped up beside me and gazed out at the road.

"What are you looking at?" he asked, and looked, too, only there were no cars going by.

"I'm waiting for someone," I said.

"Who? Big John's not coming back until next Tuesday."

"I'm waiting for a girl about my age who could become my friend if only her father or mother stopped the car and she came out to meet me."

He grimaced as usual when I mentioned being with other kids our age.

"You think someone is going to just pull up and get out to meet you? That could never happen, anyway, Faith. What would make someone stop and let their little girl out of the car? Unless," he said, thinking a little more about it, "Mama had invited them."

"Maybe there's someone who needs a friend, too, and Mama's finally decided," I said, excited by the idea. "She knows that girls need girlfriends, right? She'll find a suitable boy for you to have as a friend, too."

He stared with that "spy" face of his and then shook his head. "I don't know how important she really thinks that is. She never talks about any girlfriends she had in school or even afterward in college and when she worked. Did you ever see a picture of her with a girlfriend?"

I shook my head. What he was saying was true; it darkened hope for us, especially me.

"You'd better stop looking for something that won't happen. That's like trying to stop the rain by holding your hands up. Remember?"

I didn't say anything. I continued to look through the window. He stepped forward and closed the blinds sharply.

"Don't upset Mama," he warned, and walked out to start back up to our classroom.

I hurried after him.

"Why would that upset Mama, Trevor? All I'm doing is looking."

He didn't answer, but I kept after him. I waited for him to enter our classroom and sit behind his desk.

"Why would it upset her if I had a friend or you had one?" I asked, more insistently.

"She was a schoolteacher. She said other kids could be like a disease right now. We're not prepared for it. She wants us to be older before we get friendly with any other kids."

"I never understood that. What did she mean they could be like a disease?" I was usually explaining things to him, even if he didn't ask me to explain them. I just knew he hadn't understood whatever it was. But this was different, and maybe I was wrong about him. Maybe Trevor was just as smart or smarter than I was after all.

"Selfish parents brought them up wrong, and they have bad ideas in them. They could spread those ideas to us. Peer pressure, remember?"

I nodded. I remembered, but I didn't want to hear it. "If we believe that, Trevor, we'll never have any friends, ever. Mama would first have to live with their parents to be sure they taught them the right things."

He didn't answer. He started to read our English literature assignment. I stepped up to him and forced his book closed.

"So we'll never have any friends? It will just be you and me forever and ever? Is that what you're saying? Is that what you really believe?"

He shrugged. And then he looked up at me and said, "We will. When we're smart enough to avoid any bad things."

"When is that?"

"I don't know. Soon." He thought a moment. "Maybe sooner than Mama thinks."

That had sounded like he would defy Mama Eden if he could. He could have been saying it just to please me, but it still filled me with an excitement I never thought I'd have. I smiled, and he returned to what he was reading, but that thought didn't disappear. It was like a seed now, and it would grow into something.

It grew with every step we took whenever we walked away from the house. For most of our lives here, we were so afraid of going beyond the boundaries of our property that we didn't even get within a dozen yards of the stone walls on either side. I was jealous of our cats, Becky and Moses, who often walked the walls and hunted on the other side. As Mama said, they were house cats but at some point became more like two feral cats. Becky was a blanket merle, and Moses was black. They seemed indifferent to Trevor and me. Because Mama fed them, she was the only one they were even a little close to, and they literally ran from Big John.

When I mentioned that to Trevor, he started to give his usual shrug but stopped and said, "So?"

"Don't you wonder about them? They never come into our room," I said. "They never follow us or rub against our legs to get us to pet them and pay attention to them."

"Because they live outside, they can't trust us; they can't trust anyone or anything."

"But we wouldn't harm them. You'd think they would know that by now."

"That's the way it is. You're the one who once said nature can fool us for spite. It certainly could fool them, then. Sometimes coyotes come into our woods, and they wouldn't stand a chance against a pack."

"We're far from being a pack of coyotes, Trevor."

He grunted.

"Why aren't they afraid to go beyond the walls, then? We've seen them do that."

"Oh, they're afraid. They have to be always afraid. That's the point. Critter wasn't afraid enough, so he's dead and buried."

"Well, we don't have to be," I insisted. "We're smarter than dogs and cats. We don't have to be so afraid of where we go."

Even though I had said it and he had looked like he wanted to believe it, too, whenever we drew closer to the stone walls, either Trevor would look at me or I would look at him, and without either of us saying a word, we'd turn and move closer to our house. It was as if there were invisible chains tying us to it.

But Mama did encourage us to go into the woods to study plants, insects, and animals. When we were ten and eleven, she had Big John stop on one of his trips and buy us a microscope. It was important then that we brought back a good specimen. Trevor used it far more than I did. Nothing fascinated him more than looking at tiny things. I wasn't as excited about seeing worms and ants, spiders, and beetles so close up especially, but I forced myself to like his discoveries and at least pretend to be as excited as he was. He knew it, but he didn't care as long as I pretended.

Our woods were perfect for all this. We had thick forest on both sides, amounting to a total of almost three acres of our property. Mama was right when she told us that all sorts of creatures, big and small, lived in it, especially beautiful deer that would sometimes venture out and come right up to our house. And there were birds, sometimes birds that built nests high enough to keep their chicks safe. Some lived on our roof.

"No one who goes to public school can get the kind of education you two can get out there," Mama said proudly. "They have to look at pictures in textbooks. You see everything live, as it happens. Children in the cities and towns are lucky to see flies." She laughed at how clever she was.

"Don't they have parks to go to?" I asked.

"Yes, but they're nothing like this. This is untended nature. In some schools, they hire buses to take the children to places like your own backyard. You can wake up every morning and see the seasonal changes firsthand and exactly how all the animals and insects behave. Why, either one of you could soon be hired to lecture other children in public schools."

Could we? She did make it sound very exciting, and I believed our woods were truly special. No one else ever walked through them. It seemed like there were *No Trespassing* signs every twenty feet. No hunters ever came here during hunting season. Mama always reminded us to be cautious nevertheless.

"You have a special responsibility to protect each other, too," she said, "especially when you're outside of this house." She smiled. "Think of it as being like swimming in the ocean. As long as you're not too far from shore, you're safe. It's when you go out too far that you put yourselves in danger," she warned. She often warned us about that. "The moment you're out there, you're Trevor's lifeguard, and he's yours."

It wasn't difficult envisioning our forest the way we might envision the sea. Someone going too far in to see any signs of our house or the road would feel or should feel like someone who had lost sight of land. In the spring and the summer, our woods were full of shadows cast by the heavy foliage. Every pocket of darkness housed some mystery. Something was born in there; something lived in it and, from it, watched us.

Here and there, the sunlight streaked through the tree limbs and leaves, working like spotlights to help us capture something about which we had just read. Trevor would suddenly stop, get on his knees, and search with a magnifying glass for interesting things to bring to our little laboratory. I would walk around in a circle, daring myself to go farther and farther away from him, through darker areas and into places we had never entered. Usually, he didn't notice.

I'd pause and look through the woods, past the stone walls, dreaming of what lay beyond. It was over there where we would more likely find all the wonders and mysteries we could otherwise see only through books and pictures. I would tell myself that I wished we weren't so special. I wished we were more ordinary and therefore in public school. Mama would be so angry if I ever told her or if she overheard me telling Trevor such a thing. She never stopped telling us how special we were and how if we lost sight of that, it would be the beginning of some family tragedy.

"We'll be such a special family, and you will keep us special."

"How, Mama?" I asked.

She smiled. "You'll know," she said. "When the time comes, you'll know."

I never told Trevor; I even tried not to tell myself, but somehow, that sounded frightening.

four

It finally happened the third week of one June, late in the morning. I didn't recall a morning since I was twelve when Mama didn't ask me about it, either in a direct question or with her eyes after I had dressed and gone down to help with breakfast. Even if I didn't want to think about it, I couldn't keep it from hanging over my head and following me everywhere like an invisible balloon tied with invisible string around my neck. If I put my hand on my stomach, Mama's eyes would widen in expectation, but I had nothing to tell her. She wore such a look of disappointment that I started to worry that something might be wrong with me because it was taking so long to happen.

Finally, I asked her, and she said, "No, but I'm sure you're orbiting the moment."

Trevor overheard her and laughed about it later when we were alone. "She makes you sound like a satellite."

Today I was thinking about it almost from the moment I awoke. My stomach was moaning and groaning right through breakfast. I had been woken with expectations all night. I couldn't help but be nervous even after all the preparation, the reading about it, and Mama's descriptions and instructions. As she once had said, "Expectation will always first travel through the tunnel of panic. Even though it's common for all women, it's natural to feel tension because it's happening to you."

There was something in her eyes at dinner the night before that gave me the firm feeling it was all imminent. It was why I believed Mama could look at us and know everything about us instantly. Trevor certainly believed that and repeatedly told me, as if he was afraid I would doubt it or I would get into trouble being skeptical. He made me terrified of lying even in my thoughts. Mama would see it.

I tried not to think about having my first period when we awoke, but I could feel the trembling inside me as we began our lessons after breakfast. I read the same lines repeatedly. I couldn't concentrate and fought back tears. Finally, a cramping pain became so intense that I moaned, leaped out of the desk chair, and hurried to the bathroom to do all Mama had instructed. It was important to her, and she assured me that it would be to me, that I do all this without her help. She had lectured me privately again about it just two days ago, emphasizing my need to act grown-up.

"I don't want you getting hysterical over this," she had told me, her eyes wide with emphasis and fear. "I saw a girl do that in my classroom when I taught. I suspected it would happen. She was maturing quickly, but it wasn't a pretty scene. And it greatly disturbed the other girls, especially the ones who still had some time before they would experience it. I could have wrung her neck when I dragged her to the school nurse."

"What did she do?"

"Never mind. If I told you, you would get nightmares about it, and I would not like you to frighten Trevor with your complaints, moans and groans, even though he knows exactly what is supposed to happen to you, as well as you knowing what happens to him as he gets physically mature."

"Why would he be frightened at what happens to me?" I asked.

"Boys can have a worse reaction to what happens to girls than girls actually do themselves. From what he's read and heard me say, he knows all about your moods and aches, but I don't want him treating you and thinking of you as if you were some fragile little doll, do you understand? He'll be afraid to be around you. For a week every month, you'll be a monster to him," she said, "and I don't want either of you to ever be unpleasant to the other because of changes in your bodies as you mature. Especially now."

"Why *especially now*?" I asked. She just turned away. Something flashed in my mind, and before I could stop myself, I blurted, "Is that why Big John blames things you do on your time of the month?"

She spun around on me. Her eyes had taken on that explosive look again, only more emphatically this time. Unconsciously, perhaps, I stepped back.

"Have you been listening in on our private conversations? I warned you both about doing that."

"No, Mama. I just heard him say something to you in the hallway."

She had tapped her right foot as she thought about what I had said, and I knew that meant something horrid could come pouring out of her mouth. Often, she said things that in and of themselves gave me nightmares. Of course, I would never accuse her of it. I didn't even mention it to Trevor. Despite how much we depended on each other, I always had a suspicion that he would or did tell Mama things about me, especially anything I had said about her.

"God made the mistake of providing men with an easy way to blame us when we criticize stupid things they do or complain about something or another that could very well be their fault," she said, and then she added, "But men are weaker."

"Weaker?" Now I was confused. "How can they be weaker? They can lift so much more and—"

"There are other ways to be weak. Enough! You know what to do when the cramps turn into the flow. Everything you need is in the bathroom. Just take care of it if I'm not right there at the time. Come to me to tell me about it as soon as it does and you've taken care of yourself. If Trevor wants to know what's wrong with you afterward, you can just tell him 'female things.' He'll understand, and that's all he needs to know for now, anyway."

"For now?"

"For now. Just be sure to tell me immediately," she said, and just as if there was a zipper between us, she closed our conversation and walked off.

If anything, after that talk, I was more frightened of getting my period than I had been. She had wanted to wring the neck of a girl in her classroom? Ghoulish, ugly things came to mind. How did this girl behave afterward, or didn't she return to her class? She must have been too embarrassed to show her face. I wanted to know more, and yet I didn't really want to know, because I was afraid of the details.

From the way she had described it every time, my body wouldn't just undergo physical changes. I would become a different person. It was as if some unexpected part of my character was waiting to be born, and I very well might not like it for a while every month. She made it seem as if Trevor wouldn't like it, either, and if I wasn't careful, it could change his entire opinion of me.

The whole thing was making me more than just a little angry.

Boys can have a worse reaction to what's happening to girls?

They're weaker?

As far as I could tell from anything she had said or taught and from anything I had read, nothing that happened to boys was as terrible. Maturity didn't bring them cramps. It only brought them pleasure.

It wasn't fair.

Lately especially, there were many times when Mama talked privately to Trevor, too. She'd pull him aside or take him into another room, where her voice would drop quickly into a whisper. From the way his face would redden when I asked him what they talked about, I knew it had something to do with sex. But when I turned twelve and she had already begun having private talks with me about the "changes," I suspected her talks with Trevor might be more about me than him, just from the way he would look at me afterward and how he would be alert to any moan or groan.

He would certainly not reveal anything to me about what she had told him about himself when I asked, even though I told him things about myself, like the sensitivity around my nipples or the cramps I'd feel bubbling as if something or someone inside me was starting to emerge.

He did say, "I hope it will be all right," which made my heart race. Hope? Why did he have to *hope*?

"Why shouldn't it be all right? Did Mama say something to you about me? Did she tell you to watch me and go to her if I don't look all right?"

He made a face as if I was asking the dumbest thing.

But that didn't keep me from being suspicious. More and more, I was feeling that Mama was closer to him than she was to me. He was only a year and four months older, and she was always telling me girls matured faster than boys, anyway. Something was different.

"You're sharing secrets," I accused. "Secrets about me?"

He gave me that quick headshake and walked away. If anything made me want to have a girlfriend my age, it was this. There was no one I could call, no one I could ask if she was going through anything similar. I only had Mama and the textbooks. How I wished I had made contact even with a female ghost.

Mama had been out of the classroom when it began today, but she was standing there in the hallway when I opened the bathroom door, so I was convinced Trevor had gone looking for her.

"Well?"

"It happened, Mama. Just the way you said it would, and I'm okay. I'm sure I did everything right."

She nodded, looking pleased.

"Of course you did. You're a woman now," she said. She

reached out and stroked my hair. "I'm proud of how you took care of yourself." She drew to attention. "Never again think of yourself as being a little girl. Come with me. I have a present for you to mark the occasion."

I followed her to her room. A present? For having my period? She went to the closet and took out a sheer, light pink nightgown and held it up.

"Time for some grown-up clothes, for a woman's clothes," she said, and handed it to me. "Don't wear this until your period is over. I'm going to buy you another one, a different color, and here," she said, going to a drawer to take out a box, "are the panties for you."

She put it on her bed and opened the box to take out a pair.

"What are they?" I asked breathlessly.

"Lace panties."

"They're so small."

"They're all you need," she said. "Your period will take a while to get used to, I'm sure. It did for me, too. But eventually, you'll awaken and suddenly realize that what has happened to you is more than just a biological event. Now you really are a woman. You'll see all sorts of changes, even in the way you look at things. It'll be as if your eyes grew different lenses, and your body will tingle in different places. Sometimes it will just happen, and you'll wonder why. The why is simple. You're maturing. In some countries, girls not much older than you are married with a family. We'll talk about all that later. For now . . . Oh. There are these matching slippers for your nightgown, too."

She piled everything in my arms.

"I'll tell you exactly when to start wearing this. Take it all to your room, put it away, and then return to your studies. I'll be right there. There's something I have to do first. I have a calendar I'm keeping for you."

"Calendar?"

"So you'll know what's going on in your body all the time. Don't suddenly become a dullard, Faith. You are a lot more intelligent than most girls your age, and you will be a lot more mature much sooner. Go on back to the classroom," she said, flicking her wrist.

"Shouldn't I rest or something?"

"Rest? No!" she exclaimed, her face twisting and wrinkling into her rage mask. "I told you. Don't treat it as an illness, Faith. Treat this as a grand opening, a beginning, even a rebirth. I expect you to think like a woman now, not a child, and a real woman thinks before she blurts some giggly stupidity."

I stared at her blazing, happy eyes. If I had ever had any doubt that she thought of herself as my mother, my real mother, this smothered it. And yet when her face softened, her look was so different, even a little crazed with joy. Because I had my first period? Her excitement actually frightened me, but I was sure not to reveal that. I was just . . . a little stunned.

"Didn't you hear anything I just said? Go back to work. And remember what I told you: be sure you don't moan and groan like some child looking for sympathy, especially from Trevor. Most men are quite uncomfortable with it. They like to pretend it doesn't happen."

"Why?"

"Why, why." She leaned into me. "There's blood, Faith. In some religions, the man won't dare touch you. They think of you as . . . as dirty."

"*Dirty*? Why do they think we're dirty?"

"Forget about that. Just think about how you and Trevor behave toward each other after this."

"What about Trevor? If I've become a woman, has he become a man? He is older, and he's getting some peach fuzz over his upper lip. You said so yourself."

She smiled, but it was a cold smile.

"That doesn't make him a man. I've told you. Men take longer to mature, even though their bodies might be racing along."

She nodded. "You'll know when he starts to act like a mature man. Don't worry about your missing it. You won't miss it. You have a woman's intuition now. You can depend a lot more on your feelings and your thoughts. Go on. Put everything away until I tell you it's time for you to wear these things."

"When is that?"

"Soon. I'll be getting you other womanly things, and after you start wearing them, I doubt anything or anyone will stop you."

I looked at what she had given me. Why did she think it was all so magical?

"Stop me from what?"

Her expression changed even more, seemed to calm. She smiled as lovingly as she had ever smiled at me. I felt guilty for being afraid, but was it her fault? Was she expecting too much of me too soon? What had I done really to bring such happiness to her? It was all biology, beyond my control. She had taught that to us herself.

"You'll know when the time comes. Trust in time. And don't act childish about it. Ever."

Perhaps she was right. I should be acting more mature. I should already be behaving like a woman. Was I ready for and capable of putting away childish thoughts for good? Wouldn't Trevor think I was stuck-up or something if I acted older?

After I had folded my new things into my drawer, practically hiding them, I reentered our classroom. Trevor looked up at me with curiosity spinning in his eyes. I had probably frightened him by the way I had leaped out of my seat and run. I thought he should know exactly what had happened, even though Mama had said I should just say "female things." Only a child would hide behind those code words, and whether I liked it or not, I was no longer a child.

"Well, as you know," I said, taking on Mama's teaching voice, "I had my first period. Blood from my uterus is dripping out of my vagina. There are all sorts of changes occurring in my body."

He shrugged, of course. He wouldn't be frightened, and he certainly wouldn't think it was funny. Mama would be very angry if he had reacted like that.

"Did you hear what I said?"

"I heard. So? You know about it more than I do," he said. "I wasn't paying that much attention to what happens to girls when Mama explained it more." He looked at the math problem he was solving.

"Mama warned you, though, didn't she? She told you what to look for in me. I know she did. When you had your secret little talks with her."

"Maybe she did. So? Big deal."

"You were like her little spy, watching everything I did."

"What? Oh, stop," he said, looking down at his book again. "It's no big deal."

What bothered me the most, I think, was that he wasn't embarrassed as much as he was indifferent. He didn't have to be like that all the time. I never really heard him cry. He smothered his sobs. And he didn't whine and moan for things the way I did, not even when it was about going with Big John. Sometimes he turned into that Trevor shrug. He had a way of shrugging in words, too.

"Then you know I'm going through my period," I said, again sounding as mature as I could.

He was trying hard not to hear me.

"It can last two to seven days," I added.

"I know," he said sharply. "Stop lecturing me. I read the same biology book, don't I?" Then he relaxed and looked more interested. "What difference does it make, anyway? Unless . . ."

"Unless what?"

"You're complaining about it. I heard Mama out there talking to you when you came out of the bathroom. Was she upset with you? Did you say or do something stupid?"

"No. I knew what I was doing. Actually, she was proud of the way I'm handling everything. She gave me presents."

"Presents?" He sat back. "What do you mean? What presents?"

"More feminine things, a nightgown, panties, slippers."

He smirked.

"So you see, there was nothing wrong with how I took care of myself," I said, maybe a little arrogantly. I gave him my best scrutinizing look. "I know why you're asking me that. You told her I ran to the bathroom, didn't you? You made it seem like I was panicking."

Without answering, he returned to his math textbook.

That was all he was going to say? He wasn't even going to deny it.

"Well, there was no panic, and I did everything I was supposed to do. Now that you know what's happening, I can give you even more details," I said. "You don't know everything from reading the biology text. Mama did give me that extra pamphlet and didn't give it to you. Unless, of course, it embarrasses you to hear about it."

He looked up, thought, and shook his head.

"Why would it embarrass me? There was enough about it in our biology textbook. I don't need to know much more or read any pamphlets."

I took a step back. *Why would you be embarrassed?* I thought but didn't say. *It's in the textbook? Because this is happening to us*, I wanted to say. *It's not some pages in one of our textbooks about women in general. It's about me.*

Why was he so afraid of making it personal?

Mama was right about what to expect from him, I decided. Boys could be weaker. Sometimes I thought he was more like Mama, wishing we'd be children forever. Everything was less complicated when you were a child, especially your feelings. Mama had told us more than once that children could be more selfish, caring only about their own happiness, and what made Trevor and me so special was that for us that wasn't true. If he was unhappy, I was unhappy, and vice versa. But although I thought she was right, I was not always completely sure when Trevor was really pleased these days.

I suddenly realized that was why Mama said boys were weaker. They were afraid of their feelings and far more afraid of showing them. I had no way of knowing, of course. I hadn't been around any other boy for years, really, and those were infants and some six- and seven-year-olds at the Wexlers' foster home, but I was convinced Trevor was extra shy about everything, especially himself and me. Of course, he wasn't always like that.

When we were first brought here, Mama had us take baths together. Nanny Too would never do that. Mama acted as if there was nothing unusual about it. I remember Big John looked in on us in the tub and said something that made Mama shout, "That's disgusting!" She chased him away, but I heard him laughing in the hallway.

As we grew older, I thought more about the differences between Trevor and me, not that I wasn't always aware of them. Trevor was so busy with his toy boat that he missed it all, missed my reactions. When Mama made him stand up to wash him, his penis dangled in front of me, and I had a new fascination with it. I wanted to touch it and tried to find awkward little ways to accidentally do so. He was totally oblivious. He could just as well have been alone.

One time when Trevor and I took a bath together, I glanced at Mama, who was staring at me as she washed Trevor. There was a look in her eye that stirred something inside me that I really hadn't felt as intently as I did then. She knew my thoughts, and that embarrassed me. I felt a wave of heat rise up my neck and into my face, warmer than the bathwater.

Trevor sat, and she urged me to stand. I kept my eyes on Trevor, but he was still far more interested in his toy boat than in my vagina. I thought Mama was a little rougher on me than she had been on Trevor. When I moaned, Trevor looked up and watched Mama scrub.

"This is how you will take care of yourselves when you're a little older. Both of you make sure the other does it right."

I looked at her. How long were we going to take baths together, and when we didn't, were we supposed to watch each other wash and go running to her if either he or I didn't do it correctly? Once I heard Mama and Big John in the shower together laughing. I wanted to go peek in, but I was too frightened. I had seen Big John in his underwear a few times, and once I saw his naked rear, but I hurried away before he could see me watching him.

Trevor had no interest in seeing either of our parents nude. He paid attention in class when Mama explained how animals and insects create babies, and without my help, he did well on the tests she gave us. But I could see he was two inches away from boredom most of the time. What he'd rather do was rush outside and pretend to be someone he had seen on television. I'd stand off to the side most of the time and watch him drift in and out of his fantasies, fantasies he could create and perform with or without me.

Even before all this was happening to me, I was constantly watching for him to stop being a little boy. Maybe he would be like someone who had been tapped on the shoulder, surprised, and turn to look at me differently. When I recall those moments now, I think I was waiting for him to think about how other animals concentrated on creating more of themselves and then see his face, especially his eyes, have a new light that was focused on me. From what we had both read and understood when Mama explained them, there were small things happening within us both that would change us.

Trevor did become more self-conscious. Something simple like his hesitating to zip down his fly in front of me and take a pee in the forest would occur, perhaps barely noticeable at first. But at least he was thinking about it, which naturally made me wonder if he was thinking more about me, too.

I was always eager to show him I was sensitive to anything he did and said, especially any changes in him. But I was also quite aware of saying or doing something that would embarrass him. Although I would never admit to speaking in codes, that was what I was doing. I was hoping he would soon have the awareness to realize it all himself. Sometimes I told him something like, "Your eyes are bluer," or "You look taller, and you have more muscles." I could have said "The sky is blue," for all that mattered. Finally, I got braver and said, "I heard you moaning last night. In your sleep, I think."

"Was I?"

"Yes."

He simply shrugged like it wasn't important.

"Maybe you were hearing yourself."

"I was not. Why would I?"

Trevor rarely mentioned anything about me physically except to say I was too weak to lift this or that. He seemed oblivious to the changes that were occurring in my body, happening faster and faster now, just like Big John had said. I didn't need Trevor to confirm it, but I couldn't help wishing he would. The truth was that I was angry at him for being so oblivious.

I took more time looking at myself after a shower or a bath. I was almost five foot four, and my breasts were growing more and more each day. It was as if the older me was already inside me and finding little ways to emerge, pulling the child I was deeper and deeper into me until I'd wake up and find I could see that child only in photographs.

My hair felt thicker, too. Up to now, I normally had been so unconscious of my appearance. Maybe that had been part of being a child, being unaware of how you were maturing or unconcerned about it. I didn't think hard about being pretty or grown-up. But now that I was looking at myself more in the mirror, I realized so many things were changing on my body, demanding I pay more attention. My thighs were thicker, and my rear had a curve in it that seemed to have developed overnight. I actually looked at myself in the mirror and asked my image, "Are you getting to be pretty?"

And then, for the first time, really, I wondered if my real mother was pretty. Didn't children start to look more like one of their parents as they grew? Would I ever find her, see her even without her knowing? Would she come looking for me, perhaps awakening one day and feeling the terrible guilt and sin Mama said she was enduring? Or maybe she was dead and in hell, what Mama had described as the destiny for all our parents. If Mama even suspected I had these thoughts about my mother now, she would go into a rage. I tried to drive them from my mind.

However, the more I saw the changes in myself, the more I felt annoyed with Trevor for not saying anything about me, even when I subtly, as subtly as I could, pointed them out. One day, I even said, "I wonder when Mama will think I need a bra."

We were too old to take baths together, but if one of us was in the tub, the other might very well come in to get something or wash up at the sink and brush his or her teeth. When I did it lately, most of the time not deliberately, he would turn his back on me. I thought if he was finally getting embarrassed at seeing me, then surely he was thinking of me in a different way. But if he was, he didn't want me thinking about it. And he especially shied away from my talking about it.

But how could I not?

He looked at me when I mentioned a bra, and for a moment my breath caught. He was going to say something, maybe about how mature I was looking or how pretty. I waited, only he didn't. Instead, he gave me his Trevor shrug and then added, "Whenever. You know Mama. One day, it will just be there."

I felt a splash of rage and quickly looked away.

However, after that, whether I was imagining it or not, he did come into the bathroom as soon as I got into the tub. He would glance at me, and just in the way that he quickly turned his eyes to something else, I felt he was feeling different. What made him want to hide it so much? Did he think I would make fun of him or complain to Mama or Big John about it?

Recently, when he came in, I deliberately closed my eyes and lay back, fully exposing myself. I didn't hear him turn on the faucet or open a cabinet. Moments later, he left without doing anything. Was I teasing him or myself?

He had yet to walk in on me again since then. I did catch him staring at me more often, but when I looked back at him, he turned away or continued to do whatever it was he was doing. And in bed, he turned on his left side as soon as he could. He was never as dramatic about ignoring me. He was surely suffering by stifling his feelings. At least, I hoped he was.

All this made me wish even harder that we were allowed to go to a real school. I wanted to look at other girls my age; I wanted to compare myself. And I wanted to see how other boys looked at me.

"Don't you wish that you could meet and be with other girls sometimes?" I asked him recently.

"Why?"

"You know why," I said. "I see the way you look at pictures of beautiful women in Big John's magazines. You dream about them."

"Do not," he said, blushed a little, and avoided me as much as he could that day. I felt a mixture of satisfaction and guilt, like some bee that just had to sting him. I hoped I wasn't a honeybee, because they die after they sting, but on the other hand, I would hate to be a hornet or wasp. Mama spent so much time teaching us about insects, animals, and birds that it wasn't hard envisioning ourselves just like one or more of them.

In fact, thinking about this made me long to be around other girls and boys my age even more. Except for some of the silly teenagers I saw on television occasionally, I had no one to look up to, to model myself after or dream of becoming like. Why didn't Mama realize that we needed to be around other children our age, especially now? Maybe she was right, and most of them would teach us nothing but bad habits and ideas, but surely there were those we could or should strive to be like. Didn't competition make you stronger? It was hard, if not impossible, to run faster than someone you could only imagine beside you.

Minutes after I had returned from putting my new things in the bedroom and Trevor and I had spoken, Mama came into the classroom and looked at us, more suspiciously at me.

"What did you talk about just now?" she asked. Was she going to be angry because I had said more than "female things"?

"I told him what happened and explained it so he would realize it's more than a textbook lesson," I added pointedly. Maybe it was my period, but I felt like my emotions could explode. I was actually feeling more like crying, the one thing I knew Mama would hate to see. My throat ached with effort to swallow back my feelings.

She stared at me, probably easily reading my thoughts, just as Trevor believed she could. I held my breath. Would she accuse me of doing precisely what she had warned against, frightening Trevor? She might take back all her presents.

But she totally surprised me. She smiled.

"That's the way I want you two to always be, honest about everything, especially yourselves. Now you know Faith is a woman, Trevor. Everything I've been teaching you both will become more vivid. That is not bad. I simply want everything to happen at the right time and in the right way. This is the age and the time you could be wonderful or dangerous to each other."

She thought a moment, losing herself in whatever she was thinking. I looked at Trevor to see if what she was saying bothered him at all. He looked as indifferent as ever. I continually wondered why Trevor was pretending none of this mattered. It mattered to me almost more than anything. Despite what Mama had told me, it didn't seem like he was that far behind me when it came to our maturing, at least physically. Trevor had become so much taller this year. I had, too, but he seemed to be growing faster. He was almost five feet seven inches. We knew every inch we grew, because Mama would measure us before she went out to buy us clothes. She even had a shoe store foot-measuring device. When I asked her why she didn't just take us so we could try them on, she said it was faster and more efficient for her to just do it this way.

"And people jabber nonsense wasting your time. If they saw you, they would unload so many stored-up thoughts about their own youth that your heads would spin. Also, you might look at things you don't need and moan for them. That's what children of bad parents do, and then the bad parents decide to spend the money, waste the money, to shut their children's mouths. I saw it so many times when I was a teacher. I saw all the things those kids had when they came to my class, expensive watches, clothes, and jewelry that really were meant for adults. It was sickening."

Why was that sickening? I wondered but didn't ask. What was wrong with having pretty and expensive things as long as you could take care of them properly? Almost anything either Trevor or I had was in some way connected to our education or what Big John brought back for us from one of his trips. Sometimes Mama would forbid him to give something to us. It was either "too old" for us or in some way "improper." She was especially critical of anything that in her mind belonged with someone much younger. Big John would protest to no avail. If he pointed out that it said on the box that it was for children our age, she would tell him, "Yes, but thanks to how they are being brought up and taught, they are way beyond that age."

He'd give up and throw it back into his truck cab. Trevor would be upset, but he kept it to himself as always. He knew better than I did that nothing would anger Mama more than either of us whining for something. We swallowed unhappiness as easily as we swallowed milk.

Anyway, Trevor found ways to create his favorite toys for himself from things he could find around the house or in the woods, like a sword, and then imagine he was on a pirate ship. He wanted me to pretend and be in his action scenes, but I thought it was boring and usually walked off to find something interesting for science class or just something pretty in nature that I could wear on my wrist, on my dress, or in my hair. Sometimes Mama would rip it off, saying that I was being too absorbed in my own appearance for someone my age. So in some ways we were too young, and in others we were too old or, in my case, in danger of becoming conceited.

Trevor didn't feel sorry for me. *Pretty* wasn't in his vocabulary yet, anyway. Even the word seemed hard for him to say. If I said something was pretty or showed him a pretty dress or model in a magazine Big John had been reading, he would nod. The most he would say was "That's nice" or "She's okay."

"Not beautiful?"

"I guess," he'd say.

Would he ever say I was? No matter how many times I suggested he make some comment?

"Our time and our money should be important to you as well as me, Faith," Mama had said when I longed for something special, something to make me prettier, just like the spoiled girls in her classroom. "Children who want those things are selfish. Every member of the family has to look out for the family. If I waste any time and money, it's not good for the family, and you want only what's good for the family, too, right?" She looked at Trevor, who was always the first to agree with her. "Trevor?"

He nodded quickly, and she turned back to me.

"Yes, Mama," I said, even though one of my dreams was to go to a big department store and see all the new clothes and shoes myself.

She smiled, but I wondered if she could see how unhappy I was about it. Trevor was right, I decided. She saw practically everything either of us was thinking. Now, often, that frightened me, and I would deliberately try to think of something else when she was near us. Like counting the nail heads I could see in a nearby wall or rattling off algebra equations.

Despite Mama's assurances and Trevor's obedience and acceptance of everything Mama said about us, I had the ever-growing nagging feeling that everything wasn't all right. We weren't as perfect as Mama claimed. Maybe it would come out of the dark, or maybe it would come out of us, something terrible, something neither of us could imagine.

five

"Actually, this is a perfect time to move to your science homework," Mama said, nodding to herself like she always did when she was sure about something. "We were studying beetles. All beetles reproduce sexually the way mammals do. The offspring are created by the joining of sperm from the father and eggs from the mother. You might see this . . . when a male locates a female, he will usually start to court the female in a very specific way. He quickly strokes his antennae and his front pair of legs on the female's back while crawling on top of her."

"So, when their beetle babies are born, do they become a family?" I asked. "I mean . . . the father . . ."

"Ha!" she said.

Trevor smiled, but I was a little frightened by her reaction.

She had lifted and then waved her arms as if she was going to fly off. "No. The male, like most species, even humans, leaves the female and does not give any help in raising the offspring. Men run around planting children like Johnny Appleseed planted apple trees. He didn't wait around to watch them grow, did he?

"Trevor," she said, gazing at him lovingly, "will never be that sort of male."

I looked at him. How could she tell? And why even talk about that now?

"Anyway, children in public school seventh, eighth, or even ninth grade wouldn't ever be taught about all this the way I'm teaching you," she said. "Go on outside, see what you can find; see what you can learn on your own. It's the beetles' time to reproduce. Bring a male and a female back."

"What?" Trevor asked. "You mean, while they're reproducing?"

"Exactly. Go! Do as I ask," she commanded.

Trevor rose quickly and scooped up a petri dish. We started out.

"We'll have to hurry," he said. I grimaced. I wasn't that comfortable rushing. "Those clouds are looking like rain." He nodded to the sky as soon as we stepped out of the house.

"You know when Mama says she's happy we're being honest with each other, she means you should be, too?"

"So?" he said, pausing at the start of the woods.

"You never tell me about the things she told you privately about yourself, but I tell you what she tells me privately, and I tell you what's happening to me."

He stared, unmoving. "I tell you stuff."

"Stuff. You had what's called an orgasm last night, didn't you?"

His face reddened.

"I heard your moaning."

He turned to keep walking into the woods.

"Honesty," I called after him. "We have to be honest with each other. Mama just said so."

"It just happened," he said, pausing. "I didn't do anything."

"We read about that," I reminded him. "How you could. I think you did!"

He kept walking until he found a dead tree. I walked past him.

"Well?"

"You're supposed to help with the beetles," he said, instead of answering.

"I need to walk a little and think."

"About what?"

"Everything," I said, surprisingly angrily. I didn't know myself why I was growing into a rage.

He grunted, and I began my usual circle. A few minutes later, I heard the sound of someone chopping wood. It echoed again and again, faster and more than we had ever heard it before. It was coming from our neighbor's property. I looked at Trevor.

There was something about his expression that told me he was more curious than ever about the noise coming from just beyond the stone wall. We didn't have to say a word to each other. He saw my agreement in my eyes, and he rose. We walked through the forest toward the sound. It wasn't until we drew closer that we realized there were two people splitting logs on the other side of the wall.

Trevor moved to our right where we could see through the bushes on the other side and went to the wall. I stepped up beside him. There was a boy who didn't look much older than Trevor striking at a log with our neighbor, Mr. Longstreet. They seemed to work perfectly together. When one split a log, the other put his up instantly and struck it. Mr. Longstreet split his with one blow. The boy had to hit his twice sometimes. They wore matching dark blue coveralls with similar flannel shirts and dark brown shoe boots.

Mr. Longstreet paused to wipe his face, and the young man stopped, picked up a jug of water, and took a long drink. When he did, he turned slightly and saw us.

Trevor pulled back as if a snake had struck, but I kept looking. I saw him smile. He looked to be about Trevor's height but wider in the shoulders, with hair a shade darker than hay and almost as long as mine. He wiped some strands away from his eyes and mumbled something that caused Mr. Longstreet to look our way, too. Almost immediately, he started to gesture for us to come over. Trevor had leaned forward and could see him, too.

I started to climb over. Trevor seized my left leg.

"What?"

"We have to ask Mama first," he said.

I looked at Mr. Longstreet and the boy, who was smiling and turned in such a way that his face seemed to glow in the sunlight.

"No. It's okay," I said. I pointed to the left. He looked.

Becky and Moses were lying side by side, not more than ten feet from them.

"And you know how cautious they are. You told me."

"We still should ask Mama first."

"I'm already over the wall, Trevor," I said, pulling my leg out of his grip. "I'm tired of asking Mama's permission for everything. Next, we'll be asking her when to breathe."

"Faith!"

I didn't look back and walked toward Mr. Longstreet and the boy. Both kept smiling. Maybe Trevor had run back to tell Mama, I thought, and took a deep breath. I would be in great trouble, but she did tell me I was a woman now. I could decide more things myself, couldn't I?

"Well, howdy do?" Mr. Longstreet said as I drew closer. He leaned on his log splitter. His partially bald head had curly thin ember-gray hair on the sides. He was clean-shaven, and his bright greenish-brown eyes helped him look quite spry. Although nowhere near as tall and wide in the shoulders as our Big John, he was clearly not the dotty, sad old man Mama had implied he was, an elderly sort who sat by his windows longing for friends and family. I remembered almost crying when she had described him.

The man I now saw had rosy Santa Claus cheeks. His face was just a bit flushed from the work, but the lines in it were remarkably shallow. In some ways, Big John's face looked more worn and aged. As we drew closer, Mr. Longstreet's eyes held on to that youthful glint. The warmth in his welcoming smile eased the tension that had me holding my breath.

I looked back. Trevor had reluctantly followed, remaining at least six feet behind me.

"Hi," I said. My heart was thumping as I envisioned Mama coming after us, screaming, "Don't you dare talk to my children!" I actually glanced back in anticipation. No matter where we were, in the house or outside it, I always imagined Mama was watching us and aware of what we were doing.

Trevor edged closer, looking more worried. His eyes were ablaze with fear.

"You're the Eden kids," Mr. Longstreet said. "You two are sprouting like beans. Last time I saw you, you were both knee-high to a grasshopper. 'Bout time we said hello. This is my grandson, Lance. He's visiting for the summer."

Trevor stepped up beside me.

"Hi," Lance said.

I had thought no one but Trevor could light up not only his own face but the faces of everyone around him when he smiled. Although I had obviously seen few people in my life compared to most girls my age, I had never seen violet eyes. The way the light caught them, Lance's were somewhere from a pale silver to a light purple, really.

For a moment, I was hypnotized.

I realized I was staring, which only widened Lance's smile.

Although he didn't look that much older than either of us, everything childish had slipped out of his face. There was tightness in his cheeks and chin that made him handsome but also added a firm, mature look. Trevor could look as mature sometimes, but maybe because we were so close, I still saw his innocent wonder and thought of ourselves as children, even now, even after my period and the lines of sexual development each of us had crossed. From what I had seen on television and read, I knew that teenagers despised being thought too young for this or for that. Although he didn't complain, I knew Trevor hated being treated like a little boy of late. Lance didn't look like he would be thought too young for anything.

There was a lively twinkle in Lance's eyes. He wasn't looking at Trevor at all, and the feeling that it stirred in me was something I hadn't felt as much from any sneaky look Trevor had taken at me, even when I stepped out of the tub or the shower lately and he was gazing through the open door. I crossed my arms over my breasts, feeling a little naked before him.

"Hi," I said, so softly that I wasn't sure I had said it. Maybe I had only thought it.

Trevor said nothing.

Lance's grip on the ax emphasized the muscle in his forearm as he lifted it to point to the woods. I thought he was close to six feet tall. His hair was as long as that of some of the teenage boys I saw on television. I knew Mama didn't approve of the style. She kept Trevor's short.

"It's really like raw nature here," Lance said. "I'm sure I saw a bobcat the other day come out of the woods right there, cross the field, and disappear in the woods behind the house. At least, that's what my grandfather said it was."

"It was. They're out here often," Mr. Longstreet said. "They have no interest in you as long as you don't bother them."

"So you guys live on the other side of the woods?" Lance asked. "Do you feel safe walking through it? How far away are you? Any bad snakes? Have you seen bobcats, too?"

He asked his questions quickly, as if he thought we might bolt and run home. Trevor probably was giving him that feeling. I didn't have to look at him to feel how anxious and uptight he was.

"Lance is from New York. Manhattan," Mr. Longstreet said, because both of us were still staring and silent. "He's only seen trees in Central Park. He keeps looking for Tarzan."

"Oh, c'mon, Grandpa," Lance said. He did look a little embarrassed.

Mr. Longstreet laughed.

"We're not afraid of walking in the woods," Trevor said, his voice tight. He sounded angry, annoyed that anyone would think he was fearful of our woods. He surprised me by taking my hand and giving me just a slight tug to get me a little closer to him. "Yeah, there could be a rattlesnake or a bear," he continued, his voice very different. I glanced at him. He looked like he was enjoying putting some fear into Lance.

"Bear? You never mentioned a bear, Grandpa."

"Well, the likelihood of seeing a bear—"

"One killed my parents' dog years ago," Trevor said, practically shouting.

"Yeah?" Lance's eyes widened.

"Sorry to say, that dog wasn't the brightest," Mr. Longstreet said. "He was over here quite a bit. He probably terrified some bear's cubs, and mama bears don't take too kindly to even a suggested threat to their young."

"Those your cats?" Lance asked, nodding at Becky and Moses, who were still just lying there watching us with what I thought was boredom.

"They're not bobcats," Trevor said, with a sharp, sly smile.

"Yes, they're our cats," I said quickly. "They live outside most of the time."

Lance tilted his head a bit. "So they're safe wandering through the woods? Bears don't scare them?"

"They're very careful," I said. "But very curious, as are most cats, usually. Is this your first time here, visiting your grandfather?" I asked. I knew I sounded more critical and amazed than curious.

Lance looked at his grandfather to answer for him. My question had hit the bull's-eye of a sensitive subject.

"Lance's parents just began their divorce proceedings. His mother decided he needed fresh air. People in the city need to take turns breathing."

Lance laughed. "I was here when I was very little," he said. "What grades you guys in?"

I was still thinking about divorce. That was just what Mama told us about families today.

"We'd be in tenth and eleventh," I said, realizing the silence. Trevor wasn't going to answer. "Trevor would be in eleventh."

"What's that mean, 'would be'? You quit school?"

"No. Our mother is our teacher," Trevor said.

Lance looked at him and then nodded. "So you're home-schooled, huh?"

"Yes," I said. "Our mother was a teacher in the public grade school. We're on a twelfth-grade reading level."

"Wow. I'm in eleventh grade and on an eighth-grade reading level," he joked.

His grandfather poked him.

"He's a straight-A student. Probably graduate early," Mr. Longstreet said.

"Not too early. I don't like getting up with the sun."

"He's getting used to that," Mr. Longstreet said.

Lance nodded. "I think my grandfather is part rooster." He looked around again. "How deep are these woods?"

"They go a few miles on the west side," Trevor said, sounding knowledgeable, even though we had never walked through the woods that far. "Supposedly, there's a way to the lake if you keep going."

"Oh, there is that," Mr. Longstreet said. "Been on it in my younger days. Your dad should take you hiking. When he's home, that is. Truck drivers need walking. Their dad drives a semi. What, an eighteen-wheeler?"

"Yes," Trevor said. "He's driving to North Carolina at the moment," he said proudly.

"Well, you tell your mother if she ever needs anything while he's away, I'm here," Mr. Longstreet said.

"My mother doesn't need anything," Trevor said. He looked up at the gathering clouds. "Let's go, Faith. It's going to rain, and we got things to do."

"That's your name? Faith?" Lance asked.

"Uh-huh," I said, resisting Trevor's tug.

"I believe in you," he said, smiling.

Mr. Longstreet laughed.

"What?" I said.

"You know, like you have faith."

I just stared at him with what I knew was a soft smile. I liked the way his smile settled around his eyes. My heart wasn't just thumping; it was racing as if I had just run a few miles.

"Don't tease," Mr. Longstreet told him.

Trevor tugged me harder, almost knocking me off my feet. "C'mon."

He let go when I started after him. I followed him to the wall but looked back. Lance watched us for a few moments, still smiling at me, and then started splitting wood with his grandfather again.

"Do you think he's nice?" I asked Trevor as soon as we crawled over the stone wall.

"Who? Mr. Longstreet?"

"Yeah, and Lance?"

"I don't know. Mr. Longstreet's okay, I guess, but you heard him. Lance's a city kid."

"What's that mean?"

"I don't know." He walked faster and then paused. "Don't tell Mama we were over there and met him."

"Why not?"

"He's a *city kid*," he said a little louder.

"He might be fun. I'd like to hear about the schools in the city. New York City looks so big in the pictures of it. Don't you think you'd like to go there someday?"

Trevor didn't reply; he kept walking with his head down.

I looked back.

"Becky and Moses are coming home," I said.

Trevor glanced at them. "They know rain's coming. They can sense it better than we can."

"You know, you split wood better than he does. I saw some of the pieces looked like less than half a log, and you know how particular Big John can be about it. Mama, too."

"It's probably his first time," Trevor said, with a little more charity than I had anticipated. He paused. "Maybe his grandfather didn't teach him right. Let's go back to that tree stump. I think there were beetles reproducing."

Beetles reproducing, I thought. How boring that suddenly seemed to be.

I followed him, but while he looked, I kept gazing back at the stone wall.

"Mama's not going to like him just coming over here," Trevor said, without turning or looking up at me. There was that "uncanniness" again. He could sense what I was doing and what I was wishing. He didn't have to look.

"That's why we should tell her we met him and Mr. Longstreet. Maybe she would invite them to dinner. She told us he used to come to dinner when her parents were alive."

Trevor looked up this time, the right corner of his mouth tucked into his cheek.

"You really expect Mama would invite them?"

"I just thought maybe," I said. "Her parents did have Mr. Longstreet over for dinner. Maybe she'll feel sorry for Lance because his parents are divorcing."

He didn't respond.

He scraped the beetles into the petri dish and stood up, glancing back toward the stone wall.

"That was then, when her parents invited Mr. Longstreet to dinner; this is now. I'm not going to be the one to ask her," he said. "And besides, how are we going to have known Lance's parents are divorcing? She'd figure out we were there for a while. Better leave it be."

He started for the house.

"It's just being polite, isn't it?" I said.

He didn't even shrug.

"I mean, Mr. Longstreet offered to help her in any way he could. It's not easy for him suddenly having his grandson to cheer up."

"This is exactly why she doesn't want us, especially you, attending public school," he said, pausing and looking at me.

"What? Why?"

"First boy you see . . ." he said, and walked faster toward the house.

First boy I see? Maybe he'd noticed how Lance had been looking at me. Could he see how excited I was? It really bothered him, I thought. Was he jealous?

"What does that mean? First boy I see?"

I knew what it meant, but I couldn't help playing dumb, maybe because I didn't like him reading my thoughts and feelings the way we both now thought Mama could.

"Figure it out. You're smarter than I am, even though I'm more than a year older. Mama's always saying so."

"She's just trying to get you to work harder."

He grunted.

Clouds were sliding in quickly from the west, some of them looking bruised and stained. A summer thunderstorm was marching toward us. I could feel the breeze get stronger. Leaves began to tremble. Trevor went up the side steps quickly and, without looking back, entered the house, slamming the door closed behind him. The snap seemed to echo all around me.

Was Trevor right about me? Was that it? I wondered. The first boy I saw was attractive to me, or was there something special about him? How did you know, especially if the only boy you really knew was your adopted brother?

I heard thunder rolling over the mountains and saw the lightning stinging trees, which were fortunately too damp to catch on fire. Moses and Becky hurried toward the rear of the house, barely glancing my way. They had places to hide under the foundation if Mama didn't see them and open the door. I embraced myself and walked with my head down. I could hear the trees in the forest behind me swaying harder. Tiny branches and dust began to dance. Birds seemingly burst out of nowhere to seek their hiding places. Everything that lived shuddered and hovered under or behind something. I wondered if every living thing out there thought God was angry at them or if it was just capricious Nature having some fun.

When I reached the top of the stairway, the door opened. Trevor was standing there.

"Why are you diddle-daddling? The electricity's just gone off," he said. "Mama is lighting candles, because it's going to get pretty dark in a few minutes with those clouds sweeping in over us. She wants you to help."

"Not you?"

He didn't answer. He turned and headed for the stairway to put his beetles under the microscope for later. I stood there for a moment, thinking. *Trevor really is suffering jealousy, the sort of jealousy that is a doorway to anger. He doesn't want me even thinking about Lance. He wants me in the house, the door shut, and every moment of our visit to be forgotten, forever.* I didn't know whether I should be happy or upset that he was so possessive.

I turned and looked back at the woods and the rain now falling on a slant as the wind began to play havoc with the downpour. Lance and his grandfather surely had to rush into their house. Probably they were lighting candles, too. It occurred to me that until this moment, I really never thought much about anyone else besides Trevor, Mama, Big John, and me. Maybe I thought about a boy or a girl I had seen on television, but all that was in the realm of fantasy and lasted for a dream or two. This was real.

I decided I was happier than I expected about Trevor being jealous. It was as if when I had gone over that stone wall, I had stepped into my maturity, my being more of a young woman, and Trevor knew it, too. Just that realization made me tingle with excitement. I was sure a chick bursting out of a cracked egg had a similar feeling. It was as if we could be born more than once, maybe even more than twice, just as Mama had suggested.

"Put this in the living room," Mama said when I walked into the kitchen. She handed me one of our kerosene lamps. We had six of them made of brass, each over fifty years old. "Be sure it's put on a stable place."

I took it and hurried to the living room. Trevor had returned and was setting one in the downstairs powder room. Mama put one in the kitchen and then brought another to the living room.

"We won't put any upstairs," she said. "I like keeping my eye on them. My great-aunt Mary Dowd set her house on fire in a rainstorm. Even though the house was soaked, it still went up like a stack of hay."

"What happened to her, Mama?" I asked. She had never even mentioned a great-aunt Mary Dowd, but she did seem to have a relative to illustrate any story or warning.

"She went up with it," she said. "She was living alone at eighty-nine. A stubborn woman. My father took care of her as best he could, doing all that had to be done to maintain her house. He tried to get her to move in here, but she'd never slept in a bed other than her own for over sixty years. Her husband died young," she continued, and flopped onto Big John's chair.

"How did he die?" I asked.

"Unexpected heart attack while he was shoveling snow off their front walk. Storms like this could give you heart failure," she said, gazing at the rain pounding the window. It sounded like the sky was falling all around us, rapping on the roof.

Whenever anything threatened us, like a rain that resembled a hurricane or a tornado-like wind, and we hovered in the living room, Mama clung to anything that had anything to do with Big John. She never said it, but I sensed it gave her a feeling of safety and security. We had even seen her put on one of his sweaters or a jacket. It was like he was here, protecting us. After a while, I felt that way, too, and was happy she had done it.

A crack of thunder rattled the windows. The rain had begun as a heavy downpour and now was continuing even harder than I could ever remember. Trevor came in and quickly lowered himself to the floor near her.

I had started to approach the window to look out when she shouted.

"Get away from there! Lightning can come through the window."

Could it? I wondered, and quickly backed up to the sofa. When I looked back at the window, it looked like the rain had turned to hail and then rain again in a matter of seconds. Even so, the drops were as heavy as hail, tapping so hard on the glass that I thought it might shatter.

"How long will the electricity be out?" I asked, not disguising my fear.

"Who knows? Lucky I never went for that electric stove your father wanted. I can still warm up our dinner. He's always looking to replace things around here. Sometimes the old is better than the new. So," she said, obviously wanting us to think of something else, "how did you do with the beetles?"

"Got good ones, Mama," Trevor said. "Reproducing, just like you told us. I put them in the classroom by the microscope."

"Yeah, well, you were out there long enough," she said. "You went pretty deep in?" she asked suspiciously. Had she been watching us through the living-room windows after all? Did she know we went to the neighbor's house?

Trevor looked at me. He would never lie to Mama, not Trevor. Mama's comment about the world being harder for people who couldn't lie suddenly flashed in my memory.

"We walked up to the wall," I said. "Because we heard more wood being chopped than usual and wanted to see what was happening."

That was the truth, just not all of it.

The lanterns flickered, bouncing the light off her face, especially the sudden new darkness in her eyes. It was as if her skull was illuminated for a split second and then again and again. We could hear the rain pounding the roof, sounding, as Mama often said, like "devils with small hammers."

"And?" Mama asked after a long, silent moment.

"We saw Mr. Longstreet," I said. I wondered if I could stop there and get away with a half-truth by not mentioning our climbing over the wall and meeting his grandson Lance. Trevor was staring at me. He looked like he was enjoying the tension I was feeling. *He can be such a little imp*, I thought.

There was another flash of lightning and then another. In the flickering light, Trevor was smiling, or was it just the light's effect?

Mama stared, waiting. I had the clear, cold feeling that she already knew the rest. Had Trevor told her everything while I had taken longer to get into the house? Had he rushed right to her and confessed?

"There was someone else chopping wood besides Mr. Longstreet," I said.

"So? Why was that your business?"

"Mr. Longstreet beckoned for us to come to say hello."

She looked at Trevor. "Did you?"

"Yes," he said immediately.

"It was his grandson," I said. "He wanted us to meet him. He's in the eleventh grade."

Thunder rolled so hard over our heads that we all anticipated the roof caving in. I folded my legs and sat on the floor, leaning against the sofa. I couldn't recall a harder, faster rain. I was afraid to look out again. The rain and thunder were all that broke the heavy silence among us.

"Damn it!" Mama suddenly cried. I had thought she was talking about Lance and Mr. Longstreet, but she leaped to her feet. "It's leaking in the pantry again. Don't you hear it? It's far worse."

She picked up the lantern she had brought into the room and hurried out.

"Did you tell her before I came into the house, tell her about meeting Mr. Longstreet's grandson?" I asked Trevor.

"Nope," he said, standing. "But you could see she knew something."

"How?"

"Better see what's happening in the pantry," he said, and started for it.

I rose and walked slowly, thinking so hard I almost walked into Big John's chair. I could hear her screaming to Trevor to get a bucket, and then I hurried to the pantry.

"I told your father we needed that fixed. He kept putting it off. There's some leak by the gutter on this side of the roof. The water is running straight down, making the hole wider and wider. It's going to get worse."

Trevor returned with the bucket.

"Go get the mop out of the closet," she told me.

It was raining harder than I had ever seen it or heard it, coming down in torrents, a regular full-bore summer rainstorm, hitting the roof so hard those imaginary small hammers were more like regular-size ones. By the time I returned, which was in only seconds, there was a big puddle on the floor and water streaming down over food shelves. Mama began pulling off boxes and cans of food and just tossing them wildly out onto the kitchen floor, nearly hitting both of us. I knelt down, went around her, and started to take things off shelves, too. Trevor joined me, and we were all emptying the pantry into the kitchen. The water cascaded over the shelves. Our hands were soaked.

"This is no good," Mama said. "We'll soon be swimming in here, and it's going to spread to the kitchen!"

We followed her out. She started stuffing old towels and rags into a garbage bag.

"What are you doing, Mama?" Trevor asked her.

"I have to get it plugged," she said, and went to the back door. As soon as she opened it, Moses and Becky, soaked and looking more like big rats, charged in.

"Where are you going, Mama?" I screamed.

Trevor and I went to the door. She had already gone around the corner of the house. We looked at each other and charged out to follow her, protecting our eyes with our hands opened on our foreheads over our brows. Our clothes were instantly soaked, as were Mama's.

She struggled to lift a ladder that was lying beside the garage. Trevor rushed ahead to help her.

"What are you going to do?" I shouted. "Are you going up on the roof? You could fall, Mama."

She didn't answer. It was raining so hard that it was difficult to keep my eyes open if I took my hands off my forehead. With Trevor's help, she guided the ladder against the house and seized the garbage bag.

"Maybe I can do it, Mama," Trevor said.

She didn't look back. She continued to climb up the ladder. As difficult as it was to believe, the rain was growing even more intense. It was almost impossible to look up at her. We were all soaked through and through. My teeth began to chatter. Trevor started up the ladder, too, but she turned and shouted down at him.

"No! Just hold the ladder steady," she said, and took another step.

Trevor stepped down, and I shot forward to hold it on the other side, but before he and I could steady the ladder, it shook a little too much, and Mama slipped on a wet rung. Because she was holding the garbage bag in her right hand, she could only grab the ladder with her left.

"Mama!" I screamed.

She dropped the bag as her left hand slipped off the ladder rung. It was like grabbing onto ice. She started sliding down the ladder, grabbing at the rungs, but not getting a solid enough grip on any one of them to stop her fall. Before either of us could move, she hit the ground between us, breaking her fall with her left leg first and then sitting down hard and falling back.

Trevor and I were stunned and frozen for a moment. It seemed unreal. The rain pounded us. Mama struggled to sit up. Trevor rushed to help her. When she sat, she immediately reached for her left ankle. Her face twisted with the pain shooting up her leg, rain streaked down her cheeks, and her hair looked like it was plastered to her head.

"Get me into the house!" she cried, and Trevor stepped closer for her to put her arm around him. I moved for her to put her right arm around me. We helped her stand on her right leg, and the three of us headed back toward the rear door, Trevor and I really carrying her between us, all of us oblivious to the rain, which was still quite steady. With the wind not as hard, the rain was not falling in torrents, at least.

We didn't look at Mama's ankle until we were inside and had her lying on the sofa. Mama had her eyes closed and moaned.

"Get those old towels I have in the kitchen closet and throw them on the puddle in the pantry," she said without looking at us. "Quickly!"

"Maybe you broke your ankle," Trevor said.

She opened her eyes and looked at it. "Don't worry about me. Get the towels," she said. "Both of you. Hurry. Just toss them in to soak up some of the water. It'll be running into the kitchen and under the stove and the refrigerator, and we'll have rot throughout."

We turned and went back to the kitchen. The entire floor of the pantry was covered in at least two inches of water. It was maybe a quarter of an inch away from rushing over the bottom of the pantry doorframe and onto the kitchen floor. Towels weren't going to help much, I thought, and the water was still running down the sides of the shelves, as if someone on the roof had turned on a hose and aimed it directly at the leaky area.

"We'll have to build a dam at the door. She'll be mad, but we'll have to use good towels," Trevor said.

"But what are we going to do about Mama?" I asked him.

"She has to go to the hospital. We can call for an ambulance."

"That will take too long."

"Well, I can't drive, and neither can you."

"I can run over to Mr. Longstreet," I said.

"She won't be happy about that," he said. "I'm going to get more towels, rags, and other stuff to build a dam."

"So I should go get him?"

He thought a minute. We could hear Mama moan.

"Just go," he said. "Don't tell her first. Just go."

I hurried out the back door. And then I paused, even though I was in the rain.

Trevor had better not tell her this was only my idea, I thought. He could make it seem like I wanted to go get Lance here more than I wanted her to be helped.

It almost felt true.

six

The rain was still steady, but the wind had died down. I started toward the woods because it was truly a shortcut, but then I thought I'd get even more soaked and might get tripped up by the mud. It was better to take the road. Maybe someone would come by in a car and stop when they saw me waving. I looked back. The road was straight and probably ran for half a mile or more before it reached a turn. I didn't see any vehicles, so I started to run as hard as I could. My soaked shoes squeaked. I kept wiping the rain off my face, using my hand like a windshield wiper. I slipped once but caught myself before I fell. I almost twisted my ankle on the macadam that the rain had made more like ice.

Finally, I turned into Mr. Longstreet's driveway. His two-story redbrick house had a small porch with three cement steps. The windows were dark. If they had candles lit, they were most likely toward the rear. There was a ringer on his door, something to turn. It didn't move, so I just started to pound on the door as hard as I could, yelling, "Mr. Longstreet!"

It seemed like almost a full minute had gone by before he finally opened it. Lance stood beside him; both were still in their coveralls and flannel shirts. A candle flickered in a room behind them.

"Oh my," Mr. Longstreet said. I couldn't imagine how wild I looked, my hair streaming in strands down the sides of my face alongside my tears. My clothes were fully soaked. Because of my running and the excitement, until I was standing still, I didn't realize that I was shivering.

"We need your help," I said, catching my breath. "Mama has to go to the hospital. She fell off a ladder and maybe broke her ankle."

"Broke?" Lance said, grimacing.

"Why was she on a ladder?" Mr. Longstreet asked, stepping up. "Outside? In *this*?"

"She was fixing a roof leak because the water was streaming into our pantry and spoiling food in boxes. We took all the food out we could."

"Oh, jeez," Mr. Longstreet said, and then he really took a look at me. "You're soaked to the skin. You'll catch your death of it."

"Don't worry about me. Mama," I said. "She needs to go to the hospital."

"Let's get into the car. C'mon," he told me. "We'll go through the house to the door to the garage."

I followed them through the small kitchen lit with two good-size candles. Lance hurried ahead. When we stepped into the garage, Mr. Longstreet grabbed a towel I thought he used to wash his car and tossed it at me.

"Dry up a little until we get you home to change," he said. It smelled like the polish Big John used to polish his truck cab, but I dabbed it on my neck and hair.

"Lance, there's a cord to pull that releases the garage door, and then we'll lift it manually," Mr. Longstreet said.

Lance was already at the garage door. He pulled the cord and, without any help, lifted the garage door in one motion.

"Yeah, he's a strong one," Mr. Longstreet said. "Let's go."

We all got into his light blue SUV, me in the rear. He backed out, turned in the driveway, and started for our house.

"Shoulda called for help," he said. "I think I gave your mother my phone number years ago. Never changed it."

"She wouldn't have let me call. My mother is stubborn. She doesn't know I came for your help," I said.

He glanced back at me, amazed. "Doesn't know?"

"Our pantry is so flooded it's going to run into the kitchen. She's more upset about that than her leg."

"Yeah, well, let's look into your mother first," he said. "Everything else can be replaced."

He swung onto the side road and then stopped.

"What part of the house is she in?"

"The living room," I said, "but we can go through the back entrance."

I wanted him to see how bad the flood was, too. I leaped out, and they followed me. Trevor was building the dam to keep the water out of the kitchen. He was still soaked and on his knees. His hair was a matted amber cap. He looked like he had been crying, but with the water still dripping off his hair, it was hard to tell what was rain and what was tears.

"I'll help you as soon as we see about your mother," Lance told him. Trevor didn't say anything.

I led them into the living room. Mama was lying back on the sofa with her eyes closed. She looked like she had passed out. Mr. Longstreet knelt beside her and gazed at her ankle. When he touched her right arm, her eyes snapped open.

"What?"

She looked at him. He didn't touch her ankle.

"What are you doing here?"

"Your daughter came for us."

"She did? I don't need anyone fussing over me. I . . ."

"We got to get you to the hospital and have it x-rayed, Paula."

She looked at me. My heart began to pound. How angry was she?

"My roof and the pantry . . ."

"Let's just get you fixed up first. We'll take care of the rest. You have a nice blanket to put around your mother?" he asked me, not tolerating any more resistance.

I looked at Mama. I was afraid to move, but she saw Mr. Longstreet's determination, too.

"Take the one from my bed, folded at the foot of it," Mama said, still reluctant but giving in.

I turned and rushed up the stairs, got it, and hurried down.

Mr. Longstreet took it, but Mama grabbed it out of his hands and pushed herself into a sitting position. He froze, looking like he was afraid to touch her. She wrapped the blanket around herself.

"Be faster if you let me carry you out," Mr. Longstreet said when Mama put her right foot down on the floor.

"Nonsense," she said. "I can hobble. Just give me some support."

"I can help you, Mama," Trevor said. He had left the pantry when he heard what was happening.

"We'll be fine. You just stay on that pantry," she told him.

Mr. Longstreet helped her stand, and then Lance shot forward and opened the front door.

"After you help me get her into the car, you stay with them and help with the flood," Mr. Longstreet told him. "It's my grandson," he told Mama.

Mama looked at him and then glanced at me and Trevor.

"Both of you change into dry clothes, and don't go taking anyone upstairs or anywhere else in this house. I can't go looking after what you'd dirty up. Just keep working on the pantry, and keep that water out of our kitchen until I get back."

"We will, Mama," Trevor said.

Lance went to get Mr. Longstreet's car.

The rain finally had slowed to a steady drizzle, but the sky still looked quite gray and dark.

Trevor and I watched Mama and Mr. Longstreet making their way off the porch, her leaning on him more than she had intended, as Lance brought the car as close to the steps as he could. He hopped out and opened the car's back door. They helped Mama to the car and in. I ran back and got a pillow off the sofa.

"Use this, Mama!" I shouted.

Mr. Longstreet took it from me and handed it to her. She lay back so she could rest her leg. Mr. Longstreet said something to Lance, and then he got in and started away. Lance, Trevor, and I watched them for a moment.

"She'll be okay," Lance said.

I nodded, and we turned to go into the house and hurry back to the pantry.

"What a mess," Lance said.

"Still a bad leak," Trevor said. "Although not running down the walls as much. We can start to scoop it up and put it in a pail."

"Mama wants us to get out of our wet clothes," I said.

"Mine aren't as wet as yours, Faith," he said, even though they obviously were. "You change first. I'll keep these clothes on until I make a little more progress, because I'll be getting wet anyway."

"How can I help?" Lance asked.

"There's a pail under the sink," Trevor told him, and Lance practically leaped to get it.

"Go on, Faith," Trevor ordered. "I don't want you getting a cold."

"You can catch one, too," I said. I wasn't going to be treated like a little girl, especially in front of Lance.

"Okay. I'll change. You just go first." He looked at Lance. "Please."

"Okay," I said, glanced at Lance, and then hurried to the living room to get one of the kerosene lamps and then up the stairway.

I heard the two of them scooping water into the pail. I could hear Lance saying he had never seen a rain like this. Trevor mumbled something, and they both laughed.

I went to the bathroom first and got out of my dress. My panties were soaked as well. I slipped them off and reached for a towel. As I wiped myself dry, I realized this was the first time ever that there was a stranger other than Big John's friend Nick in the house when I was undressed and totally nude . . . but it wasn't just any stranger. It was a handsome boy who looked at me so differently from the way anyone else had ever looked at me, including Trevor.

From somewhere deep inside me, there was a new burst of self-confidence. I felt certain that Lance wasn't seeing a young girl when he looked at me. That indifference was not in his eyes. What had he seen? How quickly did he realize I was now a woman? Shouldn't I feel guilty for even thinking about this while Mama was being taken to the hospital? I knew it was wrong to have these thoughts now, but I couldn't deny them. I didn't want to deny them.

I took time to gaze at myself in the mirror, the mirror that had turned into a window through which I could see the new and older me. The flush in my face could have come from all the running and excitement and not from what I felt and what I believed Lance felt, but I didn't want that innocuous reason to be true. I wanted to feel . . . sexy. Mama never used that word, but I knew what she meant when she said I would feel more like a woman. *Mature* was her word for *sexy*.

I continued to stand there to look at myself. Slowly, deliberately teasing myself, I took the towel away to gaze at my nudity in the glowing light of the kerosene lamp. I gently lifted my breasts, touching my nipples, and then I ran my hands down my hips and in between my legs.

Did I moan? Or did I imagine it?

I closed my eyes but kept my fingers teasing and sending delightful tingles in waves up to my breasts. I pictured Lance in the doorway, gazing at me. He had slipped away from Trevor and quietly come up the steps. In my fantasy, I knew he was standing there, but I didn't try to cover my naked body. I took my hands away and held them at my sides. He smiled that smile I had first seen travel over his lips and to his eyes. Then he took a step closer, waiting. I turned and stepped up to him, and he brought his hands to my waist to gently draw me closer until his lips met mine, and his hands moved over my rear, cupping it so he could press me against him.

I sighed so loudly that I snapped my eyes open and waited for a few moments to see if they had heard me below.

Of course, it was all wishful thinking, but it had filled me with excitement.

Was this what Mama meant when she said I would see dramatic changes in myself? Thoughts like this had never been as vivid. If this was how I reacted to the first good-looking boy whom I had seen, maybe Mama and Trevor were right. It was too dangerous for me to be in a public school. I wasn't mature enough to fight off the peer pressure girls would lay on me and the temptations more sophisticated and mature boys would bring.

"You can't act like this," I told the girl I could see through my new window.

"Of course I can," she said. "This is who I've become. Grow up."

"Arguing with myself about this right now is crazy," I told my naked image, and then ran into the bedroom to find dry clothes, pausing again, this time to look at my hair after I had put on new panties, a pair of jeans, and a long-sleeved blouse and a blue sweater. My hair looked like it was drying in clumps. I returned to the bathroom and rubbed it dry with the towel and then ran a brush through it before heading downstairs again. It felt good to be a little vain, even though I knew Mama would pounce on me for it, especially with a new boy in the house, one I had hardly met.

Trevor and Lance had picked up everything we had thrown into the kitchen and had it all piled on the kitchen island neatly. They had scooped a lot of water out. They both turned when I appeared.

Lance's pleased expression made me blush.

"Supergirl couldn't have done it any faster," he said.

"What?"

"The change."

"Water's running under the pantry floorboards and into the basement," Trevor said, before he could explain any more. "But we'll check it later."

"We can take a look at it now if you want," Lance said.

Trevor looked at me. Surely he saw how much I wanted to do it.

"My mother said not to go wandering around the house," Trevor said. "And we'd have to bring lanterns down and everything. If one of us got hurt . . ."

"Right. Well, what exactly was your mother trying to do when she fell? Maybe I can do it."

"You can't do it. She shouldn't have even tried it. My father will fix it or get someone who knows what he's doing to do it," Trevor said. "You have to patch a roof correctly, or it will just happen again," he added, sounding more like Big John. Mama had made him the man of the house for now, and that was who he was going to be.

"When's he coming home?"

"Not for another two or three days," Trevor said. "He hasn't reached North Carolina yet. I know how far he has to go in the state and how long it takes, dropping off his load and all," he added proudly.

"Maybe my grandfather can find someone to fix the leak after the rain."

"My father can do it when he gets back."

"It might rain again tomorrow or the next day," Lance said. "Might as well fix it."

"He's right, Trevor."

"Mama will decide," Trevor said, not liking my taking Lance's side. "She'll think about it when she gets home. As long as the rain keeps slowing down . . . And we'll worry about the basement later," he insisted.

I saw how he was closing the argument, slamming the door on it like Mama would. There was no sense arguing about it now. I didn't like the deep moment of silence, afraid he might tell Lance he could go home.

"Meanwhile, I can make us something to eat, warm up the stew. Mama makes great stew," I said. "We have a gas stove, so the electricity doesn't matter."

"Sounds good to me," Lance said. "Dinner by candlelight." He smiled. "This is great. I've never been in a summer storm like this. Real country life. My city friends would have run for the hills by now."

I looked at Trevor. He gave his Trevor shrug, but he looked a little proud.

"Yeah, well, you get used to more things out here, I guess," he said.

Lance nodded.

"You'd better go change into dry clothes, Trevor. You'll catch cold for sure," I said, turning the tables a little.

"No, I won't," he said sullenly. He looked at Lance and then relaxed, realizing I was right and that he was looking like a sullen little boy.

"I left one of the kerosene lamps in the bathroom for you," I said. "You said you would, but if you're not going to go up . . ."

"I'm going. I'm going. I'll be right back," he said, making it sound like a warning.

"We'll be here. We've put off all other appointments," Lance joked.

Trevor almost smiled. He hurried away, and I went to the refrigerator to get out the pot of stew Mama had prepared.

"How can I help you?" Lance asked.

"You can set the table, I suppose. Put that lamp on it first. Wait, use this," I said, taking out one of the old, even a bit worn tablecloths. "We don't need to spoil one of my mother's special tablecloths, even though she usually would when she entertained a stranger."

"Boy, you think of everything. I bet you could run this house yourself," he said. "Like some pioneer girl." He looked serious and then laughed at my expression.

Pioneer girl? If anything, I wanted to be as sophisticated as any city girl he knew.

"I'll get busy," he said.

"That would be nice," I said. I knew I was borrowing Mama's penchant for sarcasm, but it didn't sound mean.

I widened my eyes when he just stared back at me.

"Yes, boss," he said. He saluted and started to turn.

"Remember to be careful with the kerosene lamp when you put it on the tablecloth."

"No candlelight?"

"The kerosene lamp gives more light."

"But not as romantic."

His smile was like a broken egg yolk spreading over his face. I couldn't keep my smile from coming, even though I told myself again that it was not the time to be happy and excited.

"We'll manage. Go on and do that. Then take the dishes out of this cabinet. Napkins are over there," I said, nodding at where they were on the counter, "and the silverware is in this drawer."

I opened it. The way he was watching me made me nervous now, making me conscious of every move I made. I usually was not this stiff and stern. Was I behaving too much like a child trying to be an adult, imitating Mama?

"Well, get going," I said, flicking my wrist the way Mama would.

"Yes, ma'am," he said, and left for the dining room.

Both Moses and Becky suddenly appeared. I realized Mama usually fed them at this time, so I paused to get their food. They watched me suspiciously as I filled the bowls and provided bowls of water, too.

"Don't worry. It'll taste the same," I told them.

Lance returned to get the napkins and silverware. I kept my back to him and worked on dinner preparations.

"How old are your cats?"

"We think twelve. My mother got them from one of those save-a-pet places."

"I wanted a puppy once, but both my parents were against it. They said I would neglect it and they'd end up with all the pet chores."

"You could have gotten a kitten. Cats are independent."

"My mother has allergies."

He returned to the dining room. Moments later, I heard Trevor and Lance begin talking. Trevor had really rushed his change and probably hadn't dried his hair. As I stirred the stew, I heard Trevor asking Lance questions about his school.

"He's in a class with over eight hundred students," Trevor said when they returned to get glasses.

"That must be one big classroom," I said, and Lance laughed.

"No, we're not in one room. There's only about twenty-five of us in each classroom, depending on the subject. History class is closer to thirty."

I looked at Trevor. Despite Mama's descriptions of her teaching career and how she categorized other kids, how we saw them on television, and what we had read, neither of us really did know what the world outside was like. Trevor wore the same look that I'm sure I wore, a mixture of embarrassment at our ignorance and yet curiosity.

"How big is the whole school?" I asked.

"We're about thirty-five hundred," he said.

"Thirty-five hundred go to the same building?"

Lance laughed again. When I didn't, he stopped.

"Sorry. Yes, New York City schools are that big. I'm on the

basketball team, by the way," Lance said. He turned to Trevor. "I saw you have a hoop on your garage. No net?"

"There's one in the garage, I think," Trevor said. "We haven't used it in a long time. My father used to shoot some hoops with me, but he's been working more lately."

"*A lot* more," I said. Trevor gave me a surprised look. He could hear my underlying meaning. Big John used to hate to leave us; now he seemed to jump at every opportunity.

"Well, maybe we can locate it and I can help put it on. My grandfather doesn't have one, and I don't want to get out of shape," Lance said.

"Are you his only grandson?" Trevor asked.

"No. I have a cousin two years older in California."

"You've been to California, too?" I asked, maybe too quickly and too wide-eyed. Trevor smirked. I guess I sounded either childish or stupid, and suddenly that embarrassed him.

"About five times," Lance said. "He lives near the ocean, so we go surfing."

Both of us stared at him now. I didn't know what Trevor was thinking, but I imagined he was thinking again about traveling with Big John and being able to brag about things he saw and did.

Lance smiled. "I think your stew is boiling."

"Oh!" I rushed toward the stove. Both Trevor and Lance were laughing. "Get something to drink and the bread, Trevor," I ordered, angry and self-conscious.

"Will do," Trevor said. Everything in the refrigerator was still cold, but I could hear Mama saying, "Don't open it too much. The electricity is still off." So I said it, too.

They moved quickly, leaving the kitchen with the glasses and a jug of Mama's homemade lemonade.

"Get control of yourself, Faith," I whispered.

I couldn't believe how excited I was and how wonderful it made me feel.

What a terrible thing to think, I told myself, but I was almost happy Mama had slipped off the ladder.

seven

What surprised me the most was how quickly Trevor had gone from not wanting to have anything to do with a "city boy" to being intrigued by his revelations about city life and public school, especially the social life. He rolled out one question after another. I never knew these thoughts weighed so heavily on his mind. He always either ignored or belittled my curiosity about public school and getting to be with other kids our age. Big John was right about him: he had a "poker face," but now it was dropping. You didn't have to be a genius to sense how much Trevor wanted to be with other boys.

I listened without interrupting. It certainly sounded like Trevor wanted friends even more than I did. He had questions about the privileges public-school students had while they were attending, what a lunch hour was like, how friends stuck together and planned their weekends, what happened after ball games, and what kinds of things kids got in trouble for at school. I knew he was wondering if they, especially city kids, were as bad as Mama had made them seem.

Lance told him anecdotes about him and his friends pulling pranks on girls in his class and some of the older girls. Nothing sounded especially terrible. Some of it was very funny. Those who were caught received reprimands and in some cases were assigned detention. Lance was more amused than shocked at Trevor's needing to have detention explained.

"So they're forced to sit in a classroom and read or do homework?"

"Yeah. Some detention monitors are a bit more severe. They won't let students do anything but sit with their hands clasped on the desk."

"And then what?"

"They go home."

Trevor looked at me, but I didn't say anything or ask any questions. Mama never mentioned this when she was teaching, but she taught younger children who probably couldn't be kept after school. When we were little and we did something she didn't like, she had us sit quietly and think about it, sometimes for an hour. She called it a "time-out."

Just like Trevor, I had wondered about how students in public school were punished, of course, but Trevor was always afraid to ask Mama any details about her work in the public school and especially the big question: when would we be attending? Whenever I asked him why he didn't ask her, his one response was always "We'll see about all that when Mama thinks we're ready."

Ready? I would think. Why did we have to be more ready than any other kid? Just because we were adopted? We passed all the tests we had to take. We were certainly not going to fall behind academically. How could we ever be socially ready if we had virtually no contact with anyone else our age? How would we know how to recognize bad behavior if we had never seen it? We'd never trust anyone we met.

"And that's that? That's how they get punished?" Trevor asked Lance, still sounding incredulous.

Lance laughed. "You sound like you expected them to be hanged upside down. Of course, someone who does something really bad could be suspended or even expelled. But that rarely happens, at least at my school. It's a private school. We're sort of the crème de la crème."

"What's that?"

"Best of the best," I quickly said.

"Yeah, that's right . . . although not the best basketball team," Lance said.

"That crème de la crème thing. That mean girls, too?" Trevor asked.

I know my eyes were as wide as they could be. Was this my shy brother asking about girls?

Lance glanced at me.

"You mean, is there a girls' basketball team? There is."

"No, not that." He glanced furtively at me. "I mean . . . when you said 'best,' you included girls?"

"Some really smart ones, yeah. There are some very pretty girls, too."

Trevor was trying so hard to look sophisticated.

"I would imagine," he said. "You have a girlfriend, then?" he followed, practically pouncing on him. Lance looked at me. I hoped I didn't look as interested in his reply. I tried to act as if I didn't hear Trevor's question.

"No, no one special," Lance said, looking at me.

"You go on dates, though?"

"Dates?" He smiled.

"Yeah, I mean . . ." Trevor looked to me to help. Mama had called her dating of Big John their "courting," and from what we understood, he was the only man she had courted. But Trevor and I knew enough from what we had read and watched on television that *courting* wasn't a word anyone now used for dating.

"Ask someone out, go to her house and pick her up, maybe bring flowers, meet her parents, especially her father," I recited. It was what we had seen watching some of the old movies Mama liked.

"Oh." He smiled at me, but I looked down. "Sure. We don't call it dates, not the way you are thinking of them, I think. We meet at malls and places, usually in a group with our other friends. Sometimes we do that, too," he said, "actually call and ask someone out. Most of the time, it's done through text or messaging. Mostly it's just hanging out rather than 'dating.'" He kept looking at me.

"What do you mean by just meeting at malls and places?" Trevor asked.

Lance looked from him to me. He could easily see I was a little embarrassed by Trevor's interrogation. I realized how naive we both sounded. I almost expected Lance to ask if we were from this planet.

"He means they just meet and talk to see if they like each other, right?" I said.

"Sure." He did look a little dumbfounded by what we were asking and saying. "Some also meet online, I guess."

"Meet online?"

"On the computer."

"Oh. We're permitted to use our computers only for research assignments," Trevor revealed.

"But don't you get to go to malls or something and still meet other kids?"

"No," I said sharply.

He nodded but looked amused. "Well then, I guess you don't have the opportunities to meet other kids and start messaging, anyway," he said. "But I think you'd like some of these apps," he added quickly. "I know some guys who met girls totally that way."

"Met? How do you meet online?"

"Someone responds to something you said in the comments of something you post, and you start a conversation, or you text on your phone. Stuff like that."

I could tell Trevor was having a hard time following all the terms, just like I was, but Lance was patient.

"That's it?" I asked.

"If they think they really like each other, they meet for real. Dangerous more for girls than guys," he said, again looking at me. "But there are so many fun things to do, games you can play. The reach is international."

"What's that mean?" Trevor asked. "Reach?"

"You communicate with someone far away. You actually could play a game against someone in Spain, anywhere."

He rattled off some of the more popular apps and sites.

"Yeah, well, our mother doesn't approve of those things. She says they waste time we could be applying to more intelligent pursuits," Trevor said, sounding arrogant.

"Pursuits?"

"Research," I said. "More information about subjects in our textbooks."

Lance's amused smile faded. "Sounds like you two never get out of homeschool."

We were both quiet. He looked sorry, like someone who had blurted a criticism would.

"I mean . . . it's probably good. It's just that everyone needs some relief, entertainment, that sort of thing, right?" he asked, looking from me to Trevor.

"Our father set up a pool table downstairs," I said.

"Really? I've played a few times at a friend's house. I bet you guys are good."

"Trevor's better," I said. "He beats even our father. There's a dartboard, too."

"That sounds like a fun place. Maybe we should take the lanterns and make sure nothing got damaged from the leak, and if it's all right, we can play a few games."

"We gotta wait up here for Mama," Trevor said.

Lance nodded. He thought a moment. "Right. But maybe we should check to see how much water ran down there anyway? If the three of us carry lanterns . . ."

I looked at Trevor. I was ready to go. Hopefully, Lance would look at it and at least be more enticed to return.

"It can wait," Trevor said. "There's a lot to do up here first."

Lance nodded. "I tell you what. Since you clearly don't have cell phones, I'll give you both my email address, and we can keep in touch that way. Do you have one?"

We both shook our heads.

"You don't have internet friends, and you don't order anything over the internet?"

"No," Trevor said.

Lance was silent. I doubted that he would come right out and say we were weird, but I could clearly see that he couldn't fathom how isolated we were, how we had never been to any sort of sporting event or even, when Trevor revealed it, to a shoe or clothing store, not to mention a food store or out to do small errands.

"I don't get it," he kept saying. "You don't leave your house and grounds much? Your mother has been buying you everything for . . . how long?"

"Since we were brought here," I said. Trevor looked sharply at me, as if I had revealed some deep, dark secret.

"Brought here? From where?" Lance asked. He smiled, hoping to ease some humor into it. "Don't tell me from Mars."

Neither Trevor nor I laughed, however, and he lost his smile.

"So . . . what's the story?"

I paused, waiting to see if Trevor would answer. His hesitation surprised me. He never seemed embarrassed or thought less of himself or me because we had been adopted. Of course, strangers visiting us were few and far between. We never had to explain our history to anyone. But I'd never heard him say anything negative about us. I didn't think it ever would occur to him that we were less than any other kids our age. He never mentioned them having more love or fun in their homes. Who would tell us that if we didn't, anyway? What little we did realize about other families came from what we saw on television, which Mama said was simply fantasy.

"No one lives like that," Mama would say. "They should call it dreamvision. There's nothing for you to regret not having. I assure you. I never had more than you two have growing up."

For a while before Mama and Big John had legally adopted us, there was a woman from social services who came to speak to us, searching, as we eventually realized, for something terrible that might stop our parents from having us as their children. Sometimes I thought she was upset because we had no complaints. What, I wondered, would happen if she came back now? Would she sense our growing desire, even growing need, to have friends? Where else could we find them but in school? We didn't belong to any church group, and neither Mama nor Big John had friends or relatives visit with their children. As far as we knew, we had no cousins, not even second or third cousins.

Maybe we did live on Mars.

This wasn't something I felt from the beginning or even as intensely in the past year as I did now, maybe because we had met Lance, and that was like opening a magic window and seeing the outside world up close. If you don't know what you're missing, have it in your face daily, how can you regret not having it?

When our adoption was official, Mama and Big John had a beautiful dinner and our favorite cake and ice cream. And then she surprised us with presents, a new dress with matching shoes for me and something Trevor always had wanted, a really powerful telescope with which he could see the rings of Saturn. He was always intrigued with the stars and planets, because our night sky, especially at the rear of the house, was truly spectacular some evenings.

"This is better than our birthdays," I had said, more or less blurted. Everyone laughed.

"Oh, it is. From now on until the day you die," Mama had predicted, "this day will be your real birthday, because it's the day you were given the hope of a real life, a happy life. It's our birthday, too, because we have the children we always wanted."

She looked at Big John for agreement.

"Absolutely," he said. "You did real good finding them both, Paula."

"Well, John. Not *good*," she corrected. "You did *really well.* Every day is school here. For them, especially," she added, looking at us.

"See how she picks on me," Big John said. "She's a bully," he added, feigning being upset for a moment and then smiling.

We all laughed. It was truly the happiest day of our lives.

Why were we both hesitant to reveal it all now?

"Mama found us at a foster home," I told Lance. "We're adopted. Legally," I added.

It did feel like some sort of a confession. I looked at Trevor. He had quickly put his poker face back on.

"Oh," Lance said. He looked a little stunned. And then he smiled. "I thought you two didn't look much alike. Grandpa never told me about you. He just said there were a couple of kids living next door who were about my age."

"If he had told you we were adopted and made it sound like we were inferior or something, and Mama found out, she'd probably shoot him," Trevor said.

"Really?"

"Yeah, she knows how to use a shotgun. She'd march over there."

"Oh, she wouldn't," I said.

Trevor just shrugged.

"Why is she so sensitive about it?" Lance asked.

"She says some people treat adopted children as less important, without souls, because they have no family," Trevor said.

"Huh? Really?"

"Yes," Trevor said. "Really. She was a teacher, so she should know," he said firmly. "She had a couple in her classes and saw the way they were looked down upon by the other pupils, and even how their parents wanted to keep them away from those kids."

"That happened?"

"That's what she told us," Trevor added firmly, clearly implying that if Mama had said it, it was gospel.

Lance nodded, thinking. "Is that why she doesn't want you to go to public school? She's worried about how you would be treated?"

"No," I said, but I didn't sound confident, I'm sure. I looked at Trevor.

"Mama's never said that was the reason," he said. "She's giving us a better education here. We told you our reading levels."

"Mama's not fond of how other children are reared," I said.

"Reared?"

"Brought up, taught."

"Oh. What does she think they're taught?"

I let my eyes drift from him.

"Not enough. Little religion, and what they are taught are bad habits," I said. "She said the most dangerous thing is peer pressure and it was better that we weren't exposed to it yet."

"Really? Peer pressure?"

"She says you just have to look at how Eve influenced Adam."

"Huh? You mean, like in the Garden of Eden?"

"Yep," Trevor said. "And no matter how pure of heart you are when you enter public school, you will be influenced. Just like some of the friends you were describing even in your private school, how they do things to impress each other. I bet if you didn't tease girls and pull off some of those pranks, your friends wouldn't have liked you."

"Or trusted you," I added.

Lance looked from him to me, obviously expecting us to laugh, thinking we were putting him on. I actually felt bad that we weren't.

"So Mama wants us to remain in homeschooling until she thinks we're old enough and mature enough to resist the bad influences," I explained.

Even though I said it firmly, it sounded empty.

Lance nodded, looking thoughtful. I was afraid he would be insulted and leave, but suddenly, he smiled.

"Your last name is Eden. You're like Adam and Eve. Is this the Garden of Eden?" He laughed.

I think we both blushed at the same time.

Lance saw we were embarrassed. "What I mean is you've got everything you seem to want, and you don't have much to do with the evil outside world."

He smiled, hoping that had pleased us. It didn't, because it was too true.

He dropped his smile. "Actually, my mother has similar ideas. The few times I did something that resulted in detention, my mother told me it was because of the guys I hung around with. But I don't know that she would want me homeschooled. She says I get in her hair too much as it is."

"Hair?" Trevor said.

"You know, get in her way, play music too loudly, have noisy friends over, mess up the house, stuff like that."

Trevor smiled enviously, as if he wished we could do some of that.

"That's probably the main reason she sent me to stay with my grandfather during this divorce proceeding."

"Needless to say, you're the first kid from divorced parents we ever met," Trevor said.

Lance laughed. "Actually, you're the first adopted kids I've ever met. I mean, I'm sure there are a number of them at my school, but I'm not friends with any. Not deliberately avoiding them, of course," he quickly added.

"Be careful. We're going to grow horns, you know," I said.

"Huh?"

I laughed at the expression on his face. Trevor laughed, too. Then Lance realized what I was saying and pressed his lips together so hard that his cheeks bulged.

"You two are real wise guys. Reassure your mother. You'd do well in public school. Nobody's going to get the better of you."

"Maybe. Before you ask either of us," I said, getting serious again, "we don't know anything about our biological parents."

"Biological? Oh, right." He looked like he was peering at me. "You weren't left on a doorstep, were you?" he asked with a timid smile.

"Something like that," I said.

"Really?"

"It doesn't matter how we got here. We couldn't love any parents as much as we love ours now."

I looked at Trevor. We both knew we'd never describe our biological parents the way Mama had: dangling over the mouth of hell.

"That's nice," Lance said. "Besides, when it comes to parents, I'm not particularly going to brag. I'm not adopted, but now I'm a child from a broken home and a lot less happy about family life than you guys seem to be here."

Everyone was quiet, and then Lance, who had gone into deeper thought as all of us had, obviously regretted the dark turn our conversation had taken. Sadness always opened the doors for ghosts. They hovered as though they fed on unhappiness. Mama told us that so convincingly that I had thought I did see one once when I was melancholy. I knew she told us that so we would always try to be happy and mentally, if not actually, bury sad things.

Suddenly, Lance looked like he had just woken up and snapped out of the dark mood shadowing us all.

"It stopped raining," he announced.

We turned to the window. It had. And then the whir of the refrigerator told us the electricity was back. The lights that had been on in the dining room went on as they did everywhere they had been on throughout the house.

I rose and turned off all the kerosene lamps.

"Thanks for a great and fun dinner," Lance said. "Tell your mother I thought this was a delicious stew. I don't get that many home-cooked meals," he added. He looked despondent and again lost in his own deep, dark thoughts. Trevor and I glanced at each other.

"Let's have some ice cream for dessert," Trevor suggested. "We earned it."

"Don't ask me to wash dishes," Lance said. "My mother says I don't concentrate on it and always start wiping before they're clean."

"You don't have a dishwashing machine?" Trevor asked.

"Yeah, we have one of the most expensive ones, I'm sure, but she doesn't use it when there are only the two of us eating, mostly takeout, mostly using paper plates, which was something she would never do before all this. Lately, that's been it, the two of us. She actually took the chair my father usually sits in away from the table. I think it makes that empty spot worse. But she's so angry at him."

"Why so angry?" Trevor asked.

"Did your father cheat on your mother?" I asked.

Trevor looked surprised at my forwardness, but I sensed we were all beyond being shy about ourselves.

"Looks that way. She has had my aunt over a couple of times, and I heard them ranting about it. She's my mother's unmarried sister, and occasionally she invites one or more of her friends, but I haven't invited any of mine over yet. Most don't even know my parents are breaking up. Life in the city is different. You can be a couple of doors away from someone and not know they've been dead a week, even a year."

"That's not so different," I said, almost under my breath. "If something had happened to your grandfather, we wouldn't have known."

"He told me that your parents don't speak to him that much, especially your mother."

"Our father travels a lot, and my mother just leaves to do errands and stuff," Trevor said. "We rarely see anyone," he added, looking like he was saying it more to himself, as if he had just realized it.

"No relatives coming over?"

"No."

"He has a friend we see occasionally, another truck driver, and that guy's younger sister; they play pool and drink beer, and we watch. I play them sometimes. Darts, too," Trevor said, as if somehow that was enough.

Lance thought and stared at us a long moment.

"But my grandfather's never been over when your father is home? He likes a good beer."

"Apparently, a long time ago, he came to dinner with our grandparents and our mother. That was a long time before we were adopted," I said.

Lance nodded, looking more disturbed than surprised. "Yeah, he's alone, too, mostly. He has some friends his age, but I think he's got to visit them. They don't get around."

"Your grandfather is in pretty good shape," Trevor said.

"Yeah, but I guess I should have visited him more," he said, looking down and guilty.

"So what about your father? When do you see him?" Trevor asked. "Or are you mad at him, too?"

"I try not to take sides, which is what makes it harder. That," he said, "is really why I'm staying with my grandfather so long. The divorce will be over by the time I return. I hope."

"I never asked," I said, "but from what your grandfather said, I guess he's your mother's father?"

"Yes. I wouldn't call them that close. They were always arguing about something. I don't think my grandfather wanted my mother to marry my father. It's one of those 'I told you so' things."

Both of us just stared for a long moment. That was quite a confession, I thought, embarrassing. Lance looked away.

"So you don't see your father?" Trevor pursued. I tried to signal him to stop with the personal questions, not only because it was embarrassing Lance, but also because it resulted in more personal questions about us.

"He takes me out to dinner on the weekend . . . sometimes," Lance said. "And we went to a Yankees baseball game a few weeks ago. He has box seats."

"What's that mean?" I asked.

"They're the best and most expensive seats and always reserved for him and his guests. There are four seats, but it was just us last time."

"Wow. What does he do?" Trevor asked.

"He runs a hedge fund in New York."

He could see from my expression that I didn't know what that was, and neither did Trevor.

"Hedge?" Trevor asked.

"It's a fund wealthier people invest in. The stock market," he added.

"So is he very rich?" Trevor asked.

"Kinda. We live on the East Side in what they call a classic eight apartment. I heard my parents say it was worth about seven million."

"Dollars?" Trevor said.

Lance nodded.

"It's part of their proposed divorce settlement. We'll live in it. My father will have a different place. But not too far away," he quickly added.

No one spoke for a moment. We were the ones who were trying to be silent about ourselves because we were afraid of how Lance would react, but now it looked like he really was the one who felt strange.

"Okay," I said, standing. "You guys bring everything to the kitchen. Nobody has to wash dishes. I'll take care of them, the glasses, and the silverware," I said. And then, sounding like Mama, I added, "Once the table is cleared, and everything is organized, Trevor can get out little bowls for the ice cream. We have some whipped cream, too."

"And chocolate sauce," Trevor added.

"Once we take care of everything. We want it all spick-and-span for Mama when she comes home."

"Is the hospital far from here?" Lance asked.

"No," Trevor said. "Five or six miles."

"I can call my grandfather and see how it's going."

"Great," Trevor said.

Both of us waited nervously. Lance tried, but his grandfather didn't answer.

"I'll leave a message," he told us. "Call when you can, Grandpa, and let us know how Mrs. Eden is doing," he said, and then turned to us. "Probably can't have the phone on in the hospital or something."

"We should call Big John," I told Trevor.

"So Big John is what you call your father?"

"Most of the time," I said. "But not to his face. I mean, we call him Daddy."

"When you meet him, you'll see why we call him Big John," Trevor said, sounding proud. "From what you told us, I guess you're staying a while, right?"

"Until the first week in September, actually."

"That's great," I said, before Trevor could. He looked at me as if I had given away a secret.

"I'll call him," Trevor said when we were all in the kitchen. I stopped washing dishes.

Trevor went to the phone on the wall. The moment he lifted the receiver, he smirked.

"What?"

"Dead. That happens often with heavy rainstorms, even though we have electricity."

"Use my phone," Lance said, and then thought a moment and asked, "You guys really don't have one?"

Trevor shook his head. He looked afraid of answering.

"We aren't away on our own, so we don't need one yet," I explained.

Lance nodded. "Sure. Here," he said, offering his phone to Trevor. Trevor looked at me. I stepped forward quickly and took the phone.

"We don't have Big John's mobile phone number memorized,"

I said. I went to a cabinet drawer by the sink and looked for the slip of paper I knew it had been written on. Mama had done it as a precaution, which proved to be very wise now.

"Maybe you should wait to call him, Faith," Trevor said when I had found the number.

"What? Why?"

"We don't know how she is yet and what they had to do. He'll just ask lots of questions we can't answer."

I thought for a moment.

"Trevor is right." I handed Lance his phone.

"Well, just ask when you want to use it," he said.

"Let's have dessert," Trevor said. He got the plates, the ice cream, and the whipped cream.

I suddenly felt a loss of appetite, even for this. We should be thinking and worrying more about Mama, I thought again, and not be so happy, treating our dinner as if it were a party.

"Maybe I'll just watch you two," I said. "I'm just a little nervous now."

"Sure," Lance said. "I mean, if no one else wants any, I'm fine." He looked at Trevor, who shrugged and started to put it all back.

"Might as well just go into the living room and wait, then," he said.

"Check the pantry first, Trevor."

"Just a slight trickle," he said from the doorway.

"We'll wipe the shelves down later and wait to see what Mama wants to do before we put everything back."

"I could help now," Lance offered.

"We should wait for it to stop leaking, or we'll be like the boy plugging a hole in the dike with his finger."

"Who's that?" Lance asked.

Both Trevor and I laughed.

"It's a famous legend in the Netherlands, which has much of its area below sea level," I explained.

Lance still looked lost. Then he brightened.

"Maybe you guys are really getting a better education. I should see if I can enroll in your homeschool."

"Are you serious?" Trevor asked. "You'd live with your grandfather?"

"No, no. I'm just kidding," Lance said.

I saw the disappointment in Trevor's face. He really, even desperately, wanted a friend, despite the act he put on and how vehemently he insisted he could wait until Mama thought we were ready for school and friends.

"I'll finish up here, and we'll wait in the living room," I said.

They left, and I wiped down the counters, rearranged some of the boxes from the pantry on the counter, and put away everything I had used in the kitchen, getting it as spick-and-span as I could so Mama would be pleased when she returned.

Lance and Trevor were talking, but their voices were so low that I couldn't hear much. I paused and embraced myself. It felt as if the house was closing in on me, the walls inching closer and closer. What if what had happened to Mama was far more serious than we thought? Somewhere I had read that household mishaps were a major cause of accidental death and severe injury. I often had nightmares about something happening to Mama, especially when Big John was away. Would some social agency come to take us away? Would we end up back in a foster home like the Wexlers'?

I'd sooner run away, I thought. Trevor would, too. We'd pack what we could, and we'd leave.

Maybe we were like Adam and Eve after all.

We'd be tossed out into the world.

eight

After drying the dishes, glasses, and silverware, I started for the living room. When I heard Lance's phone ring, I hurried in. He was just listening and looking at me.

"Okay, Grandpa. I'll let them know. Oh. Tell Mrs. Eden we ate her stew and all is well here. The rain stopped, and it's not leaking much in the pantry. It's just a trickle. Right," he said, and ended the call and turned to us.

"She's in a cast. It was a break. They fit her for a crutch, but she has to be careful and try to stay off the foot for a few weeks at least. They should be here in less than an hour. They gave her something for the pain. She's going to be a little out of it, my grandfather said at the end."

"Meaning what?" I asked.

"The medication makes you sleepy, in a daze."

"She's on a crutch?" Trevor asked.

"For quite a while, I'd say," Lance replied.

Both of us stared at him. For the first time since everything had happened, I felt weak and afraid. Nothing ever happened to Mama. She didn't even get a cold. Tears peeked out under my eyelids. I felt my body trembling.

"Oh," I moaned. I actually felt a little dizzy, maybe I even swayed.

Trevor looked frozen in place, but Lance rushed forward and gently took my arm. "Hey, sit down, Faith."

I let him lead me to Big John's chair.

"Sorry. Got a little dizzy," I said as they were both standing there looking at me.

"You're just coming down from this whole shocking event," Lance said. He looked at Trevor. "Both of you. You guys have been through a lot. I'd have been on my ass long ago. I mean my *rear end*," he said, smiling. "And most of my friends, too. You guys are tough."

Trevor smiled.

I took a deep breath. "Call Daddy now, Trevor," I said. "You heard what to tell him."

Lance pulled his phone out of his pocket quickly and handed it to Trevor. He took it, but I could see he wasn't happy about being the one to do it.

"You want me to call him?" I asked.

He looked at Lance, then said, "Naw, I'll do it. Oh. Where did we put the telephone number?"

"It's still on the kitchen counter, Trevor. I'll do it if you get it for me."

He hurried back to the kitchen.

"You should ask your dad if he wants that leak fixed. My grandfather can get it done, and I'll be around to help you two in any way I can."

"Thank you."

Trevor handed me the phone number and the phone. Then he stood back as if there might be an explosion. I pressed the numbers and waited.

And waited.

"He's not answering," I said.

"Does it go to voicemail?" Lance asked.

I shook my head. "It just stopped ringing."

"He might have blocked it."

"Blocked it?"

"He's not recognizing the number," Lance said. "Often, people don't pick up because they think it's some kind of scam. They just click it off and block it."

"What do we do?" I asked.

"You'll have to wait for your home phone to be fixed. Maybe check it again," he told Trevor, who hurried to do so.

"No," he called from the kitchen. "Still dead."

"Does he call in?"

"When he stops for the night," I said. "I'll try again."

I did, but this time it rang only once and stopped.

"Blocked," Lance said when I told him. "Doesn't your mother have a cell phone?" he asked, brightening with hope. "He'll recognize her number if you use her phone."

"No," I said.

"No, what?"

"She doesn't have a cell phone."

He looked amazed. I handed him his phone. He backed up and sat on the sofa.

"Why doesn't your mother have a cell phone?" he asked Trevor.

Trevor gave him his Trevor shrug.

"She's not away that much," I said.

Lance nodded but still looked incredulous. He peered around our place.

"From the way my grandfather described her just now, it won't be easy for her going up and down those stairs. I guess that's where all the bedrooms are, huh?"

"Yes," I said. "Thanks for thinking of that." I thought a moment. "She could stay in Big John's den. There's a sofa that opens."

Trevor nodded. I stood up. "I'm going to get her bedding and set it up so she can go right there," I said.

"Need help bringing it all down?" Lance asked.

I looked at Trevor. He shook his head emphatically. He looked fearfully at me. Why? There was nothing unusual upstairs except . . . he didn't want Lance to know he and I shared a bedroom. Lately, we were anticipating Mama finally separating us and having Big John fix the Forbidden Room's floor, but she still hadn't done it, despite Big John's frequent comments. Was this also why Mama didn't want us taking him upstairs?

"No, thanks," I said, and before he could ask again, I hurried to the stairs.

"I'll get the sofa opened," Trevor called.

"Okay," I called back.

When I brought everything down, Lance and Trevor both helped with tucking in the sheet. I fluffed the pillows and folded the blanket neatly, as Mama liked it to be when she made a bed.

"This is a nice man cave," Lance said, looking around.

"What?" I asked.

He laughed. "You know, a place where men escape."

"Mama doesn't want Big John smoking his cigars anywhere else. That's why he comes in here and watches television while he smokes."

"That's practically the only time he does," Trevor said.

"Sometimes he falls asleep on this couch," I reminded Trevor.

Lance sniffed. "Doesn't smell like cigars. Smells nice. There's a smoke shop near us in New York, and you can smell something when you walk by it."

"My mother gets rid of the odors five minutes after he leaves on a trip," Trevor said. "Airs it out and scrubs the smoke off the walls. She sprays her favorite scent, lavender, practically bathes the place in it."

Lance nodded, smiling. "My mother would probably do the same if my dad smoked. Not that she'll ever have to worry about that now. I won't smoke. Basketball. Got to keep my wind. I guess a lot will change, though."

It was obvious that his parents' impending divorce bothered him more than he'd like to admit. I felt like I should say "I'm sorry," but I didn't know if that would sound right. It would sound like his father had died.

Just as we left to return to the living room, we heard Mr. Longstreet sound his horn. We all hurried out as he parked right by the front steps. It would have been easier to bring her through the rear to Big John's room, but I imagined she wanted to get out of Mr. Longstreet's car quickly.

However, when I peered in the truck, I saw that Mama looked asleep in the rear seat, her head on the sofa pillow.

"That sedative took effect," Mr. Longstreet said when he stepped out of the car. He reached in for her crutch and handed it to me. "Don't let her go too soon or too quickly with that."

"We fixed the sofa downstairs in my father's den so she doesn't have to go up the stairs," I said. "If you drive around to the rear . . ."

Her eyelids fluttered.

"No worries. I'll carry her in," Mr. Longstreet said. "She's confused enough. Hey, Paula," Mr. Longstreet said, putting his hand on her shoulder. "We're going to help get you out and resting. You'll be up on your feet in no time if you behave yourself."

He practically pushed her into a sitting position.

"What?" She looked at us.

"I fixed Daddy's den sofa for you, Mama," I said. She really looked dazed, unable to understand. "I opened his sofa and put on your bedding and pillows."

"Whaa."

"Let's just help you get out, and if you don't mind, I'll carry you in, Paula," Mr. Longstreet said. "Don't you worry. I carry a load of logs twice your weight."

I looked frantically at Trevor and at Lance, questioning if he was strong enough to do that. Even though Mama did weigh very little, he was still an elderly man. And Mama would absolutely hate any man but Big John carrying her. I was sure of that.

Mr. Longstreet turned her gently and helped her out of the car, scooping her up in his arms, sweeping her up as if she was a little girl, just as easily as Big John would surely do.

She didn't put up any resistance.

Lance smiled, looking proud of his grandfather, who obviously still had the strength of a younger man. Trevor and I rushed ahead, with me carrying the crutch. Mama still looked quite dazed as Mr. Longstreet carried her up the steps. She turned her head into his chest and, maybe not realizing it or maybe just too weak to care, let him carry her into the house with her eyes closed. He followed me to Big John's den, and carefully, as carefully as he would lower a baby into a crib, he put Mama on the sofa bed. I quickly moved to take off her right shoe, gingerly working around the cast, afraid to touch it.

"Is she still in pain?" Trevor asked.

"Oh, yeah. That's why they shot her up with the painkiller," Mr. Longstreet said. "That's one of the worst breaks I've ever seen. Good doctor, though. Haven't been to one myself for about ten years."

I brushed her hair away from her eyes.

"Just let her sleep a while now, I think," Mr. Longstreet said as I fixed the blanket. He reached into his pocket and took out a pill container, handing it to me. "These are for pain. She had two about an hour ago. Try to keep it to every four hours as needed, just as it says, and be sure she drinks lots of water. The doctor said she'd heal faster if she's not in pain."

He took out another container from another pocket.

"She had one of these just before we left, too. The next one of these is in about three hours, but the doctor said it's all right if you give it to her when she wakes."

"What is it?" Trevor asked him.

"It's her antibiotic, to keep the ankle from getting infected. She might get hungry, but I doubt it for a while," he said.

He looked down at Mama. I could see the sympathy in his eyes. "Must have taken quite the fall to suffer such a serious break."

"It was," I said. The image of her sliding down that ladder made me grimace.

"Okay," he said, turning to the doorway. "We'll get along and leave you two. You're both old enough to handle things, I'm sure."

"We still have some stew I can warm for you, Mr. Longstreet."

"No, thanks. I'm fine. Had one of those health bars at the hospital. Rarely eat them. They're okay. Lost my appetite a bit, anyway. Hospitals do that to me." He looked at Lance. "Your grandmother was held up in one for weeks before she passed. You were too little to remember."

"I remember," Lance said, almost angrily. "I just don't want to."

"Right." Mr. Longstreet nodded at Mama. "She'll be aching more in the morning, and as the doctor said, she must stay off that foot. Let's go, Lance."

I looked at Mama, asleep, and followed Mr. Longstreet, Trevor, and Lance out to the kitchen.

"You call us if there is the slightest problem," Mr. Longstreet said. "Got Lance's phone number and mine?"

"Our phone's dead, and I imagine yours will be, too," I said.

"Here," Lance said, handing me his phone. "I'll write down my grandfather's cell number. Actually, it's on the list of the most recent calls," he continued, leaning to turn the phone in my hand. "See, it says 'Grandpa' next to it. Press this and then this, and his phone will ring. I unlocked it so it won't be a problem."

"Okay. Thanks," I said. His face was so close I could see how long his eyelashes were. When he turned, our eyes seemed to float into each other's.

I glanced at Trevor guiltily, but he wasn't watching us. He was still looking toward Big John's den. He seemed perfectly terrified.

"She's going to be all right, Trevor," I said.

He looked at Mr. Longstreet quickly and regained his composure, shifting from a little boy to a young man.

We followed them to the door.

"You know, I have no problem hanging out here tonight," Lance said. "I can crash on their sofa."

"Let 'em get some rest, Lance. You can come over tomorrow," his grandfather told him.

He had said it too quickly. I had been about to invite him to stay and do just that, sleep on the sofa. But he nodded and followed his grandfather out.

"'Least it stopped raining." Mr. Longstreet pulled his collar up around his neck. "What a storm. Enough rain for the rest of the summer."

"They probably need that roof leak fixed, Grandpa."

"Oh, right. When you talk to your dad, tell him if he wants, I know someone good."

"Use my phone tonight, and keep trying your dad. Maybe he'll realize it's not a scam call when he stops to call home and sees your landline is out," Lance said.

"I will," I said. Trevor stepped up beside me to watch them go to their car.

"Oh, thanks for dinner."

"No, thanks for helping us."

They got into Mr. Longstreet's car. Lance waved, and they drove off.

Trevor looked at me with the same thought forming in his mind: for the first time in our lives, with Mama sedated and Daddy on the road, we were truly in charge of everything, including ourselves.

As soon as we reentered the house, we hurried to see if Mama had awoken. She hadn't.

"I guess I'll sleep on the living-room sofa myself," I said. "For when she wakes, so I can give her the antibiotic."

"I'll sleep in Big John's chair right here," he said. He wanted to be closer to her than I was.

"Okay. I'm going to change into my pajamas."

He thought a moment and then just plopped into Big John's chair.

"Don't need to change," he muttered.

"I'm leaving Mama's medicine on the kitchen counter."

He nodded. I knew he wouldn't give her anything without me. He tried not to show it, and he would never say it, but all this frightened him. It frightened me, too, but as Mama had told me many times, girls matured faster.

"Some men never grow up," she had said, "but you don't realize it until it's too late too often." I was afraid to ask if she meant Big John.

Mama moaned, but she didn't wake up.

"I'll try Daddy again when I come down," I said.

I put Lance's phone next to Mama's medicine and hurried up to brush my teeth, wash up, and change. Boys just tolerated being grimy more than girls, I thought. Mama had told me that once, too.

After I changed, I put on my robe and slippers and headed downstairs. When I looked in on Mama, I saw she was still asleep, and now so was Trevor. I practically tiptoed back to the kitchen, where I thought to check the telephone there. It had a dial tone.

Daddy picked up after the second ring, and in practically one breath, I described everything that had happened. He said he had been just about to call us.

"I can park my truck and get a flight back to Pennsylvania if Mama gets worse or anything," he said. "Thank Mr. Longstreet for me, and yes, ask him to look into having that roof fixed. It's my fault. I neglected it. It's all my fault . . ."

"No one expected it would rain that hard, Daddy."

"No one expected it *never* would," he replied. "Call me anytime, night or day. I'll call you in the morning before I drive on." He paused, as if thinking. "I'll turn around as fast as I can and head back. You're a good girl, Faith. Your mama was right to bring you both up to be adults faster than most kids your and Trevor's age, for sure."

"Okay, Daddy. Oh. Those earlier calls were from Mr. Longstreet's grandson's cell phone, by the way. You have the number now on your phone, Lance says."

"Yeah, that's right. I didn't know who it was."

"You can call it. It might be easier for Mama if I can bring the phone to her. He left it with us because the phone was still dead at the time."

"Good. Nice of him. How old a boy is he?"

"A year or so older than Trevor."

"Is he?"

"Yes, and he's on the basketball team."

"Seems you learned a lot about him. Where's Trevor now?"

"He fell asleep in your chair in the den."

Big John laughed. "Don't let him smoke any of ma see-gars," he joked.

After he ended the call, I checked on Mama and Trevor again, and then I went into the living room and fixed the sofa with the blanket and sheet I had brought down. It wasn't until I actually lay back on the sofa pillow I was using that my fatigue hit me, climbing up my legs as if I had stepped into it and was sinking. I kept fighting it so I'd be alert if Mama needed me, but the reason I really fought it was that I wanted to think about Lance. His expressions, especially his smile, lingered on my eyes the way a flash of light did for a split second. I was afraid to blink and wash it away.

Through the living-room window, I could see the clouds being torn apart as if God was wiping them from the sky. One of Trevor's stars or planets twinkled. Maybe that meant things would get better and even be wonderful.

I fell into a deep sleep until I heard Trevor waking me just at dawn. He wiped his eyes and waited for me to sit up.

"She's awake," he said, "and trying to get out of bed. I had to give her the crutch. I told her about the antibiotic, and she said she'd take it but not the pain pill."

I rose quickly and saw Mama hobble her way into the bathroom.

"I reached Big John," I told Trevor. "He'll call this morning. If something else happens, he'll fly back. He said to get Mr. Longstreet to look after the roof."

"Oh."

"Go wash up a little, Trevor," I ordered with Mama's firmness. "I'll start on breakfast and make sure she takes her antibiotic pill. Go ahead."

He hurried to the stairway. As soon as I heard the bathroom door open, I rushed to help Mama. She paused, her hair looking like a smashed bird's nest.

"You have to stay off your broken ankle, Mama."

"Did you do anything with that boy?" she asked.

"What?"

She started past me, into the kitchen. I hurried ahead to get her a glass of water.

"You have to take one of the antibiotic pills," I said. She slipped onto a kitchenette chair. "Do you need a pill for pain?"

She looked up quickly. "I'm not taking those. Pain's pain. It will go away," she said. "You don't have your wits about you when you take those."

I took out one of the antibiotic pills and handed it to her with a glass of water.

"I want to know everything that you did here last night," she said, as if that was far more important than what had happened to her.

"We did what we could about the pantry. As you can see, we organized the boxes and cans on the center island, and then I went up and changed out of my wet clothes. After I came down, Trevor changed his, and I warmed up your stew, and we ate dinner. I tried to keep Trevor and me busy because we were frightened. Lance was very nice and helpful."

She narrowed her eyes. "Lance. What kind of name is that? I don't want you becoming too friendly with him, neither of you, but especially you."

"Why, Mama? He's only been helpful."

"That's how they open the door."

"What door?"

She smiled, but it was a scary, cold smile.

"You'll know. You'll know faster than I did."

Faster than she did?

"What's that mean, Mama?"

"Never mind."

She took her antibiotic.

"Want some eggs? I can make them just the way you like them with toast and coffee."

"I don't know. Yes," she said. "Where's that boy from?"

"New York City. His parents are getting a divorce, so his mother sent him here to spend time with his grandfather until it's over."

"Why doesn't that surprise me?" she said. "That's Lyla's son, then, that boy?"

"He never told us his mother's name, but if that's her . . ."

"If that's *she* . . ."

"She. Yes, Lance would be her son."

She looked up at me sharply.

"What else did he tell you?"

"Just told us about his school. He's on the basketball team, and he and his mother live in an apartment worth millions of dollars."

"Trying to impress you," she muttered. "That's what they always do first."

"What?"

She looked down, thinking.

Having changed and washed up quickly, Trevor came into the kitchen.

"How do you feel, Mama?"

She looked from him to me and then back to him.

"You'd better be on your toes, Trevor," she warned him. "This isn't the end of it."

"Why? Oh, you mean the roof leak."

"Daddy told me to tell Mr. Longstreet to have someone fix it, Mama. He's sorry he didn't," I said.

"I'll bet. Men are always sorry afterward, when, as my father said, the chickens come home to roost. Okay, make the eggs," she told me.

I nodded and quickly began her breakfast and ours.

"So why do you want me to be on my toes?" Trevor asked her. He looked so confused and afraid that I felt like hugging him.

Mama didn't answer.

Neither of us could tell which was stronger, her pain or her anger.

Suddenly, Lance's phone rang. Mama hadn't noticed it on the counter until now.

"Whose is that?"

"Lance's," I said. "Our phone was dead, so he left his here for emergencies."

I picked it up before it rang again. "Hello."

"Didn't know if your phone was working. Thought this would be easier. How's everything?"

"We're fine," I said quickly.

"How's your mother doing?"

"She's okay. Everything's okay."

"Well, good. Your phone work yet?"

"Yes, it does."

"Okay. I'll stop by to pick up mine. You need anything?"

I paused and looked at Mama.

"Do we need anything, Mama? It's Lance. He can get it for us. He drives Mr. Longstreet's car."

She just stared at me. And then she shook her head.

"No, nothing from him."

"My mother says we're fine. Thanks."

"See you in a while," he said.

I put the phone on the counter.

"Trevor," Mama said, and he quickly stepped up. "You take that phone and run it over to Mr. Longstreet's house and give it back to that boy. Then you come right back."

"Lance will come to get it, Mama," I said.

"Go on, Trevor. I especially don't want to see any company here while I'm in this state."

He scooped up the phone, looked at me sympathetically, and hurried out.

"Wait!" I cried. Trevor stopped. "Remember? Daddy said to tell Mr. Longstreet to get someone for the roof."

He looked at Mama. She muttered to herself but didn't tell him anything different.

After Trevor left, she told me to go upstairs and get her a change of clothes. "Everything," she said, "and bring down my toothbrush and my skin cream."

"Okay, Mama. Why don't you take one of those pain pills, at least for a little while? I can see you're in pain. You don't have to suffer. Mr. Longstreet told me the doctor said you'd heal faster if you're not in pain."

She stared at me and then grimaced, nodding at some thought she thought was right. "You'd like me to be in a daze, huh?"

"What? Of course not, Mama."

"I know the itch when I see it," she said. "I know exactly how it starts."

"What itch?"

"Just get my things," she ordered.

I hurried up the stairs to get the things she wanted and to get away from the mad look in her eyes. She was just upset at herself for getting so injured, I thought, and upset at Daddy, too.

When I gathered all her things, I stood there questioning that anger in her eyes. Maybe I just wanted it to be her disgust about the roof and Daddy's neglect. Maybe it was a side effect of her medicine and her pain. No matter how small and uncomplicated your world appeared to be, mysteries and tension slithered in like baby snakes. Sometimes, although I couldn't pinpoint why, I'd stop and think that I would never again feel the sunshine on my face the way I had when I was just a child, holding Mama's hand and watching Big John roll Trevor along in the wheelbarrow to gather kindling for our fireplace.

Christmas was always around the corner then.

This was all just a result of the changes in my body and the sensitivity of my emotions, I decided. All of them were turned up like the flames on a stove. It seemed so logical to believe you were more fragile as a child.

But children could simply retreat to fantasy and do away with anything unpleasant, anything threatening. They could turn down the flames. It was harder now. I had a woman's sensibilities. Surely, I would learn how to adjust to that and bring the sunshine back through the dark clouds, and then all would be as it was.

How else could it be?

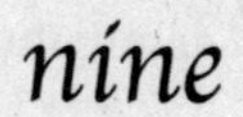

nine

As I was returning to the kitchen with Mama's things, Daddy called from wherever he was on the highway. She had gotten up with her crutch and had answered the phone on the wall. She was wobbly, but she looked so enraged I was afraid I'd burn my hand if I touched her shoulder to steady her. When I went for a chair to get her off her good leg, she shook her head. I brought her things into Big John's den. I knew from the way she was listening that Daddy kept apologizing to her, but she didn't forgive him and go on to something else the way she often did when he admitted doing something she thought was wrong.

"I'll tell that to my ankle," she said. "Next time, when I ask you to fix something, John, maybe you'll listen. Foresight is always better than hindsight. Anyone who knew your personal history would expect you to know that, too."

I could almost hear the silence on the other end. At the moment, I was feeling sorrier for Big John than I was for her, even though it was obvious that she was still in lots of pain. After she hung up, telling him to finish his trip and that she would do just fine, she moaned to herself and started back to the sofa bed in Daddy's den. Her neck strained with what I imagined was the agony shooting up her leg.

"The doctors said you should rest, Mama. When did Daddy say he'd be home?"

She grunted instead of answering and collapsed onto the sofa bed, dropping the crutch. I hurried to pick it up and place it nearby where she could reach it. Mama kept her hand over her eyes.

"Did he say?" I asked softly.

"Day after tomorrow," she muttered, and closed her eyes.

I kept listening for Trevor. He was taking much longer than I had expected. I was afraid Lance might have convinced him to let him come back here with him.

After a moment, I thought Mama had fallen asleep.

"Do you want me to get you something?" I asked.

When she didn't answer, I hurried to the front windows to look out at the road. There was no sign of either of them. I thought about calling and started toward the phone in the living room.

"Faith," Mama called. I rushed back to her. She had sat up again. "Where were you?"

"Just in the living room, Mama."

"Start wiping down those shelves in the pantry. I have some shelving paper in the broom closet. We'll have to put it over them before we put anything back."

"Okay, Mama." I started to turn.

"Wait. There's that small electric heater in the garage. Get that first. Ask Trevor to help you turn it on in the pantry so it dries up before we get mold."

"Okay, Mama."

She didn't realize he wasn't home yet, and I didn't want to tell her.

She closed her eyes and lay back again but then snapped them open and looked at me because I hadn't moved. "Where's your brother?"

"You told him to take Lance's phone back," I said. "And get someone to fix our roof." I smiled. "Mr. Longstreet can talk and talk."

"He should have come right back to help." She thought a moment. "Did he like that boy?"

"Oh, yes, Mama. They got along very well. They might fix the basketball net and play."

"No!" she snapped. "I don't want that. Your brother is too young yet to recognize deception and dishonesty. Boys his age from the city could very well be into drugs. You make sure that ends," she demanded. "Makes me even sorrier I slipped on that ladder."

I wanted to tell her she was wrong about Lance, but I didn't say anything. I knew what she would say. If I argued for him, she would tell me he'd already been a bad influence. Instead, I hurried out to the garage to find the heater. I was more angry than disappointed in Mama's lack of appreciation for what Lance and his grandfather had done for us. Mama was surely wrong about him. He was so nice, so considerate and polite. She would see that if she let herself see it.

As I started out of the garage, I saw Trevor jogging back to our house. He looked excited, pleased, smiling like I rarely saw him smile.

"Trevor!" I called, surprising him.

"Hey," he said, coming up to me. "What are you doing with that?"

"Mama wants us to plug in the heater and start drying up the pantry shelves so we can put new shelving paper on them and begin to load everything back. What took you so long? What did you do?"

"Lance wanted to show me his laptop computer. He has some great stuff on it." He looked at our house as if he anticipated Mama watching us from a window. Instinctively, he lowered his voice to just more than a whisper.

"He set me up with an email address and is going to email some apps over to me—he showed me how to download and open them," he said, his eyes still fixed on the house windows.

"You're going to do email?"

He turned to me. "If you want, I'll show you how to get an email address, too."

"Why? Is he going to send me apps, too?"

"Maybe. If you want them. Actually, he said . . ."

"What?"

"He told me a few times that he wanted me to show you how to get email."

"He did?"

"Yeah. Maybe he'll suggest a girlfriend for you to get to know over the internet."

"A girlfriend. How can you have a girlfriend over the internet?"

"You'll see. Maybe it will be someone he knows from his school. You can learn more about the things you're always wondering about." He looked at the house again. "But you have to be sure Mama doesn't find out."

"You don't have to tell me that. She was getting angry about the possibility you were doing something with him, and she said she didn't want you playing basketball with him here. She thinks he might talk you and me into taking drugs."

"What? That's stupid. If she meets him . . . maybe later."

"You heard her. She said she doesn't want him coming here now while she's sick. She doesn't trust him because he's just what you said: a city kid. And according to her, city kids are deceptive and dishonest and do drugs. You made a big thing out of his being a city kid after we first met him, too," I reminded him, wondering why his opinion had so shifted.

"I was wrong. You can't lump everyone from the city into the same pot. Don't worry. We'll get her to change her mind."

Of course, I was surprised by this. Trevor rarely went against anything Mama wanted or did.

"You really like him, don't you?"

"He's okay, and he wants to learn things from me, too, especially about nature. I told him about my bow and arrow and how I made a real one. I told him a little bit about how we use the forest as a classroom."

He leaned in to whisper again, as if Mama was nearby.

"He thought it would be cool if the three of us went on that hike through the woods down to the lake. He has a nice camera and wants to get some good pictures to bring home."

"How could we ever do that? It would take hours. We can't leave her until Daddy comes home, and it could be impossible without lying then, too."

"We'll figure it out," he said. He started for the house and then stopped. "Meanwhile, Mr. Longstreet arranged for someone to fix the roof. He'll be here tomorrow morning. I'll tell Mama. Give me that. It's too heavy for you."

"No, it's not."

He laughed. "Pretend it is. You're a young lady now, remember? You acted dainty around Lance."

"*What?* I did not."

He took the heater from me. We started back to the house.

"Lance said he wanted to drop by later."

I paused. He realized that I had and stopped.

"What, Faith?"

"Are you just being a dunce, Trevor? I just told you Mama doesn't want him here, especially while she's sick. You heard her say the same thing. She would send him right home, even though he helped us so much. It would be embarrassing for us, as well as for him. Why didn't you discourage him?"

He thought a moment. "We don't have to tell him that. Maybe we'll meet him outside."

"How are we going to know when he's coming?"

"I'm going to send him my first email, asking. You figure out a way to explain to him why we're meeting him outside," he ordered, and continued to the house.

"Me? Why me?"

"You're better at lying. Liars have to have good memories, and yours is better than mine."

"What? When have I lied, Trevor?"

He raised his hand and kept walking. I looked up the road in the direction of Mr. Longstreet's house. What would I tell Lance if I couldn't explain even to myself why Mama didn't want him around without her ever really meeting him? I'd sound ridiculous if I told him that she was afraid he would contaminate us with evil city boy ideas, even if he agreed there was something like peer pressure. It made it sound like Trevor and I were like putty, gullible and stupid. Why didn't she believe we were strong enough to resist any bad influence, anyway? We never had done anything to give her an opposite opinion. How old did we have to be to meet new people? When would it be safe?

I hurried into the house to work on the pantry. Trevor helped but then snuck away to work on his computer when Mama fell asleep. I couldn't keep my mind off meeting Lance. Was he more interested in talking to Trevor or to me? Why would he be more interested in me? I thought. He surely knew far prettier girls back in New York, girls who had more to say.

That was probably the reason he had told Trevor he would find me a girlfriend on the internet. She would teach me how to not sound and act like some country bumpkin.

He had only been polite when he was here, I decided. Everything else I had thought was just a fantasy. Maybe I wouldn't even bother to go out to meet him. I would probably stay back in case Mama awoke. That was what I was determined I would do until Trevor returned from our classroom upstairs and changed my mind.

"I set up your email name, too," he said. "Faithless."

"What?"

"That's your internet mail name. Kind of a joke. I did what he said and sent him an email from you, too, so we'd both have his name and email. His is Lanceomatic, by the way."

"I don't know what to do with it," I said, acting not very interested, when I was really dying inside to go up and read what he had written.

"It's easy. You go to this website, log in, click on his email, read it, hit reply, write something, and send. C'mon, Faith, you're just as good at computers as I am, and you're always showing me how to research, too.

"He told me he'd be here about five. He's still helping his grandfather with some chores. He wanted to know if he could buy us all pizza for dinner. He asked me what I thought of Mamma Mia's Pizza. I didn't tell him we've never been there or ordered any."

"How can we do that? Why do you keep ignoring what Mama said?"

He shrugged. "I said he should ask you."

"Trevor! Why do you think I'll come up with all the things to do and say? And don't say I'm a better liar. We don't lie to Mama or Big John."

He shrugged. "You've lied to me."

"How? When?"

He shrugged. "You're not a better liar, exactly. You're smarter than me, and sometimes that's the same thing. Besides, Mama once said she pitied people who couldn't lie."

"I can't. Not when it comes to Mama," I said.

"At least you should go look at your computer in the classroom to see what he wrote to you."

He started for the stairs. I looked toward Big John's den to be sure Mama wasn't up, and then I followed. He checked my computer first.

"There it is," he said. "He wrote back to you already. Look. He's looking forward to seeing you again. And asked again about bringing us pizza."

I stared at the monitor screen as if I could have him leap out of it the moment I wrote back to him.

"Well? What do we do?" Trevor asked, folding his arms. "You want to tell him Mama doesn't want him near us? Go ahead."

I sat, thinking. "All right. Here's what we'll do. I'll make Mama an early dinner. He can bring the pizza at six, not five."

"So you think Mama will just be all right with it once he appears?"

"No," I said, starting to write back to Lance.

"Well then . . ."

I paused and looked at him. "When I give her dinner to her . . . I'll make sure her pain pills are included."

His eyes widened. "You mean, poison her?"

"It's not poisoning her, Trevor. It's helping her deal with her pain. You saw her. She'll be dazed and sleepy. Just for tonight," I added. I held my fingers above the keyboard. "Okay?"

He looked a little frightened but then smiled with surprising excitement.

"She'll be really angry when she realizes it."

"Maybe she won't realize it, and besides, by then it will be too late. So?"

He took a deep breath, thought, and nodded. I wrote back

to Lance as if I had been receiving and sending emails for years. Then we hurried downstairs so I could prepare dinner. Mama loved the way I made mashed potatoes with butter, parmesan cheese, chives, a little cream cheese, and garlic with just a pinch of salt and pepper. She had taught me this recipe and then said I was better at it than she was. I took out some hamburger meat, which she liked with a little Worcestershire sauce and onion. Trevor stood by watching in awe as if I was some gourmet chef.

"I didn't realize how good you were at all this," he said.

"I hope I am. Mama will know, and in the mood she's in, she'll tell the truth even more quickly and sharply than she always does."

We heard her moan and hurried to Big John's man cave. She was struggling to sit up and grimacing with the effort. I rushed to help her. Giving her the pain pills might not be such a bad idea after all, I thought, and gave Trevor a look that he understood.

"Bathroom," she said.

Trevor got her crutch, and we helped her to her feet, escorting her to the bathroom. She paused at the doorway and turned, mainly to him.

"My wonderful children. I just knew you'd be up to the challenge. We'll get through this together. As long as you both do as I say," she added firmly, looking more at me.

"Of course we will, Mama," I said. Trevor nodded. "I'm working on your dinner, too, making your favorite mashed potatoes with some hamburger and salad. Okay?"

She smiled and touched my face. "Our little girl, already like a little mother. Thank you, dear."

"And Mr. Longstreet's roofer will be here in the morning tomorrow, Mama," Trevor said. "We'll get the pantry back in shape by then, too."

"I know you will. My little man and my little woman," she said, and went into the bathroom.

Both Trevor and I released a sigh of relief. I returned to my work on the dinner, cutting up the salad ingredients.

When Mama came out of the bathroom, I thought she was going to stand over me and watch me prepare everything and ruin my plan, but she didn't. Trevor helped her back to her room and set up a small table by the makeshift bed. She took her antibiotic, and then Trevor put on Big John's television set for her so she could watch some news and one of her favorite programs. After that, he strutted and paced around me as I worked on the mashed potatoes. Mama had just assumed we'd be eating the same things, so just in case she looked, I made enough for all three of us. I thought Trevor was going to stop me when I took four of her pain pills and ground them to put them on her mashed potatoes, but he just sucked in his breath.

"I guess you really want pizza," he said. I looked at him. He seemed like he was kidding, teasing me, but I couldn't be sure, as usual.

He followed me when I carried the tray into Big John's room and set it on the small table. I fixed Mama's pillows so she could sit up.

"I'm actually a little hungry," she said. "And this looks very good."

"You should be, Mama. You haven't really eaten much since the accident."

"Yes," she said, scooping up some mashed potatoes just where I had placed the pills. I sent Trevor out for another glass of cold water, because he was gaping too much and could easily cause some suspicion.

"It's delicious," she said. "You could take care of us all already."

"Thank you, Mama. I'll just have Trevor help me with our dinner," I said, as soon as he brought in the water.

"Good. Men should help. They always expect to be waited on hand and foot. It's in their DNA."

"We'll get it out of Trevor's, Mama," I said, looking at him.

She actually laughed. He smiled nervously, and we left her eating. We both sat in the kitchen and waited without saying a word.

"How many pills did you give her again?"

"Four of them."

He went from terrified to astonished at my courage. I was surprised at myself, too, surprised at how far I would go to see Lance again.

"Is that all right?"

"Sure," I said with absolutely false confidence. "It will only make her sleep longer," I said, and we rose to go check on her.

"Want more, Mama?" I asked when I went back in and saw she had eaten everything on the plate.

"No, thank you," she said. "I'll just rest a little."

I quickly picked up her tray and fluffed her pillows. She lay back, looking contented.

"I think my foot is improving already," she said.

"That's so great, Mama. We'll just eat in the dining room. Don't worry. We won't make a mess," Trevor promised.

"Oh, I know you won't. Our little mama won't let you," she said, her eyelids fluttering.

Trevor, maybe out of fear more than anything else, quickly retreated to the kitchen. I stood there watching her close her eyes. She fell into breathing softly in and out. What if we had gone too far? If she realized it, she'd be so furious. It wasn't something I could change, however. What was done was done. I hurried out to the front entrance, because I could hear Trevor opening the door for Lance and whispering to him.

"Our mother's trying to sleep," he told him. "We have to be very, very quiet."

Lance nodded and widened his smile when I appeared.

He was wearing a light turquoise sweater with a black shirt beneath it, the collar making for a stunning contrast that brought out more of the violet in his eyes. His hair was brushed back but wavy on top. His tight jeans emphasized his sleek, firm physique. His white running shoes looked brand-new. I saw he was wearing a gold watch with a black leather band. It looked expensive.

From the expression on his face, Trevor revealed how much he was in awe of Lance's outfit. There was a dramatic contrast with his well-washed and faded blue shirt and baggy black pants. Neither of us had a watch. Mama had promised Trevor one on his sixteenth birthday and me one on my fifteenth, but I knew she would never give me a watch and not Trevor. If she was going to do it, it would be on his birthday, I thought, not mine.

Trevor glanced at me, urging me with his eyes to explain more and take control of our situation. Lance was holding the pizza box on his extended arms.

"I think, so we don't disturb Mama, that we should eat dinner in our classroom upstairs. Put our desks together to make a table, Trevor, but first, go get some cans of soda, and then show Lance where to go. I'll bring up the salad, paper plates, plastic forks and knives, and napkins."

Trevor hesitated.

"Just show him the classroom," I emphasized, still speaking in a loud whisper. He nodded and rushed back to the kitchen.

"Is your mother really all right?" Lance asked in his subdued voice.

"Yes," I said, "but she's very cranky."

He nodded. "Yeah, I guess I'd be, too."

"You look very nice," I said. There was a faint blush in his face. "I'm sorry I haven't had time to put on anything nice," I added, even though I knew I had nothing that would stand out. Our clothes were almost hand-me-downs.

"You don't need much window dressing, Faith."

I simply stared stupidly, I was sure. Somewhere, floating in my mind, was the realization that this was really the first compliment I had received from a boy. Getting compliments from Trevor, if I could even call them that, was like pulling teeth.

A surge of tingling warmth moved up from my stomach, circled my breasts, and flowed softly into my neck and then made my cheeks feel warmer. Inside, I was stuttering and stammering for the right words, words that wouldn't sound childish or conceited. I had to reach into places that were just opening for me and leap over the narrow canyon lying between being a girl and becoming a young woman, ironically the woman Mama believed I had become.

Thank you would sound so inadequate and much too formal.

Do you really think so? would put my childish immaturity in bold print and also sound very insecure.

And then it came to me as if I had truly grown into it.

I simply smiled, but my smile wasn't something found on the face of a giggle or a laugh. It was an adult smile with just the right touch of yes, a smile that would make him feel confident of my welcoming his flattery, a smile that told him I wanted it from him, wanted even more.

He sensed it. There was an excitement in his eyes, a glitter as his face folded into a deeper smile than mine.

Trevor returned, oblivious to what had gone on between Lance and me, and led him up the stairway, giving him some history of our house and family just the way Mama would have if she had welcomed him here and was showing him around.

I hurried to the kitchen to get everything else. Before I returned to the stairs, I looked in on Mama. She was in a deep sleep, her mouth slightly open. She looked so helpless and fragile that for a moment, I regretted doing what I had done. But I told myself it was for the best. She wasn't in pain, and no one had to be upset. I remembered how often Mama would tell us that excuses were like soap washing away the smudge of guilt. "When it's a deep stain, nothing but confession will fade it away."

Surely, this wasn't a deep stain.

Not yet.

I hurried up the stairs.

Trevor was showing Lance our microscope and explaining a slide. Lance looked up when I entered and put the bowl of salad on the table Trevor had formed with our desks.

"I didn't realize how complete a classroom you guys have," Lance said, looking around. "A blackboard, DVDs, telescopes, microscopes . . . looks like you have as many books as my school library."

"Not that many. Mama gets some delivered, and there are some from her own library. She gets us whatever she thinks we need when she thinks we need it. Let's eat," I said.

They sat down quickly.

"And there's even a bulletin board with your recent science tests. A hundred on intermediate algebra? Both of you? I don't take that for another year."

"Trevor cheats," I joked.

"I do not."

"Who sees that bulletin board?" Lance asked, a sillier smile on his face. Of course, it was embarrassing to me now. When I was much younger, Mama putting stars on my work or pinning it to the board brought me great pride and satisfaction. I knew what Lance's smile was clearly saying: it was childish now for kids our age.

"Whoever Mama wants to see it," I said, perhaps too sharply. I certainly didn't want to talk about it.

"So she and your father have a lot of friends she brings up here?"

"Not a lot, no . . ." I said.

I looked at Trevor. He was either oblivious about how it looked for us or smart enough to come up with something that would get the topic off the table.

"I'm starving," he said, which proved to be enough.

"Me too," Lance seconded.

I was aware of how Lance was staring at me as I portioned out the salad and put slices of pizza on all our plates. I was afraid to look directly at him, because I was sure I would blush. Maybe there was something instinctive about it, but I felt I had to keep my feelings and reactions from being too obvious. I might have been afraid I'd be laughed at, too.

How I wished I had a girlfriend, internet or otherwise, who would tell me about the first time a strange boy had looked at her as a girl and she had felt the sexual excitement. Was it the same for her, a little bit of pleasure mixed with a little bit of fear? Did she smile or keep her eyes averted? Was she embarrassed by the flush in her face, or did she clamp down on her feelings and pretend indifference? All I knew was it felt quite different from the way I had reacted to Trevor seeing me naked or what I knew to be the surprised feelings he had when he looked at me becoming a young woman. Our closeness closed the curtain, and although there was nothing incestuous about it, it felt like there was.

"I hope you don't mind eating in our classroom," I said, looking for safe places to go with my thoughts.

He gazed around and then leaned in as if someone was nearby and could hear us.

"To be honest, I'd eat anywhere. Grandpa talks my ears into exhaustion. Everything I see or anything we do leads to one of his long-winded stories. I know he's happy to have someone to listen to him, and it's probably not nice to complain."

"Maybe he talks so much because he thinks you're nervous or uncomfortable," I suggested.

The way he was looking at me changed. It was as if I had just revealed I had brains.

"Yeah, I bet," he said. "We skirt talking about my parents, but you can be sure the nasty divorce hovers over us like some rain cloud. Speaking of which, Grandpa and I will pop around to see how his roofer is doing for you in the morning."

Whether he saw something in my face or not, he quickly added, "I'll stay out so as not to make your mother feel uncomfortable. My mother is like that, actually. If a blemish appears on her face, she won't go out until it is gone. She isn't confident in her makeup covering it." He paused. "My mother could have been a Miss America contestant," he said, finally revealing some pride in at least one of his parents.

"She's that beautiful?" I asked.

Trevor was eating like he hadn't for days. The conversation wasn't interesting to him, anyway.

Lance paused to take out his wallet and show me a picture of his mother. She looked much younger than I had imagined.

"Oh, she is very beautiful."

"Thanks."

Trevor didn't ask to see it, so Lance put his wallet back in his pocket.

"My father's not bad-looking either," he said with a shrug.

"Explains it," I said.

He paused. So did Trevor.

"Explains what?"

I looked at them both. I felt like a diver who had gone off the edge of the board just a little too soon. There was no going back.

"Well, you're not bad-looking, Lance," I said, trying to make it sound as inconsequential as I could.

It was too late, of course. I was off the diving board. I lowered my head and ate.

Trevor, either trying to save me from embarrassment or because my complimenting Lance annoyed him, started to talk about how he could show Lance where certain animals were or had been in the woods, even the now infamous bobcat.

"Yeah, that would be fun," Lance said.

"I can meet you at the stone wall, maybe tomorrow in the afternoon, if the roofer finishes, and we'll take a walk through the woods."

"Sure," Lance said.

Trevor looked at me with an expression that seemed to be a boast. Lance was more interested in being with him than he was in being with me.

Everyone ate silently for a while.

"So what do you guys think of the pizza? It's not New York pizza, but it's pretty good."

I looked at Trevor.

"We don't have pizza much. Mama doesn't think it's a real meal, even with salad," he said. "But she can make it," he quickly added.

"Make it like this?"

"Oh, yeah. Better," Trevor said.

"Wow. That's neat," Lance said. "My mother took cooking lessons just for fun with her friends, but"—he leaned toward me—"I'd rather get takeout anytime."

Trevor ate his last piece. "Anyway, this is a meal for me. Especially with your great salad," he told me.

"Thank you."

I started to gather the plates, knives, and forks.

"I'll be right back," Trevor said, and hurried out to the bathroom. I paused and looked after him.

"Something wrong?" Lance asked when I didn't turn back.

I thought a moment and then sat again. His eyes widened with expectation.

"We lied to you," I said. "We aren't eating up here just to keep from waking my mother."

He smiled but without any confidence.

"What do you mean?"

"My mother thinks you might be a bad influence."

"Bad influence? Why? What did I do?"

"Nothing you did. It's sort of like you might bring bad habits to us from the city school. You know, things everyone encourages others to do or they won't be friends."

"Oh. You mean that peer pressure thing?"

"Yes. She'd rather . . ."

"We didn't hang out?"

I nodded.

"So that's why I feel like we're sneaking around," he said.

"Of course, we both disagree. We just don't want . . ."

"To rile her up," he said, nodding, adding what he hoped were the right words. "Don't worry about it." He thought a moment and leaned toward me. "My grandfather said she's a bit weird, practically a hermit. She really doesn't have any friends come around, does she?"

"No, but I wouldn't call my mother weird. She's just . . . worried. She was a teacher, and she saw bad things in the school. She hated the job because parents weren't very cooperative and spoiled their children."

He stared a moment.

"Well, you two don't seem so weird," he said. "I mean, it's odd some of the things you didn't know and don't do. But . . ." He shrugged. "Believe me, I have a lot of much, much odder friends in New York."

"I'm not sure I like being thought odd."

"Oh, I don't think you are. In fact, I kinda like your . . ."

"What?"

"Not knowing stuff. It makes you . . . fresh. My grandpa might say like the air up here. Pure."

Now I did blush.

"I'm only fourteen," I said. "Why shouldn't I be like that?"

He laughed. "Some of the fourteen-year-old girls I know were born R-rated."

I looked toward the bathroom. Where was Trevor? Did he go into our bedroom and leave the door open?

"I hope we can still figure out a way to hang out," he said. "I mean, unless you don't want to."

"No. I'd like to meet you whenever we can."

"Okay. I'd like that, too."

"But I don't want to make my mother sicker than she is."

"Sure. I get it," he said, smiling. "I guess I'd better sneak out."

He stood up.

"We'll check," I said, when Trevor reappeared.

"Check what?" he asked.

"Mama might have woken. Let's bring everything down before we bring Lance down. Just in case," I said.

Trevor looked from me to Lance and back to me.

"What did you tell him while I was in the bathroom, Faith?"

"The truth, Trevor."

He looked angry for a moment.

"Lance is good with it, Trevor. We'll meet just the way you suggested."

He looked at Lance, who held his soft smile.

"My mother . . ." Trevor began.

"It's okay," Lance said. "She'll change her mind after a while. Meanwhile, we'll do what you said and meet at the wall tomorrow afternoon."

"You should always stay with Mama," Trevor told me. "Until she can get around more herself. That way, if I go off with Lance, you can say I'm in the woods looking for specimens."

Then how will I ever see him? I wondered, but didn't say.

"Whatever. C'mon," I said, handing him some dishes. I put the empty soda cans on top of them. I certainly didn't want to tell him Lance's grandfather thought Mama was weird. He would get very angry.

I got everything else together, and we started out, practically tiptoeing down the stairway. As quietly as possible, we put what we had to get rid of in the garbage bin and everything else in the sink. I peeked in on Mama. She hadn't moved and was snoring a little.

"We've got to get back to the pantry," I told Trevor. "We promised it would be done tonight. She's still asleep."

"Okay."

"I'll get Lance," I said, before he could, and hurried back to the stairway.

He was hovering near the top step. I beckoned to him, and he started down softly, an amused smile on his face.

"First time I had secret pizza," he whispered.

I looked back at the kitchen. Trevor started toward us.

"Start on the pantry. I'll walk him out," I said. He paused, his eyelids narrowing. Then he turned sharply and went to the pantry.

I opened the front door softly, and we stepped out. I kept my arms folded across my breasts. He started down the steps and then stopped.

"What?" I asked, when he didn't say anything.

He walked back up to me.

"I wasn't lying earlier. You are pretty, Faith, and really refreshing."

Unexpectedly, he kissed me quickly, hesitated, and kissed me again. My eyes were still closed when he stepped back.

"Promise we will keep seeing each other," he said. "We'll keep thinking of ways."

"I promise."

"Good. Secret romances are hotter," he said.

He smiled and started for his grandfather's car. I waited until he got in and even after he had pulled onto the road and the rear lights disappeared in the darkness.

I thought I could still feel his lips on mine.

I knew I would fall asleep with them still there.

Maybe he was right. Secret romances were sexier.

ten

Mama woke shortly after we had finished reloading the shelves in the pantry. She was groggy and complained, but I didn't think she was suspicious of my putting her pain pills into the mashed potatoes. Both Trevor and I helped her up to go to the bathroom.

She stopped to look at the work we had done.

"How wonderful," she said. "I'm very proud of you two."

"I should continue to sleep on the sofa in case you need something during the night, Mama," I said.

She nodded. And then she shook her head. "You've made dinner and everything. Let Trevor sleep on the sofa," she said. "Not that I expect to need anything." She smiled. She reached out to stroke Trevor's hair. "It's comforting to know my little man is watching over us."

Trevor glanced at me. He never gloated when she gave him a compliment and not me. He looked more like he was worried I'd be upset, but I showed no emotion. He continued to help Mama to the bathroom. I went up to Mama and Daddy's bedroom and got some new things for Mama to wear in the morning. I heard Trevor rush up to fetch his bedding and pajamas. After I gave Mama her things, I went to the living room, paused, and watched him fix the sofa.

"Are you really going to help her if she messes the bed or something?" I asked.

I knew I was being petulant. Usually, I contained my jealousy of what I was sure was Mama's stronger love for him than for me. He never seemed to be jealous or care when she said something nice to me and not to him, but that only made the jealousy I hid in my heart deeper and sharper. He was never jealous because he was so confident of her stronger love.

He grimaced. "She's not going to do that, Faith."

I gave him a Trevor shrug. "If you need my help, just shout, Trevor."

"I won't. Go do your dreaming."

"What does that mean?"

He turned back to me, smirked, and nodded just like Mama would when she was convinced of something she thought.

"Mama told me that often when girls become women, they become deceitful."

"What? What does that mean?"

"But it's not all your fault. There's deceit on both sides."

"What sides? What are you talking about?"

"He's just pretending to be interested in doing stuff with me just so he can get to you. I can see that now."

I stared with a strange mix of feelings: excitement and joy that Trevor saw this in Lance, but also shame, even fear that what he was saying was true. Would he get so upset that he'd mention it to Mama? Denying that I wished it would be true was pointless. Despite what he had said earlier, from the day we were brought together at the Wexlers' foster home until now, I had believed that neither of us could lie to the other successfully. Perhaps that was why Big John thought we were as good as twins.

I could see the anticipation in Trevor's face, my expected denial and surprise.

"I was afraid to think so, especially about Lance," I said instead. "I don't want us both to look stupid. You're the one who set up our computers with his email, and you've spent more time with him than I have, actually. I thought you really liked him and he liked you."

His smirk quickly evaporated.

"Well, maybe it's not just to get to you. He really was amazed at some of the things I told him we do in the woods and how much there was for him to see. He is really a city kid," he said, and completed his bedding. He sprawled out with his hand behind his head and looked up at the ceiling.

"Don't worry. I'll look after you just the way Mama expects I will."

Before I could reply, he turned to me quickly and added, "As long as you're honest with me."

"I don't know why you said I lied to you. When haven't I been honest?" I said in a small voice. I felt the tears forming under my lower eyelids.

He didn't answer. Trevor could be infuriating if I let him be.

"I'm tired. Call me if you need me to help," I said.

"Right," he said, and closed his eyes. But he opened them when we heard the phone ring. I rushed to the one in the kitchen before Mama got up to do so.

"Hello?"

Trevor came to the doorway.

"It's Daddy," I told him.

"Yes, she's resting comfortably, Daddy. Trevor told Mr. Longstreet about the roof, and he has someone coming here in the morning."

I listened and nodded at Trevor. "I'll tell her. Glad you'll be here, Daddy. Yes. Don't worry."

As soon as I hung up, I told Trevor, "He's driving through the night to be here tomorrow as early as he can. He wasn't sure of the time, but he's sure he'll be here one way or another."

"Good."

I looked in on Mama. She had slept through it.

"We'll tell her tomorrow morning."

He nodded and returned to his bed on the sofa. I stared at him a moment, still thinking about what he had said, and then I hurried upstairs. I was happy Big John would be back sooner. But I wasn't thinking of him.

Trevor's beliefs about Lance's feelings for me only enhanced my own. If I felt or believed something and Trevor did, too, it always made me more confident that I was right to think or feel it.

Oh, that kiss, my first kiss. Could Trevor or Mama see it on my lips? Could they sense that it had happened? I ran my fingers over them and then kissed the tips. Chills quickly turned to a trickle of warmth between my breasts. I closed my eyes to see his face close to mine. Would I feel this way about any first kiss? How would I know? Did it matter? I felt what I felt right now. That was what mattered.

Mama had wanted me to wait until she told me to wear it, but after having kissed Lance, the idea of wearing the sheer nightgown excited me. It was like putting thin tissue over my naked body. With the one lamp on behind me, I looked at myself in the mirror over our dresser. My nipples were stiffening, and my firm, rounding breasts looked more developed than they had looked to me earlier today. Was it merely wishful thinking, or could a boy's interest in me speed up my maturity?

My breathing, although almost unheard, quickened.

I went to the window and gazed at the road running by our house. Car lights cast a splash of white over the macadam and passed by quickly, the night rushing in behind it as if it was closing a door that had opened to reveal more and more discoveries about myself. Without anything moving and with only the glimmering of distant stars on the treetops, I felt more locked in than ever. The only real escape was the window I could open in my own mind.

Letting my imagination run wild, I envisioned Lance standing in the dark shadows of tall oaks across the way. Unable to just go to sleep or maybe because his grandfather was talking a blue streak, he had decided to walk back to look up at our windows, even though he couldn't be sure which were the ones in the bedroom, a bedroom he still didn't know I shared with Trevor. Instinctively, perhaps because Big John made such a thing of it, I knew Lance would be very upset, too, disturbed and perhaps completely turned off when he found out. I suddenly had the thought, or really the fear, that at some point, either because he was jealous or because he was following Mama's wishes, Trevor would, as innocently as he could, mention that he and I shared a bedroom and a bed.

"Oh, it's very big, a king-size, wide enough for two more of us," he might add, but that wouldn't be enough to get Lance not to think we were strange, and Trevor would know it wouldn't.

Maybe Lance would ask me if that were true. Maybe Mama was right about girls being more deceptive when they became women, but I had no experience lying, to a new boy especially. The proof of that was how I had just had to tell Lance the truth as to why we were eating upstairs. Maybe I wasn't woman enough yet, according to Mama's measurements. I half wondered if it wouldn't be better if I just up and told Lance about my sharing a bedroom with Trevor. I could make it sound innocuous, couldn't I?

Now you're lying to yourself, Faith, I thought. Who would think it was harmless, even if we were really brother and sister?

I knew what Nanny Too would think.

She'd think Satan lived here.

I didn't want to drive Lance away, not yet, maybe not ever. He'd kissed me. Did that mean he wanted to be my boyfriend, even after he left and returned to New York City? He would have more reason to visit his grandfather. He could stay in touch with me on the computer. Should I do what Trevor told me to do? Should I dream?

I ran the palms of my hands down over my breasts, closed my eyes, and wished that when I opened them, I'd see Lance down on the highway looking up at me, the twinkling stars lighting his smile.

He wasn't there. But for now, it was enough to imagine it. I crawled into bed. Oddly, not having Trevor there beside me bothered me for a few moments. I anticipated him coming through the door, following me into the bathroom, getting into his pajamas, and sliding under the blanket as usual.

"Nighty night," he'd always say, and because it had once been more than just a joke, he always added, "Don't let the bedbugs bite."

"Yes," I whispered. He always turned on his side, his back to me.

But convinced that we were safe, I closed my eyes, unclenched my fingers, and trusted the darkness. I slipped into my fantasies and reveled in how they softly led me to sleep.

Surprisingly, I overslept. What woke me was the sound of voices below. Mama was shouting out a window to someone. I heard Trevor's voice, too, coming from outside. Sitting up quickly, I listened and realized Trevor was describing our roof leak. I rushed to the bathroom quickly, washed, and then hurriedly dressed to go down.

"What kept you in dreamland?" Mama asked. She was sitting in the kitchen, a cup of coffee in hand. She still looked pale and tired.

"Sorry, Mama. I guess it was more of an exhausting day than I thought."

"Umm," she grunted.

We heard a ladder against the house.

"Mr. Longstreet's man is here?" I started for the rear door.

"Get your breakfast," she said. "And make me some eggs, too. Trevor will be hungry when he comes in. There's nothing you can do out there. Whatever the roof repairman needs, Trevor will take care of it."

I couldn't help wondering if Lance had come over with his grandfather, too, but I hurried to do what Mama asked. The phone rang. My heart started thumping, because it might be Lance, and

Mama would grow even more suspicious. It was Daddy. I told her and held up the receiver.

"See what he wants," she ordered with a flick of her wrist.

"Mama's having breakfast," I told him. He asked if the roofer had said anything yet. I told him he was just getting to it.

"I've had some engine trouble and probably won't get back until either late tonight or tomorrow morning. If it's any later, I'll call again."

"Okay, Daddy. I'll tell her." I hung up.

"What?" she demanded before I could speak.

"He has engine trouble and has to stop for repairs. He doesn't think he'll get back until late tonight or the morning."

"Broke down? In that fancy truck of his?" She looked away, thinking. "Convenient, isn't it?" she muttered.

"What do you mean?"

She gave me a little smirk. "Figure it out. You're old enough now."

"You think Daddy's lying?"

She didn't answer. Did she think he had a girlfriend, someone he visited when he was on the road?

"Maybe he pushed it too hard, Mama. He called last night when you were asleep and said he would drive all night."

She grunted, sipped her coffee, and then looked at me quickly.

"How'd he know the roofer had arrived already?"

"I told him about the roofer when he called while you were sleeping. He's probably kept in touch with Mr. Longstreet, too."

"Damn pills. Don't know where I am half the time." She thought a moment. "Don't even remember taking them."

I held my breath. "You were in and out of a lot of pain, Mama."

"Yes." She thought a moment, and then her eyes seemed to spring at me.

"Watch that those eggs don't get too dry," she said, nodding at the stove.

Trevor came in to make a report, saying it would take most of the morning and into the afternoon, but the roofer, a Mr. Donnelly, said it would be just fine. He'd check the rest of the roof for any potential leaks. I waited to see if he was going to mention either Mr. Longstreet or Lance, but he didn't and he sat for breakfast.

"Remember, Trevor likes his eggs a little wet," Mama reminded me.

Trevor nodded and looked at me. He was already acting like the man of the house, and for some reason, that annoyed me.

"Daddy's stuck on the road," I said. "He had an engine problem that's being fixed, but he's not sure if he'll get here tonight or tomorrow."

"What was it? What broke?"

"I don't know, Trevor. Ask him when he gets here," I said sharply.

He looked surprised and then drank his juice. Since Trevor had to be available for anything the roofer needed, Mama declared we had part of the day off from school. It wasn't really a free time for me, because she assigned me some of the cleaning she did daily. I did that and made lunch, just peanut butter and jelly sandwiches for Trevor and me and a can of chicken noodle soup for Mama. He insisted on heating it and giving it to her himself. She didn't want anything else.

Even though she didn't take any more pain pills, Mama slept on and off. I continually looked outside for signs of Mr. Longstreet and Lance. About three o'clock, while Mama was still taking another nap, they drove up. I couldn't help but wonder if Lance had told his grandfather that he was what Mama taught us in English class, persona non grata. However, I didn't think he would have brought him along if he had.

When his grandfather got out to talk to Mr. Donnelly, Lance got out, too, but he leaned against their car. He wore a red short-sleeved shirt and jeans. Strands of his hair danced around his forehead in the breeze. I thought he looked quite handsome and relaxed, as if nothing I had told him mattered. Yet I was afraid to step out.

If Mama awoke and somehow got to a window . . .

Trevor walked up to him, and they talked. Lance's eyes shifted to the windows, but I kept out of sight. When his grandfather returned to the car, he spoke to Trevor, patted him on the shoulder, and got into his car. Lance said something else to Trevor and got in. I watched them drive off.

Would he ever come back? What had Trevor told him? Surely, he had asked about me. But I dared not ask.

I continued dusting and polishing the furniture, stopping when Trevor came in. He glanced at me and looked in on Mama, who had woken and sat up.

"All done, Mama. He said you could mail the payment."

He handed the bill to her.

"He checked the rest of the roof and said it was all good."

"Your father will be paying this out of his account," she said, waving it. She closed her eyes. "Get me those pain pills," she told him. "They said it would feel worse before it got better, and it does, a lot worse."

Trevor turned to me, and I hurried to get them and a glass of water. Mama swallowed them and glared at me a moment with that look of suspicion either I imagined or she had.

"Go do some of your assigned math problems until dinner. There's still a good hour not to waste," she ordered. "I don't want either of you falling too far behind. It's pasta night, Faith. You do the angel hair and eggplant. Won't take too long to prepare just the way I taught you."

She lay back.

"Yes, Mama."

I hurried away, expecting Trevor to follow me up to the classroom, but he didn't. I waited at the top of the stairs and then finally tiptoed back down. He was standing in the living room, staring out the window.

"What are you doing?"

He turned. I thought he wasn't going to answer and would just turn back, but he smiled.

"Lance is going to sneak back, and we're going to fix the basketball hoop and shoot some hoops for a little while."

"But Mama will hear you."

"Not if those pills work the way they did the last time."

"I gave her more then. Two won't keep her asleep as long, and—"

"I put two in her soup, so I guess she'll sleep longer because of the ones you gave her, too."

"What? How?"

"I crushed them up, and when I gave her the bowl of soup, I had mixed them in. She had those on top of the ones you just gave her . . . well, it didn't hurt her and helped her feel better when you did it, didn't it?" he said. "Mr. Longstreet said the doctor told him that the more she sleeps, the better. She'll stay off that foot and heal faster."

I looked at him. I had never thought he would do what I had done. It almost made me smile.

"You can be a bad boy," I teased.

"Yeah, yeah. Just do my math problems along with yours. Okay? I'll do something for you."

"What?"

"I don't know. There'll be something."

I nodded and then went up. It wasn't easy doing our assignment. My mind kept drifting, and almost every five minutes or so, I got up and went to the window in Mama and Daddy's bedroom to look out at the garage. When I looked the third time, I saw Lance on the ladder fixing the net around the hoop. I watched him come down, and the two of them put the ladder aside. Lance was very good, making one shot after another. Every once in a while, he stopped to explain something to Trevor.

I tiptoed down and looked in on Mama. She was in a deep sleep, but if she hadn't been, she might have been able to hear the basketball hit the garage wall or the hoop, because I could. Trevor's courage really did surprise me.

I stepped out of the back door very quietly and stood watching them until they noticed me and stopped.

"She wake up?" Trevor asked.

I shook my head.

"Homework's done?"

"No."

"You want to take a shot?" Lance asked, holding out the ball. "I'll show you how. We have a good girls' team."

I shook my head. "No, thank you. I just wanted some fresh air," I said. I didn't know why, but I was feeling very annoyed, very angry, maybe because it seemed that he really wanted to play hoops with Trevor and wasn't using it as an excuse to see me.

I turned and went back inside. Mama still hadn't woken. I returned to the classroom and went through our assignments quickly, filling in Trevor's papers, too.

When I went down again to prepare dinner, I didn't see either of them in front of the garage. Mama groaned, and I froze. Where was Trevor? She was sure to ask. Then I heard the front door open and close.

He appeared, looking sweaty, a mud streak across his forehead.

"Where were you?" I asked in a loud whisper.

"He wanted to see that massive anthill and take some pictures of it."

"That's far in."

"Yeah. So I ran back. I think I can run faster than him. Anyway, he caught his foot on a tree root and took a real flop," he said. He looked happy about it. "City kid."

"Did he get hurt?"

"Gash in his forehead. Maybe he'll need a stitch or two. Remember when I did something like that and Mama sewed me up? I couldn't bring him back here for her to do it. Who knows how many stitches she'd put in?"

He laughed.

"But how badly is he hurt?"

"If it's bad, his grandfather will take him to the doctor or the hospital. Basketball practice at our house will be on hold, I'm sure, at least for him. City kids are kinda weak."

"It's not funny, Trevor."

"I'd better wash up. How's my homework?"

"It's all done," I said sullenly, and turned away from him.

Mama called louder. She struggled to sit up and then looked at me.

"I hate those damn pills," she said.

"But Trevor reminded me that Mr. Longstreet said the doctor told him you'll heal faster if you're not in constant pain. And you asked for them. You needed them. Don't you want to get better faster? Why do people have to be talked into doing things for their own good?"

She looked at me warily. I sounded more like her. I wondered if she was going to laugh or scream at me for talking to her like that.

"Where's Trevor?" she asked instead.

"Finishing up his math work."

We heard the phone, and for a moment, I held my breath. Was it Mr. Longstreet complaining about what had happened to Lance?

"Well, answer it," Mama snapped.

I hurried to do so and breathed relief. It was Daddy.

Mama struggled to get up before I could help her and hobbled to the phone.

"Where are you?"

As she listened, she nodded and gestured for me to start dinner.

"How would I know? We'll have to wait for the next big rain to see," she said. "Yes, yes, they're doing fine. Both of them are little adults. You should be happy about how I reared them, and you should stop complaining. Good," she said. I thought she was hanging up, but she listened. "When? Okay," she said. She hung up without saying good-bye.

"What did he say, Mama?"

"He said his engine was fixed, and he estimates he'll be here by ten or eleven."

"Oh. I'll wait up for him."

"Work on dinner," she told me.

Trevor appeared, looking washed and fresh.

"What a handsome young man we have to take care of us all this time," Mama said.

Trevor smiled like a flower bursting into bloom.

"I'm starving," he said.

"Just sit in the living room like your father does, and we'll let you know when it's ready," Mama said. He looked at me with satisfaction smeared on his face like whipped cream. Mama told him about Daddy.

"That's great. I'll wait up for him, too."

Later, Mama said I had done a good job on dinner, but she just wasn't that hungry. She blamed it on "those damn pain pills." She was practically swaying in her chair. I told her to go back to bed and that we'd take care of cleaning up the kitchen. Surprisingly, she didn't resist. She actually dozed off again.

Trevor decided to watch television. I went up to read. I had left the novel Mama had assigned back in the classroom. When I entered, I realized my computer was on and the screen had lit up.

I had an email from Lance. I looked at the door first and listened to be sure Trevor wasn't coming up. Then I opened the email and read.

He wanted us to meet tonight. He said he would wait by the other side of the garage for me if I said I would. My fingers actually trembled on the keys as I wrote back. We aimed for in about a half hour. I had to sneak out without either Mama or Trevor knowing.

It frightened and excited me. I waited until a half hour had nearly passed and went down, holding my book.

"You should watch this," Trevor said sotto voce, and looked back toward Big John's den. "Mama would never let us watch it, for sure."

"I just want a glass of milk. I wanted to finish reading this."

"Really?"

"I don't want to be here if she comes in and sees you," I said.

"Oh, c'mon. We'd hear her get up and use that crutch."

"Rather read," I said.

"Do what you want."

I went into the kitchen, got a glass of water, looked in on Mama, and made more noise returning to the stairway. Midway up, I paused and tiptoed back down. I knew I could slip out the front door more easily than going back through the kitchen to the rear. I think I spent a good ten minutes, pausing after every creak in the tattletale floorboards. I waited when I reached the front door. It was clear Trevor hadn't heard me.

I barely opened the door enough to slip through and then gently closed it behind me. I thought my racing heart would thump so loudly both Mama and Trevor would hear it. A little dizzy with my courage, I took almost a minute to go down the front steps, listening constantly for either Mama's or Trevor's voice, and then I ran to the garage.

I pressed myself against the door and looked back at the house, especially the windows to the kitchen. Then I slowly made my way around to the far side. Lance was sitting on the ground, his knees up, his arms around them.

"Hi," I said.

He turned slowly. Through the broken clouds, the starlight illuminated his face. I saw the large Band-Aid on his forehead.

"Did you need stitches? Trevor told me about your fall."

"Naw. My grandfather said it wasn't deep enough. I just scraped against some small rocks, nothing jagged. Trevor was obviously afraid to be caught out there. He didn't even pause to help me up but just waited for me to get to my knees. When he saw my forehead bleeding, he told me to go get some stitches. Then he ran off."

He chuckled. "Why is he so afraid? Why are you? I mean, what are you doing that's so terrible? Just going outside? I don't get it."

"My mother's still in pain," I said. "And she hates the pain pills. They make her groggy and cranky."

He shrugged. Then he smiled again and patted the ground beside him.

I sat, slowly, my eyes toward the house.

"Hey, I'm not Jack the Ripper. Your mother doesn't have to be that afraid. Is she really worried because I'm from the city?"

"My mother's always been very protective. Not so much our father."

"Maybe she's just paranoid. We had a kid with a mother like that in my school. His mother practically smothered him. Even on really warm days, she made him wear a scarf. He had skin like milk, so she caked him in sunscreen. He looked like something from outer space. Wasn't long before someone made up a chant that everyone sang: 'Bobby cannot play hardball. Softball yes, hardball no.'"

He laughed.

"You sang it, too?"

"Guilty. She took him out of the school a few months ago."

"That's sad, but my mother's not like that. She's just worried because of bad things she saw when she was a teacher and because . . . she feels more responsible for us than my father. She picked us out," I said.

"What's that mean?"

I explained how she had gone to the foster home and found us. I left out the crown of light.

"I know you think we're different."

"Different but not ugly," he said.

I lowered my head. He put his hand under my chin and lifted it so I could turn toward him and his lips. This kiss was longer, deeper. I felt it reach into the pit of my stomach and then fill me with waves of warmth that embraced my heart. I turned in to him to kiss him again. His hands moved off my shoulders to my hips and then seemed to glide up to my breasts.

He moaned and turned, gently lowering me as he moved over me and began to kiss my neck, bringing his lips down to my blouse. He unbuttoned it almost without my feeling him doing it.

And then his lips smoothly moved along the top of my bra.

"Faith," he whispered. "You're so pretty, so precious."

Firmly, he lifted me just enough to get his hands inside my blouse and behind me to unfasten my bra. Almost vaguely, I thought I should get him to stop, but I felt delightfully helpless and intrigued with what his lips were going to feel like on my nipples. I leaned my head back when he kissed my breasts and closed his lips on my nipples, going from one to the other in almost a frenzy.

His right hand moved up my leg.

But just then, we heard Trevor's loud whisper calling my name. We both froze.

I reached back and quickly fastened my bra and began buttoning my blouse. Lance stepped into the shadows. Neither of us moved as Trevor's call grew louder now.

"Go," I told Lance, and stood. I hurried around the garage, and with my arms folded, my head down, and my heart pounding, I walked toward the front.

"Faith," I heard, and looked up as if I had just heard him. "Where were you? She's up and asking for you."

"Just for a walk around the house. I haven't been out all day."

He looked at me for a moment and then at the garage.

"I told her you were in the bathroom," he said. "Go on in."

He stood there, still looking at the garage as I passed him and started up the steps.

"Are you staying out?" I asked when I was at the door.

He stared at the garage a moment more and then turned and joined me. I hurried around to pretend I had come down the stairs. Mama was sitting up on the sofa.

"Where were you? Anything wrong with you?" she asked suspiciously. "Your bleeding didn't start again?"

"No, Mama."

"Start taking my bedding here to the washer. As soon as your father arrives, I'm going up to our bedroom. I keep smelling his cigar in this sofa bed. Go on," she said. She had bundled up her blanket, sheet, and pillowcase.

I scooped it up and hurried to the clothes washer and dryer. Trevor helped Mama up and then helped her walk with her crutch to the living room. As soon as I could, I went to the window in the kitchen and looked out toward the garage. I was half-hoping he was still there, maybe to wave good night, but he wasn't, and I was afraid Trevor would see me looking for him.

Mama dozed on and off while we watched television and waited for Daddy. Even Trevor fell asleep, but I stayed alert, wondering if Lance would ever come back. How frightened was he? Was he afraid his grandfather would be angry, and maybe send him home? I started to doze off, too.

Hours later, we all regained our energy when we heard the sound of gravel being crushed by Daddy's truck. Trevor leaped up first and went to the rear door, calling back to us to tell us what we knew. "Daddy's home!"

"Hallelujah," Mama said.

I rose to greet him when he entered. He had no gifts for us this time and looked quite tired. He rubbed the top of Trevor's head and hugged me before going into the living room.

"Well, you and your stubborn self," he said, gazing down at Mama.

"Santa Claus was busy," she replied dryly. "I want you to carry me up and down until I can manage on those stairs myself. Your den needs to be scorched to be clean."

"Glad you haven't changed any," he said, and scooped her off the sofa.

"Easy!" she cried. "You two go to bed," she told us. "Your father will shut everything off."

He looked at us and started up the stairs.

"Your crutch, Mama," I said, practically lunging for it.

"I'll get it," Trevor said, and took it practically out of my fingers to follow them up.

"He didn't tell us about the truck repair," Trevor complained.

"She didn't give him a chance to say much, Trevor. We'll talk in the morning."

Still half asleep, he started up the stairs. When they were all out of sight, I gazed out at the garage.

Almost as if I could literally replay the scene, I saw myself in Lance's arms, felt his kiss and his touch, and then I hurried upstairs, holding the images close to my heart so I could take them to bed with me.

eleven

Both Mama and Big John were already up and at breakfast. I sat up when I heard their voices, louder than usual, and looked at Trevor, who was awake, lying there. His eyes widened as he listened. He had obviously been awake before me.

"What are they arguing about?" he asked.

"I don't know," I said, rising. I had totally forgotten that I had gone to sleep in the sheer nightgown Mama had given me to celebrate having my first period and my dealing with it well.

Trevor sat up quickly.

"What's that you're wearing?"

"Present Mama gave me, remember?"

"You might as well be naked."

"So don't look," I said, and then scooped up my robe and hurried to the bathroom.

I had just opened the door when I heard Mama yell very loudly at Big John.

"You're a liar!"

He mumbled a response.

Trevor came out of the bedroom and followed me to the stairway so we could hear more clearly.

"I want to see the bill for the repairs on your truck. Where is it?" Mama demanded.

"He's sendin' it. I didn't want to wait around for the paperwork but get here as soon as I could."

"Oh, like that ten minutes would have mattered. With all that's been going on here, with all that's been on my head . . . you'd think you'd put your infidelity on pause, but when it comes to satisfying that thing of yours, all hell and havoc could break loose around you, and you'd barely notice."

"Think what you like."

We heard him rise, go to the sink, and turn on the water.

"I see the way you are when you return from one of your trips with pleasure stopovers," Mama said. "You didn't even kiss me last night."

"Oh, stop. You were in pain."

"When do you think you're supposed to kiss someone? You're probably all kissed out."

"What? You believe you only have a certain number of kisses per day?"

I imagined Big John smiling.

"It's those pills doin' this to you," he told her.

"Oh, don't try to get out of it by using my accident, John."

"Give your imagination a vacation, will you? Look, I'm just workin' as hard as I can for us. You think it's terrible the roof leaked? Well, I got some bad news for you. There's plenty more comin' in this old place you think is some precious old palace or somethin' full of family history. We need a new water heater. We need to work on that septic tank and the leaching ditches. There's some electric work that has to be updated. I have no idea yet what the leak's done to the pantry floor, walls, and below. Afraid to look. I worry about that furnace and hoped to have it replaced before the fall. You listenin', Paula? We're talkin' mucho dinero. I've got upkeep with the business, too, maintenance on the truck, ac-countin' work, and the traffic's gettin' worse and worse. A ten-hour trip's now at least fourteen. I've got no time to be havin' affairs you dream up."

Mama didn't say anything. I looked at Trevor.

"You think he's meeting girls on the road?" he asked.

"I don't know. You always tell me that Mama can see things we try to hide."

"Yeah, but he wouldn't have wanted to take me if he was," Trevor said confidently. "It's her fault I'm not going."

"Maybe she'll let you go with him now," I said.

His eyes widened with the possibility. "Yeah."

He forgot about them and looked at me again, standing there in my sheer nightgown. I could almost feel his eyes moving up and down my body.

"I'm getting washed and dressed," I said. "Got to make sure she took her antibiotic this morning," I added, and hurried back to the bathroom, rushing away from the look in his eyes. Mama's prediction that I would sense things differently now seemed to be coming true.

Trevor was waiting at the door when I opened it.

"What?" I asked, thinking something else terrible had happened.

"You take longer and longer now getting yourself all dolled up. I don't know who you're expecting for breakfast," he said, pushing past me and closing the door.

I didn't know whether to laugh or cry. Why was he so angry? Was he angry at me or himself? I hadn't really taken extra time on my looks. In fact, after dressing quickly, I forgot about brushing my hair and just hurried down to the kitchen. They were both sitting there at the kitchen table, neither speaking, their eyes lowered to stare at their cups of coffee. It felt like something precious had died or been lost. It frightened me to see them like this.

"Hi," I said. "Did you want me to make some breakfast, Mama?"

"Just for yourselves. I don't have an appetite yet," she said, and sipped her coffee.

"You take your pills, the antibiotic?"

"See how well they look after me, John?"

Big John looked at me, smiled, and nodded.

"Yes, I took them," she said. "Except I'm not taking that pain pill. I have other pains it can't fix."

"Oh, brother," Daddy said. "If you're scramblin' some eggs, make some for me."

"Please," Mama reminded him.

"Oh, yeah, please. Schoolteacher's watchin' me."

Trevor came hurrying down. He had slapped on his pants and slipped into his shoes, and was pulling his shirt on as he entered the kitchen.

"Hi," he said. "How's the truck?"

"How's the truck?" Mama said, turning on him. "The truck? What about me?"

"Sorry, Mama. But I know you're healing, and you'll be okay."

"Yes, I'll be fine," she said. "You might as well tell them what you told me, John. Get it all out this morning so there are no surprises."

I turned from the stove.

"Don't dry out the eggs," Mama warned.

I started to put portions on dishes, nodding at Trevor to take out the toast. No one spoke as I moved around, got the butter and some jam, and scooped up the forks and knives.

"Looks good," Daddy said.

"You sure you don't want any, Mama?"

"I'll make some later," she said. "Sit. You, too, Trevor."

We were all seated. Big John buttered his toast, put some jam on it, and started eating.

"Well?" Mama said.

He paused, but it was easy to see that he didn't want to.

"I'm home only for a few days," he said. "To get some rest," he added, glaring at Mama. "If I can. Then Nick and I have a major, major bunch of haulin' to do, a major bunch."

"Where to?" Trevor asked quickly.

Daddy smiled. "That's the great announcement. This trip's long, I admit, but it will make me half as much as I make all year. We're going south first to Miami, where we pick up a load and go to San Antonio with a stopover in New Orleans. We pick up another load and head to Houston. From Houston, we go to Los Angeles. From there, we're going to San Francisco, Seattle, and stopping in St. Louis on the way back. Might get one or two more trips between there and here."

"And?" Mama said. "Tell them all of it."

"Well, all in all, with waiting for loads, stuff to do, it could be the better part of five weeks."

"That is a long time," I said.

"Stuff to do," Mama said, curling her lips. "You and that Nick Damien."

"It's a lot of drivin'," Daddy said. "Nick's a good guy to take a shift and keep me company."

Suddenly, Mama smiled as if something really wonderful was happening. I looked at Trevor. He was just as confused by her instant mood change. She slapped her hand on the table.

"Well, lucky for you, we have a new real man of the house," she said. She reached for Trevor's hand. "We'll do just fine."

Trevor looked terrified. He glanced at Daddy and then nodded to Mama. She let go of his hand and reached for her crutch. Trevor leaped to his feet to help her stand.

"I'm going out to the front to sit and get some fresh air," she said. "Been cooped up inside too long. You all finish your breakfasts."

Trevor started to help her, but she held him off.

"I can take care of myself now, as long as I don't take those damn pain pills. You'd better sit and talk to your father. You get to see him less and less these days."

We watched her use the crutch well and go to the front door. I looked at Daddy.

"Somethin' changed that woman," he said, more to himself than to us, "and it ain't just her breakin' the bottom of her leg." He turned to me. "Tell me how that happened, anyway."

I looked at Trevor and began.

"We couldn't stop her, Daddy," Trevor quickly interjected. "I volunteered to do the work."

"And?"

I finished describing the incident and how I had run to Mr. Longstreet's to get him to help us.

"Getting help from someone probably hurt her more," Big John said.

I described how much he had helped us and how his grandson had, too.

"He didn't do all that much," Trevor said. Maybe I was emphasizing Lance's contributions too much.

Afterward, I could see Big John felt sorrier for Mama, and he went out to talk to her.

"You think she'll stay upstairs after Big John leaves?" Trevor asked me.

"Probably. We'll figure it out, take turns bringing things up to her."

"I can carry her up and down," he boasted. "Don't worry about it.

"And," he added, standing up, "you'd better just behave and not get her angry."

"What does that mean?"

He started out.

"Trevor?"

"It means what it means, especially when it comes to Lance now," he said, and continued to the front door.

"What? Why?"

"I'm going to look at the truck," he said. "I want to know what went wrong. You don't have to come. It's man's talk."

"What?"

He walked out.

I knew what he meant, and it infuriated me. What Mama had told him, had been telling him, had gone to his head. For the first time, really, that I could remember, I suddenly didn't trust my brother. We had practically grown up in each other's shadow. There wasn't a secret thought I hadn't shared with him, and as far as I knew, even though he kept far more to himself than I kept to myself, he shared his secrets with me, too.

Now I had never felt angrier and more defiant.

As soon as I can, I thought, *I'm going to meet Lance again. Trevor can't tell me what to do.*

After I cleaned up the kitchen, I went up to the classroom and turned on my computer. Expecting an email from him, I was quite disappointed. There was nothing. He should have at least been asking if everything was all right.

Should I write to him first? Was he angry with me for telling him to go? I wished there was at least a pamphlet on how to properly conduct yourself with a boy you liked romantically. I knew what it meant to be coy, and I knew what it meant to flirt, but how did you know when you'd gone too far and made yourself seem pathetic?

What kind of a girl did boys like more, anyway, shy or aggressive? Lance was certainly not shy. Surely, he was used to more aggressive girls in the city, but did he like that? How would I ever meet him again if he didn't send me an email? Maybe he was afraid Trevor would see it, too. Or even Mama. Maybe I should write to tell him I immediately would get rid of any message he sent to me. I tempted my fingers for a few moments, decided to wait, and then shut off the computer and went downstairs. As I was descending, I heard the sound of the basketball bouncing and hurried to the rear door. Daddy and Trevor were playing. Lance wasn't there.

I hurried around to the front porch to see Mama. She sat staring at the road, watching cars go by. She still looked angry, glaring ahead.

"Are you all right, Mama?"

She turned and looked at me, her face soaked in rage, her eyes wide, and her cheeks tight.

"What's wrong, Mama?" I asked. This had to be more than Big John not overwhelming her with his affection the way he used to when he came home from a trip, especially one that was as long as the one he had just completed.

"That boy came over here and fixed the basketball net. Did you know that? Did you know Trevor played with him?"

"Yes," I said in a small voice.

She nodded and looked away. "Thought so. Suspected you wouldn't tell me." She turned back to me sharply. "Your father thinks that's wonderful, those two playing basketball. He said he always meant to fix that thing."

"It's exercise, Mama. You said we needed exercise."

Before she could respond, Lance trotted into our driveway.

"Your father invited him," she said. "He called Mr. Longstreet and told him to come over to shoot some hoops. *Shoot some hoops*," she said again, as if it was something so sinful she had to emphasize it.

Lance looked our way, held up his hand to wave, but kept trotting into the driveway to join Big John and Trevor. I don't think he let his eyes meet Mama's. When she was this furious, it was like waves and waves of her rage went out a mile.

"You know what children of divorce become?" Mama asked me in a quieter, softer voice.

I shook my head.

"Hobos looking for love, not food or money. I could pick out a child of divorce in my class the moment I set eyes on him or her. They always had that fish-eyed look of desperation. Once the bond holding the family is broken, they feel untethered, like they're floating. They're veterans of anger and hate. Whether they want it or not, it poisons them. Beware," she said, her eyes narrowing.

Beware of what? I wanted to ask, but didn't. I was afraid to say a word defending Lance. She didn't want to hear it the last time. Now, after not telling her he had come over to play with Trevor, my uttering one nice thing about him would surely make her super suspicious, I thought.

"Did you want something, Mama? A tea or . . ."

"No. I'll just sit here. Go read. Don't pay attention to them."

She folded her arms and looked out at the road, as if she was expecting something terrible to come around the corner. I slipped back into the house softly but hurried to the rear door. When I peered out, Big John saw me.

"Hey. Get over here," he said, beckoning with his hand. "We'll be a team, you and me, against these two sissy boys. C'mon."

I looked back toward the front of the house. Mama would not be happy, but Daddy was asking, wasn't he? *She can't blame me*, I thought, and walked to the front of the garage. Daddy handed me the ball.

"Take a few shots," he said.

Lance was smiling, and Trevor was smirking.

My first attempt didn't even reach the basket. Trevor laughed, but Daddy showed me how to hold the ball, and then I took another shot and hit the rim.

"There she goes," he said. "A little harder, higher." He handed the ball back to me, and I shot again. This time, when it hit the rim, it bounced in. "All right. We're ready. You make a basket; you keep the ball until you don't. That's the rule. We take it out first. Ladies first."

He handed me the ball. Trevor moved forward and waved his arms in front of me. Daddy moved to the right and left of Lance, who kept up with him.

"You've got to throw it to him," Trevor said, lowering his hands to his waist, "or we get it."

Daddy pushed Lance a bit with his hip, and before Trevor could start blocking me again, I threw the ball to his right. Daddy got it, but as he turned with it to shoot, Lance knocked it out of his hands, and Trevor got it. Daddy looked a little sore about it, but when Trevor shot, Daddy blocked it, got the ball, and easily put it in the basket.

I could see Trevor was getting more and more upset as Daddy made another basket and I passed successfully to him. He lunged at me when I had the ball and stole it away. Daddy declared that was against the rules, and I was given the ball again. Lance made some shots Daddy couldn't block, and then everything stopped when Mama suddenly appeared standing at the rear door.

"Take a break," Daddy said. He passed the ball to Trevor and walked to Mama.

"I have to get home, anyway," Lance said, looking at Mama. "Got to go with my grandfather to pick up things. I'll see you later," he said, mostly to Trevor. He smiled at me and then started to trot off without saying another word.

"Your mother says you have reading to do," Daddy said. "Put the ball away for now." He walked in with her.

I turned to Trevor. "That was fun," I said.

"You did all right. For a girl," he added, and walked to the house.

I looked at the road, but Lance was already out of sight.

He hadn't paid any attention in particular to me. Maybe I had dreamed the whole thing happening with him, our short romantic moments, I thought, and followed Trevor. Or maybe to a "city boy," that was nothing special.

We never played basketball with Daddy again. He left two days later.

That morning, Mama sat on the front porch and glared at the road in the direction Daddy had gone. Trevor and I went out to cheer her up, but it was as if she had shut off her ears. We were actually frightened by how stern she looked and how unmoving. She barely blinked.

"Mama, everything will be all right," I said. "If he makes so much money like he says, he won't have to leave so much."

She turned and looked at me in a cold, hard way. There wasn't an iota of warmth in her sharp smile.

"You're grown-up when you stop believing in fairy tales," she said. "Love and promises are weak sisters. When you live alone and eat wishes for breakfast, lunch, and dinner, you're starving at nighttime. Even your dreams begin to crumble. You can't live on dreams."

She turned and reached for Trevor's hand, and then she reached for mine and pressed our hands to her bosom.

"Family," she said. "Family is all you really need. Then you're safe. You can dream and lie, make promises and see disappointments, but you are always safe with family."

She closed her eyes and rocked in the chair a little. Then she let go of us.

"Go and do your assignments," she said. "I'm fine."

"Don't worry about going up and down the stairs, Mama," Trevor told her. "I can carry you."

"Of course you can," she said. "We'll do fine."

Trevor and I looked at each other, nodded, and went inside to go up to our classroom.

"She talks as if Big John will never come back," Trevor said.

"Of course he will."

"I'm not afraid if he doesn't," he said, charging up the stairs ahead of me.

He waited at the top with his arms folded, looking older and stronger. Later that night, after dinner, he did carry Mama up the stairs easily. I followed to help her get ready for bed. Becky and Moses, as if they knew Mama wasn't quite herself yet, followed us and curled up against the wall in her bedroom.

Another day passed, and Lance didn't return to play ball or send me an email, either. Trevor said nothing about it, and I was afraid to ask. Mama's pain did seem to diminish considerably. She became more proficient at using her crutch and was soon able to lean on the stairway banister and get up and down herself. Trevor actually seemed disappointed.

When she was upstairs, Trevor and I took turns bringing things to her. She still came into the classroom and picked up on our lessons, lecturing and talking as if nothing at all had happened. She even took over the cooking and dinner preparations. Our world just seemed to wind back.

I had my second period, which turned out to be a little worse than the first. I had more cramps and bleeding. But Mama still appeared to be very happy about it and how I didn't complain. She said there were things to take to ease it, but it was better for me to get used to pain and overcome it myself. She said that was what she had done and did with her periods and what she now was doing with her leg.

Even so, it left me with a deeper, darker moodiness. I snapped at Trevor often and brooded more. I began to wonder if Trevor knew more about my meeting with Lance that night. Had he seen us after all? Had he told Mama something, and had she called Mr. Longstreet and told him to keep his grandson away from us?

I chanced questioning Trevor about him, trying to hide my real interest.

"I thought you and Lance were going to do that walk to the lake," I said, as casually as I could, while we were doing our science assignments.

He gave me his famous shrug.

"Well, what happened?"

"He hasn't emailed or anything," he said. "Whatever. Daddy said we'd do the walk when he returned this time."

Mama still became tired early in the evening, and with the ordeal of going up the stairs, she usually went to bed by eight, warning Trevor and me not to stay up too late. Trevor would guide her upstairs, standing right behind her, his hands gently on her hips. She wouldn't let him carry her now, but she praised him for being her "lifeguard" and, she added, "Faith's lifeguard, too." She said as long as he was there, she had no fear. He was becoming her "Little John."

He actually began to imitate Big John in a number of ways. He sat in his seat every night and at times went to his den and watched television himself just like Big John would do when he wanted to smoke a cigar. I looked in on Trevor once and saw that he was holding one of Big John's cigars.

"What are you doing? Mama will be upset if you smoke that."

"I'm not smoking it, am I? I like the smell. As long as I don't light it, she won't get angry."

I didn't argue with him. She probably wouldn't get angry. She didn't discourage him from sitting in the den by himself. I saw that although they were too big, he was wearing Big John's favorite slippers. I didn't know why, but what he was doing frightened me.

All boys want to be like their fathers, I thought. *Why should this be frightening?*

But it was.

He seemed clear now on what he dreamed of becoming: like Big John, our daddy.

What was I dreaming of becoming?

Five more days passed without my seeing Lance or hearing from him. And then, one evening, while Trevor was downstairs with Mama watching television, I just had an urge to check my computer again, and there it was, an email from Lance: *Sorry I haven't been in touch or tried to see you. I had to go home for a few weeks, but I'm back. Let's try meeting again. I'll wait for your email. Love, Lance.*

I had a surge of excitement, the waves of heat rising up my neck and into my face. I was flushed for sure, I thought, and told myself to make sure to wash my face in cold water before

I went downstairs again. Mama would take one look at me and wonder why.

My fingers trembled as I wrote back: *I'll send you an email as soon as everyone else goes to sleep. Same place.*

Can't wait, he replied.

I left my computer on so I could send the email later to meet, went to the bathroom, and then, as casually as I could, desperately hiding my excitement, walked down the stairs. Mama looked up at me as soon as I entered the living room.

"What were you doing?" she asked.

"I had to finish *The Grapes of Wrath.*"

Mama nodded and yawned. "Let's go to bed. Trevor, you be sure you catch up to Faith with your reading tomorrow."

He glared at me as if I had intended to show him up.

"Will do, Mama," he said. He leaped up to help her get to her feet.

"The day this comes off," she said, tapping her cast with her crutch, "we'll celebrate. I'll make your favorite cake. It'll be like a birthday."

"Daddy will be back by then," I said.

"Don't be so sure," she replied. "You heard him: unless he gets another job while they're on the road home."

She hobbled to the stairway and grabbed the banister. Trevor got right behind her.

"Turn off the television," Mama ordered. "And turn off the lights."

They started up.

I did what she asked, waited, and slowly followed them up. My heart was thumping so hard with anticipation that I almost missed a step. Trevor followed Mama to her room. I hurried to get out of my clothes, bundle them, and put them in an extra laundry bag. I could hear Trevor talking to Mama about things to do around the house tomorrow, including working on the basement.

Hurrying to the stairway, I tossed the bag over.

Then I went to the bathroom. When I came out, Trevor was getting ready for bed. He looked at me.

"I know that you finished that novel yesterday," he said. "You lied to Mama," he added, and walked past me and into the bathroom.

twelve

If I moved more than inch by inch, it wasn't by much. When I stood up, I finally took a breath. As usual, Trevor had his back to me. He looked deeply asleep; nevertheless, I tried not to rustle the blanket. I remembered Mama telling us when we were very young that if we got up too early and came to her while Daddy was still sleeping, we should walk on angel feet. "Angels," she said, "are always hovering just a little over the floor or the ground. Walk like angels."

Our door, as usual, was opened nearly halfway. I didn't move it at all to slip out. Even on "angel feet," my steps to the classroom brought up little moans and groans from the floor. I quickly entered, and with only the quarter-moon's light streaming through the windows, I moved carefully to my computer, opened it, and typed *On my way* to Lance. I didn't wait for his response. I went out to the hallway again, paused at our bedroom to be sure Trevor hadn't woken, and then continued tiptoeing to the stairway.

I paused at the stairs and listened for any sounds coming from Mama's bedroom. It was so quiet that I could hear the ticking of her tabletop grandfather clock. I knew the stairway steps would creak the loudest. When Trevor and I were very little, they had always warned us that Mama was coming up to look in on us and go to bed. Remembering that, I almost slid down the banister. I was leaning on it so much and taking baby steps on my toes like a ballet dancer. When I reached the bottom, I paused, held my breath, and listened. There were no sounds of either Trevor or Mama stirring. Confident, I scooped up my laundry bag and dressed as quickly as I could.

Once again, I paused and listened hard to see if either Trevor or Mama had risen, having heard me moving about downstairs. It was as silent as when I had begun.

It was faster to go through the kitchen and then out the back door. I closed it behind me gently and took another deep breath. The moonlight seemed to get brighter for me, lighting the path to the side of the garage where Lance and I had met that night. At first, I didn't see him and began to berate myself for not waiting for his response. Maybe he couldn't come for some reason and I had risked all this for nothing. How would I explain it if Mama or Trevor saw me returning, dressed? They might think I had seen him earlier and was on my way back to bed. I'd get the blame but no reward, no exciting experience.

I sighed with disappointment at the shadows. My heart was beating even harder and faster than it had been when I had left Trevor's and my bedroom. How much longer should I wait for him? I was afraid to take a step forward or one backward.

Then I heard him whisper my name and saw him move into the moonlight like darkness sculpting itself into his shape. I hurried to join him at the corner.

Without another word, he grasped my shoulders and drew my lips to his. It was a long, thrilling kiss.

"Hi," he said, as we lowered ourselves to the ground. "I thought about you every day I was away."

"Why didn't you send me an email?"

"It was a difficult time. My father had an investigator following my mother, and he now claims it was my mother, not him, who was the adulterer. She denies it, of course, but she was quite upset. It's going to be an embarrassingly high-profile divorce. I actually fell asleep in her bed with her for the first time since I was a little boy. She cried herself to sleep."

"Oh. How sad."

"Yes," he said. "But that'll work out. It's just lawyers playing chess. Now that I'm back, I want to concentrate on you. I left New York as soon as I could. I should have called you on my way, but I wanted it to be a surprise."

"I didn't even know you had left."

"Right. A mess. I was out the door seconds after she called, quite hysterical. Let's not think about it right now. Let's just think about us."

He kissed me again and again and kissed my neck while running his right hand up to my breast. He leaned against me so I would lie back, and then he began like last time, kissing me on more and more of my exposed breasts after each blouse button he opened.

"No bra," he realized. I could see his beautiful smile of glee.

I thought it but didn't say it: *Why bother, why waste time?*

Was that terrible of me?

"Most of the girls in my school don't wear bras often, and especially not when they meet someone they like."

How would you know that? I was going to ask, but he was moving my blouse away from my breasts to completely expose them as he ran his right hand up my skirt to my panties, my new panties. When he traced them with his fingers, I could feel his excitement grow.

"Perfect," he whispered.

He ran his left hand under my skirt, too, and with both hands, he began to lower my panties. He was breathing hard and fast. I think I was a little stunned by the speed of it all, but when he leaned back to pull my panties completely off, we heard a loud metal click. He froze. The expression on his face drove a dagger made of ice through my heart. I was afraid to turn my head to see what had frightened him.

"Get off her," I heard Mama say.

He fell back on his rear and quickly zipped up his pants. I was still afraid to move. Lance raised his right hand, palm out, as he pushed himself backward with his other hand. Then he stood. In the moonlight, his face looked like it had lost all its blood.

"Get out of here, or I'll blow you out of here," Mama said.

He crouched, and then he turned and ran into the darkness. I heard him crashing through bushes.

It had all happened so fast I simply sat there stunned, hoping it was only a dream.

"Get up," Mama said, with that voice that could slice ears.

I pulled up my panties, sat up, and then turned to see her leaning on her crutch. She held Big John's shotgun with one free hand. Trevor stood beside her. He was in his pajama bottoms, and she was in her nightgown. I couldn't find any words to defend myself. Mama still had the shotgun stock tucked into her shoulder and still pointed the gun at the spot where Lance and I had been lying. In her eyes, I thought I saw that she continued to envision us there. It was truly something she could never forget, but her intensity frightened me. For a moment, when she raised her eyes toward me, I thought she might still shoot me.

Slowly, Trevor eased the gun out of her hands. Even in this darkness, he could read the question on my mind. I had been so careful, so quiet. Had Mama seen me out of a window? Had I made more noise than I thought?

"I realized you weren't in bed and waited," Trevor said. "When I knew you weren't in the bathroom, I looked for you in our classroom and could see your computer was still lit up with Lance's email and your response."

"Good he did," Mama said. "And good he came to tell me. That was a manly, mature thing to do."

I still couldn't speak. It was as if my insides had been hollowed out and I was merely a shell of myself.

"Let's go in, Mama," he said. He put his hand on her arm. She still glared at me. I couldn't find the words. An apology would only make her angrier.

"Get into the house, and stop at the top of the stairway," she ordered.

I hurried past them, practically running through the kitchen and to the stairs. When I heard Mama and Trevor start up the stairs, I crouched, burying my head in my arms. Mama poked me with her crutch.

"Get up, and go to the right," she said.

"What?" I asked as I stood. "Why?"

"Do as I say!" she screamed.

Even Trevor looked terrified, standing behind her on the steps.

I walked slowly, hearing her coming behind me, slamming her crutch harder on the floor. She poked me again.

"Stop."

I waited, my head down. We were at the locked door to the room that didn't exist for us. Most of the time, we walked past it without even glancing at the door. I heard her rattling some keys and then saw her insert a key and unlock the door.

"Before you go in, you take off your clothes," she said. "Even your shoes."

"My clothes?"

"*All* your clothes. *Now!*"

I began to undress. Trevor was still at the top of the stairway, watching. He looked as confused as I was. When I was naked, she opened the door and flipped on a light switch that made illumination explode from a four-light candle-style chandelier with pink dangling crystals at the center of the ceiling.

"Get in, and get onto the bed," she said. I looked at her. Her face looked twisted, her eyes practically lit candles.

"Get into bed?"

I looked back to Trevor. He had lowered his head.

"But I thought . . . the floor in this room . . ."

"Do as I say," she said, bringing her face very close to mine.

I entered the room, the room she cleaned secretly, the room she had kept us out of from the day we arrived until now. I stopped in amazement as soon as I took my first steps into it. It was a nursery with a bed about half the size of Trevor's and mine in the center against the wall. There was a pillow on the bed but no blankets or cover sheet. It looked recently stripped and ready to be made. Both of the windows at the sides of the bed were draped in cartoon animal curtains that reached the floor. They were drawn closed.

The walls were faded pink, and the floor wasn't wood with weak spots as she had told us. The floor was carpeted in a tight-knit cream that looked never stepped upon. There was a strange feeling of everything frozen in time.

On my left was a blush-pink crib with spindle posts. The starch-white crib sheet had a darker blue blanket tightly folded. It looked like something was bundled in it.

To the right was a small bathroom with only a sink and a toilet.

"What is this room, Mama? Is it the nursery for one of your relatives? It looks . . ."

"Get onto the bed," Mama ordered.

"Why? I can't sleep here. There's no blanket," I said.

She just glared at me. I walked across the room, my arms folded over my breasts, and sat on the bed.

"This is where you'll be until I say otherwise."

She flipped off the light and closed the door. The moon had passed to the west. It was pitch dark. I lay back and started to sob uncontrollably.

"Mama!" I screamed.

I even shouted for Trevor. I sucked in my stomach and yelled at the top of my voice.

Finally, Mama returned. She didn't turn on the light. There was enough flowing in from the hallway. She was carrying something very carefully in her free hand.

"This won't do," she said. "I need to sleep to get better. You know that. Drink this," she ordered, and handed me a glass of what looked like just water. "Go on. Drink it."

I didn't taste anything with a short sip, but she stood over me and waited until I drank it all.

"There," she said, taking the empty glass.

"Why do I have to stay here, Mama? Why did I have to drink a glass of water?"

She didn't answer; she just started away.

"Mama, can't I go back to bed? I'm sorry. I won't go out again. I promise. Can't I return to Trevor's and my room?"

"Not yet," she said, without turning, and left the room, encasing me again in darkness.

Not yet? When?

I lay back on the pillow. Crying and screaming weren't going to make a difference. I had to stay calm. I wondered if Lance would tell his grandfather what had happened. How could he? How would he explain it? Mama would probably call his grandfather tomorrow, I thought, and give him quite the what for. Mr. Longstreet might send him back to New York. Even if he didn't, how could Lance ever return, ever see me again? I had been so eager to see him, be with him, that I had forgotten to shut off my computer. *This is all my fault,* I thought, and began to sob again, but as silently as I could.

Mama's just angry for now. She'll give me a lecture tomorrow, and that will be that. But why did Trevor run to her? I wondered. Why was he so eager to tell her? Why didn't he just come out looking for me like he had the first time? Was he simply angry at me for not sharing my secret rendezvous with Lance? Or was he simply acting the part of the head of the household, Mama's little man? We never told on each other. Was that what being mature meant, never keeping each other's secrets? I tried to channel my fear into anger. This wasn't my fault; it was his. If he had not told Mama . . .

My head felt so heavy suddenly and, now used to the darkness, my eyes felt like they were spinning. I tried to sit up but felt so weak that I couldn't even push myself into a sitting position.

"Mama!" I called as loudly as I could. Even my voice felt weak. "Mama! I don't feel good. Mama."

My eyes seemed to roll back, and I felt myself drifting. It was a weird sensation. I wasn't quite asleep, but I wasn't awake, either. I know I moaned, but my voice sounded as if it was coming from someone else in the darkness. The moaning echoed. I heard a cry. I was imagining it for sure, because it was exactly like a baby's cry.

"Mama," I whispered.

The drifting continued, as did the spinning. I felt like I was floating and no longer on the bed. Vaguely, I was aware of my rear end being lifted. It felt like a pillow with a towel over it had been slid under me. I tried to feel for it, but my arms wouldn't move. The light from the opened door cheered me until I heard Mama say in a commanding tone, "Do it. Go on. You're ready. Do it."

"Mama?"

I wasn't even sure I had said it. The shadow that moved between me and the door looked like an outline of Trevor, naked. I was sure I felt his hands on the sides of my body and then something hard and a little painful being pressed into me. My body began to shake. I felt like I was on a roller coaster being lifted and dropped, flying through the darkness and then being seized.

"Good," Mama whispered. "Good."

I moaned and whimpered, but Mama said nothing else. The light from the hallway went out. I thought I was still moaning, but soon that stopped, and I dropped deeper and deeper into darkness, until a shock of light coming from the opened curtains woke me.

Mama was standing there, leaning on her crutch. Trevor was standing beside her, holding a tray on which there was juice, some eggs, and buttered toast with a pill.

"This is your breakfast," Mama said.

Trevor put the tray on the night table beside the bed and stepped back.

"Sit up," Mama ordered.

Groggily, I moved by pressing my hands to the mattress. Trevor fixed the pillow behind me and helped me sit up. Then he put the tray on my lap.

"Wha . . . happened to me?"

"To you? Do you know what you almost did to us? You almost destroyed our family," she said. "You eat your breakfast, and you stay here and think and think and think. There's the bathroom," she said, nodding at it. "Trevor will bring you a blanket today and something I'll give him for you to read and do."

"What happened to me?"

"You were saved," she said. "We were all saved, and we'll continue to be as long as we follow the calendar and we hope."

"Hope about what?"

"Eat your breakfast. There's a vitamin next to the dish. Take it with your juice."

She turned.

"But what happened to me?"

She gestured to Trevor, and he walked ahead of her, her leg with her cast swinging.

"Mama . . ."

They closed the door behind them. I heard the lock being turned. I looked at my breakfast. I wasn't really hungry, but I knew Mama would get even angrier if I did anything to disobey her now. When I looked to the side of the tray, I saw what looked like a tiny spot of blood on the mattress sheet. I touched it and looked at my finger. It had dried, but . . . I looked at my legs. I saw no cuts or bruises, but I had an ache in my vagina. It wasn't terribly painful, but it was different from any aches I had with my period.

I started to eat. *Mama can't leave me in here much longer, and why did she bring me to this room, anyway?* I looked around as I ate, and when I was finished, I put the tray aside and stepped off the bed. First, I wanted to wash my face in very cold water.

After I did that, I felt a lot more awake and moved around the room. It looked like Mama kept this room as clean as she kept any other room in this house.

I approached the crib slowly. As I suspected when I had first glanced at it, there was something bundled under the blanket. I started to reach in to see but stopped when I noticed what appeared to be very thin strands of dark brown hair. At first, I thought it might be a spider, but then I realized there would be too many legs.

After another moment of hesitation, I peeled back the blanket and looked at a pink baby blanket tightly wrapped. When I folded the top of it down a bit, I saw what looked like a tiny ear just under the small clump of dried hair. I covered it quickly, the blood rushing up my neck and into my face. Then I stepped back and screamed so loudly that I thought I might have broken my own eardrums. There was a sharp pain in my throat, too. I continued to back up until I reached the bed and curled up on it. I didn't think I had any tears left, but they came with my sobs, sobs that started in my stomach and rose up in wave after wave.

Finally, I passed out.

When I awoke, the tray had been replaced with another, upon which there was a chicken sandwich and a glass of cranberry juice, napkins, and a fork. A light blue blanket was over me, and our history textbook was there with a pad listing the assignment. I pushed myself into a sitting position and then saw Trevor standing in the doorway.

"You have to be here two more days," he said.

"Why?"

"Mama says it's what the calendar says."

"What calendar?"

He turned to leave and close the door.

"Wait!" I said, as loudly as I could without my throat hurting.

He didn't wait. I heard the door being locked and fell back against the pillow. Hours passed. I nibbled on my sandwich and, to keep my mind occupied, started to skim through the history assignment. I didn't approach the crib again but got up to look out the window. It was a partly sunny day. From this angle, I couldn't see the road, just a small area of the driveway. I saw Moses and Becky sauntering toward the forest. Never in all the time we had them did I recall either of them paying attention to the other. Watching them now, the way they moved and held their heads, I thought they didn't look part of this world. Their indifference to it was simply because they weren't part of it. Why did Mama even care for them?

I slept, read, and continued to nibble on my sandwich. When I woke again, the sun was falling rapidly behind the leafy trees. The house was so silent. I wondered if Mama and Trevor had gone somewhere. But how could they? She couldn't drive, and Trevor had no driver's license. What were they doing? What were they talking about? Was she getting him to hate me? Had she called Mr. Longstreet? What had happened to Lance? I was simply too tired and confused to cry.

A little while later, I heard the sound of Mama's crutch hitting the hall floor and then the door being unlocked. She stood there alone, looking in on me. In one free hand, she was carrying that same glass of water. I sat up quickly, holding the blanket around me.

"Now your nudity embarrasses you?" she said, starting toward me.

"I'm sorry, Mama. I was wrong, but you can't keep me in here anymore," I said, drawing up all the defiance I could muster.

She simply smiled. "You can't be trusted," she said. "If you don't listen to me, I'll call social services and have you placed in a foster home again. Trevor and I will look for another young girl to take your place."

"Trevor wouldn't . . ." I shook my head. "What do you mean, another girl to take my place? Don't you love me anymore?"

"I will if you do what I say. Tonight you just drink this. There'll be no dinner. Maybe tomorrow, if you do as I say, you'll come out and stay in the classroom all day. I think by then you'll understand." She shoved the glass toward me. "Drink."

"Why do I have to drink this water?"

She didn't reply. She held her arm steady, the glass practically in my face. I took it slowly, sipped, and then drank it empty. She took the glass and looked at the book and the pad.

"You didn't do very much. You'll have a great deal to make up." She started to turn.

"I looked in the crib," I said quickly.

She paused, thought a moment, and then turned back to me.

"Good," she said, smiling. "Then you understand already."

"What?" She continued toward the door. "I didn't look closely. I hardly looked. Understand what? Mama?"

She smiled, left, and locked the door. I heard her crutch hitting the floor, and then the sound disappeared as she descended the stairway.

Where was Trevor? I rose and went to the windows, searching what I could see in hopes of spotting him. I tried to open the window to shout for him, but it wouldn't budge. It had probably not been opened for years. I went to the door and tugged on it, but it didn't budge, and I started to feel weak again.

Understand what? I wondered.

"What do you mean, Mama?" I shouted. I could barely hear any sounds below. Taking a deep breath, I turned and went to the crib again. This time, I folded the baby blanket as far down as I could.

The tiny bones were there, the arms and the legs, even the feet. The skull was a dark gray. I felt the little I had eaten begin to come back up. I dropped the baby blanket and returned to the bed, practically falling face-first on it. For a while, I just lay there. It was still light out, but the room seemed to be darkening and darkening, until I saw nothing and thought nothing. I didn't even have the strength to turn over, but somehow I was turning over. It felt again like a pillow was slipped under my rear.

I moaned but didn't open my eyes. I felt my legs moving apart. Mama was saying, "Good, good."

And then I floated deeper into darkness and didn't open my

eyes until I heard Trevor say, "Get up and dressed. We're having breakfast. I'll put your book back. Mama's making scrambled eggs for us today. C'mon," he said.

I could barely hear him. His voice, everything, seemed so distant.

"Wait . . . Trevor . . ."

He was almost out the door. He didn't pause, nor did he look back.

"Wait!" I screamed. I groaned as I tried to sit up. My body still felt so weak. "Please, Trevor. Come back."

He didn't. I finally sat up. The room spun for a moment, and then I caught my breath. I steadied myself when I stood, took a deep breath, and then went to the bathroom, washed my face, and slowly dressed in the clothes he had left.

Mama and Trevor were at the table. A platter of scrambled eggs, toast, jam, and butter was at the center. The table had been set. Trevor was drinking coffee. I stood there staring at them.

"'Bout time you came down," Mama said. "Eat before it gets cold. We have lots to do in the house today."

Trevor poured me a glass of orange juice. I felt like I was still in a dream. Why wasn't Trevor more upset? Why was Mama smiling?

"Once, when I was very little, my mother decided we should have a breakfast picnic," Mama said. "It was very hot that summer, so when we woke and for a few hours, it was pleasant. We went out there," she said, nodding, "spread a blanket, and had her blueberry pancakes. I was very proud I could help bring it all out. Maybe I was four. Yes." She nodded. "Four. Your eggs are getting cold." She looked pointedly at me. "Sit!"

I folded myself into my chair. They were both staring at me.

"You need your strength now," Mama said. "More than ever."

Before I lifted the spoon to get some of the eggs, I felt my chin quivering. Tears burned my eyes.

"There's what's left of a dead baby in the crib in the room," I said.

thirteen

"Trevor knows all about that," Mama said. She smiled and put her hand over his. "He's known for a long time. Trevor and I have always had an extra-special relationship. I understood him; I understood the pain he endured as a child and how much he needed a mother."

I looked at Trevor, who was looking back at Mama with such adoration and pride it frightened me. Were there more secrets?

"He needed a mother even more than you did," she said, turning back to me. "Oh, I know you were deserted, too, and you felt terribly alone, especially as an infant, confused, lost, closing up inside yourself until Trevor came, right? You both gave each other love and support even though you were barely more than infants."

Trevor turned to me, smiling, while she continued.

"It wasn't amazing and curious that you two clung to each other, that you depended so much on Trevor, no matter what the Wexlers said. That's deep-down, heartfelt love. Did you know at first they tried to use that as a reason for me not to adopt the two of you? 'Those two are unnatural,' Shirley Wexler said, her ugly daughter sitting there and nodding. 'Half the time, I think they're obsessed by something evil or something. They sit for hours beside each other hardly talking. It's as if they don't need words, just looks. Oooh,' she said, shaking her shoulders, 'sometimes they give me the creeps. It'd be good for them to be separated.'

"'Never,' I said, and I remember her look of surprise. She turned to that daughter of hers you called Nanny Too, and Nanny Too nodded. 'My mother's right. Sometimes,' she said, 'when they stand in front of a mirror, it looks like one of them was absorbed into the other. I swear,' she said, shaking her head, 'if I tell them not to do something, they give me a chillingly similar look. It's like you can't talk to one without talking to the other. I asked my mother to recheck their papers in case they were really brother and sister. They're not; they're just . . . different, very different from all the other wards.'

"She thought that stupid description of you two was going to discourage me. Both of them did. I smiled at them and said that you two were different because you were perfect. You were just what I was looking for, two children who already felt and behaved like family, so much so. I told that Nanny Too, 'That you and your mother thought they might be related—how wonderful!' I exclaimed in their faces.

"I could see they were surprised, but then suddenly they were happy I was taking you and Trevor. You were too much for them, especially that Nanny Too. *Good riddance* was in their eyes, but that only made me more confident. God had chosen you for me just when I was in my deepest sorrow and depression. Big John said it was as if the sun had come up after months and months of overcast and darkness. Why, your childish laughter, both of yours, was music in this house. Do you know you hardly ever cried? Big John said you two were remarkable from the start. But . . ."

She leaned in a little, as if the three of us were to share a great secret. "As big and strong as he is, in the very beginning, he was also a little afraid of you two. Once he actually asked me if I was sure you weren't children of a witch. Imagine that. That's why he was always saying you two were uncanny. A man wouldn't understand what a woman can feel for a child, see in a child.

"Of course, in time, he came to believe, as I always had, that you two were special, but not in any dark and evil way. You were perfect little angels. In those days, he avoided some work trips just to be closer to you, be part of this amazing family. I think he was jealous of how close the three of us became. He even said once, maybe more than once, 'You and your kids don't even miss me when I'm gone.'

"Of course, I told him he was mistaken. You were just very patient, extraordinarily patient, for children your age, and after a while, he understood. But he never really and truly felt as he should, part of us.

"That's why I'm sure he's straying now," she added. "Don't either of you worry about that. We're perfect with or without him. Everything is perfect in our house, in our family."

"But the baby in the crib," I said.

Mama sat back, shook her head, and grimaced, as if she had expected I wouldn't ask again.

"That's my sister," she said.

I looked at Trevor, who nodded as if I should have known.

"Your *sister*?"

"My mother unexpectedly got pregnant in her mid-forties. Forty-six, to be exact. When my father found out, he wasn't upset." She looked away. "My father took things as they came. He loved saying, 'What will be will be.'

"I admit in the beginning, when my mother came back from the doctor's with the diagnosis that she was pregnant, I was a little upset. How were they going to care for an infant at their age? My father was in his fifties and already complaining about aches and pains. I expected it would all fall on my shoulders, and I wasn't happy about it."

She paused, looking thoughtful, and then nodded.

"I'll confess I had suffered some stupid sibling rivalry because they talked about her coming so much. You'd think an angel was arriving." Then, quickly, she emphasized, "But I never did anything to deliberately damage my mother's pregnancy. No. No. I waited on her hand and foot when she went through all those early days. At her age, it was unusually uncomfortable and painful for her right from the start. And my father wasn't going to go running up and down the stairs after every one of her moans and groans. But I was there, always. They had me."

She sat back. Trevor was staring at her with that devoted admiration again.

"I only wanted to help her, you see. What good was it for me to be so intelligent if I didn't research to find ways to make her pregnancy easier, huh? I'm not saying it was my fault, you understand."

She paused, obviously debating whether or not to say any more.

"What could be your fault, Mama?" I asked.

It was easy to see from his expression that Trevor didn't like my asking.

"I researched natural remedies," she said. "I went to a health-food store I knew in Honesdale, and the lady there gave me a combination of red and black cohosh, herbs Indians sometimes use. She swore it would help. I meant only to help."

She looked away and rubbed her right eye to prevent a tear from appearing. "That's all I intended to do, but the cohosh . . . oh, dear me, pity me."

"What did it do?" I asked impatiently.

"Give Mama a chance to explain!" Trevor said angrily.

I looked down and then folded my arms in my lap.

"I should have done more research about it, but I took that lady's word for it and gave it to Mama when she was uncomfortable. That's all I meant to do, but maybe it was the wrong dosage, maybe that woman confused me . . ."

I waited, my heart thumping, but I didn't look up. Mama

always told us to look away when you wanted someone to tell you the truth. If someone didn't have to look you in the eye, he or she would be more apt to confess. You made it seem as if you almost didn't care. It was no big deal. But this sounded like it was going to be a very big deal.

"Later, I discovered that too much can also induce uterine spasms and can cause a miscarriage," she said. "The woman in the health-food store never warned me enough about that. In fact, as I recall now, she never even mentioned it. You can't even begin to imagine how horrible I felt. I wanted to go back there and kill her. I couldn't sleep; I couldn't eat. I spent hours asking God to forgive me."

I looked at Trevor first. He was thinking about the same thing: what we had done to Mama. He seemed to be in pain, his eyes squinted, his lips tightened, as he anticipated what else she was going to say.

"She was in the nursery. My father had finished hanging those drapes of cartoon characters. He didn't have time to take her to the hospital, even get her out of the room. It happened in that small bathroom. I don't have to describe the details, the ugly details."

My face felt so hot and flushed. I couldn't swallow. I thought I was holding my breath so tightly that I might faint.

Mama looked to the side. "I know people would think it was something I had done deliberately, but it wasn't. I couldn't explain it to my father, or he surely would have thought it. The only other person in the world besides Trevor who knows what I'm telling you is Big John. When I told him, he practically cried with me. He really loved me then. He promised he would never do anything to that nursery. He assured me he would keep it the way it was, the way I wanted it to remain, because that was what Mama had wanted. And we'd never talk about it.

"My father was too devastated to oppose her wishes, and I certainly wanted whatever she wanted. She was in there night after night for months, crying and reading nursery rhymes, singing lullabies. She even bought more infant clothes. Daddy and I never said anything. We never told her to stop, that her baby was gone. I read about it, of course. It was a case of extreme denial. We could have driven her to suicide if we forced her to face the truth.

"Days before they were killed in that truck accident, she asked me to always take care of my sister, keep her room warm and clean. Do you think I would change a thing after I had made *that promise*? After all I had *accidentally* caused? *Do you?*" she practically screamed.

"No," I said, my eyes lowered.

"I know it's not right to keep everything this way so long," she said in a calmer tone. "But there was always only one way to change it, only one way."

I looked up at her.

"I tried to do it myself, but something was wrong, and then I realized what I had to do. It's like raising a beautiful tree or bush. Bush sounds more biblical, doesn't it? I prayed for direction, for instruction. I asked God to find you two." She paused. "And he did."

I looked at Trevor. He was stone-faced, emotionless, his eyes avoiding mine.

"Now you can understand and appreciate why I was so angry

about what you had almost done. Trevor was, too," she said, smiling at him. "But we stopped it, and we're fixing it so it won't happen again."

"Fixing it?"

The realizations washed over me in waves of blue and black and red. It was more like an explosion inside me, ripples of heat and ripples of cold. A hand made of ice gripped my neck. I was afraid to breathe, to move. Mama's smile seemed to fade in and out, and Trevor's face suddenly looked carved in granite, his body so stiff, his eyes vacant.

Somewhere deep down, the words began to form like the Morse code I had read about in our history text. Dots became letters, and the letters became words.

"You drugged me and made Trevor do—"

"Do what had to be done and what has to be done," she said quickly. "I didn't think it was time, either, but when we found you with that boy about to . . . and now, when you're ovulating . . . God himself shook me awake, shook Trevor awake that night—otherwise, we would never have known you were out of the house.

"'*No!*' God was screaming. 'This isn't my plan to undo your pain!' I heard him, and I was not surprised Trevor had come to alert me. He heard him, too, didn't you, Trevor?"

Trevor nodded.

"Naturally, Trevor was a little frightened and not sure, but when he looked at you and when I told him it was the time, he did as I told him to do, as I know now he wanted to do eventually, anyway. But of course, he would do what had to be done when he realized it was destined to be. I knew it from the moment I set eyes on him and you together at the Wexlers', that he would understand. I could see it all, our future, our family."

She leaned over to kiss Trevor on the cheek. All the while, he stared at me, almost expressionless again. He looked almost hypnotized or something.

Tears were freed, streaming down my cheeks.

"You can go back to your bed tonight, now that you understand," she said. "You must love each other. You loved each other from the start, but this is mature love now, love that lasts a lifetime."

She reached for Trevor's hand, and then she reached for mine and brought them together. His fingers moved first to grasp mine. I looked at him, and then I looked at Mama. Their expressions were so similar that I could easily move his face to hers and vice versa.

"Bless you both. Now, finish your breakfast, Faith," she said, releasing our hands like the matter was settled, like all was clear and right now.

Trevor's fingers uncurled, and I brought my hand back to my lap.

"We have lots to do today. We'll skip the schoolwork and concentrate on the house. I see how it's fallen apart since I've been incapacitated, but all that will change. We have a new family to bring into it. A house without a family . . . that's an empty shell, something you find discarded on the beach."

She started to lean on her crutch to rise, and Trevor jumped up to help her. She paused and smiled at me.

"By the way, you should know that I called the driving school. They're sending someone over to begin Trevor's training. He'll be old enough for his permit soon. I'd rather a professional teach him than either me or Big John, who'd start his lessons and then go off on some trip and leave him hanging, losing his skill and self-confidence. Soon Trevor will do all our errands.

"Now, as to the house . . . if you do the living room and your father's den, dust and polish and wash those floors, you can go along, sit in the rear seat of the driver education car tomorrow. I asked, and when I told them how close you two were, they said you could go if you were quiet and well behaved. I guaranteed that. You'll be proud of him, I'm sure. Clean up the kitchen first when you're done. And finish eating." Then she added, "I want you healthy and strong. I'm going up to take a short rest. Suddenly, I feel a little exhausted with all this happening while I'm still recuperating. I'll be back down in an hour or so."

She paused and thought, looking like she was hearing the voices of her ancestors. "If my father were alive and he saw how Big John is neglecting this house . . ."

She started away, then stopped. "It wouldn't surprise me if he called today or tomorrow to say he wasn't coming back. But . . ." She hobbled on. "That won't break my heart. Not now . . . now that I have you two closer than ever to each other and to me."

Trevor rushed to help her navigate the steps.

I looked at the food on the table. My stomach was so tight that I knew I couldn't swallow one bite. I rose as if I was rising out of my body and began to clear the table and clean up the kitchen. I stopped and pressed the palms of my hands over my eyes. *If I press hard enough*, I thought, *I can push all this back into a bad dream and forget it.*

Was that really Trevor and Mama I saw at the breakfast table? I didn't recognize them. Where was the Mama face I knew when I was a little girl? Where was the look of wonder and excitement for each other I found in Trevor's face when we sat together and drew things or made things with clay, even when we were outside and formed hills and castles in the dark, soft earth at the edge of the forest? Who were these strangers sitting across from me?

When I took my hands off my face, the room spun and then settled. The rush of fear that had come over me didn't retreat. I was crying again. Without knowing what I would actually do or say, I went out the back door and down the steps and started to walk quickly toward the road. When I reached it, I sucked in my breath and started to run, but I was still so tired and weak from the night before and what I had discovered and understood this morning that I had to stop, catch my breath, and walk slowly.

Cars rushed by, one driver beeping his horn because, with my eyes closed, I swayed too far into the road. The blaring sound stunned me. I stepped completely off the road and followed along the sides of it until I reached Mr. Longstreet's driveway.

Mr. Longstreet was kneeling and whitewashing the sides of his front stoop. I waited and watched, expecting Lance to come out to join him. I don't know how long I was standing there watching him before he realized it, stopped, and stood.

"Hey . . . Faith . . . something wrong? Your mother needs something?"

"No," I said. "Why isn't Lance helping you?"

He laughed. "Aside from the certainty that he's never held a paintbrush, you mean? But I'm sure he would have helped if he was here."

"Where is he?"

"He went back to the city. I think his girlfriend threatened to go out with someone else or something. You teenagers . . . life is so . . . dramatic."

"Girlfriend?"

"I don't think he'll be back before school and then maybe on a holiday. I might have to go to New York myself soon. This divorce mess . . . Sure you don't need something?"

I shook my head.

Then I turned and started back, not feeling my legs move forward or hearing the cars go by.

"Faith!" I heard him shout. "You don't hesitate to call me if you need anything. You hear?"

I kept walking.

"You hear?" he repeated, until his voice died away.

I continued walking back home. Where else would I go? I felt as if I had been hit twice in the face, once on each side.

Suddenly, a bobcat stepped out of the woods on my right. I paused. It stood there looking at me for a moment. I wasn't afraid of it; I was more in awe at how unafraid it was of me. The sound of an approaching truck sent it back into the woods. So many animals could exist alone, actually seemed to want to be alone. Another who was like it, the same species, was a threat, not a brother or sister. They'd both want the same things, so they stayed away from each other.

I wished I was like that, I wished Mama was wrong and we didn't need family, but even just having the sense of loneliness was frightening. Yet that was how I felt at the moment, terribly alone. Maybe I always was. I just never realized it until now. Right from the start, I sensed Trevor was closer to Mama and that she favored him more than she did me, but I lived with it. How could I do that now?

Thinking more about him, I realized that Trevor's shrug was just another way to help him hide the secrets. From the way Mama had talked, it seemed to me he had hidden them for a long time, maybe years. But what difference did it make? There might never be an iota of trust between us forever and ever. That realization was more painful than the lies themselves.

I was thinking so hard about him, recalling his expressions, his way of avoiding me, avoiding my questions, that it didn't surprise me to see him, standing there at the turn into the side road, waiting for me. It was as if I had the power to conjure him.

He looked so different; he looked older, which oddly made him more of a stranger. *It's what happens to all children,* I thought. *We start out so close, laughing and crying about the same things, needing each other to share our feelings. And then, almost suddenly, we shy away from each other. One of us starts to see everything we've been doing as childish. He or she wants someone else, someone who never knew that childish side of us.*

"What did you do?" Trevor asked as I drew closer. He folded his arms across his chest and smirked. "Did you go running to tell your boyfriend everything?"

"Lance returned to New York City. He has a girlfriend. He just never admitted it or talked about her. Silence can be a lie, too," I said.

He was quiet then, so I thought he was feeling sorry for me, but he wasn't. "You were too eager," he said. "You brought it all on yourself."

"Really? You believed things he said. You were excited about being on the internet with him and playing basketball with him. You took him to see things and looked forward to the hike to the lake. It's not all my fault. None of it. *You* also gave Mama those pain pills so we could have him here. You encouraged him to write emails."

His face softened, and he unfolded his arms.

"I know. It's partly my fault. But I didn't mean to hurt Mama."

"Hurt Mama? He didn't hurt Mama. He hurt *me*," I said, hoping he would feel sorrier for me and even more guilty.

"I should have listened to my instincts, my first warnings. I should have protected both of you from the city boy."

"Why are you any better? You've lied, kept secrets. You did what Mama wanted you to do, didn't you?" I asked, and walked past him.

"I wouldn't leave you, ever," he said.

I didn't turn back. I walked to the front porch and sat on the chair Mama always sat on.

Trevor stood there watching me, and then he stepped up to the front steps slowly. I avoided looking at him.

"I didn't want to hurt you. I'll never hurt you," he said. "I was afraid of losing you. Mama promised I never would if I . . . It wasn't only her making me. I love you, and I'm sorry about what happened."

He did look sorrier and, suddenly, so much smaller. His lips quivered. A voice inside me repeated, *It's not his fault. Mama did this.*

Trevor sat on the stoop and looked out at the road. There was a gust of wind out of nowhere that lifted the dust off the road and sent it in a cloud to the side. A rabbit peered out of some tall grass and then hurriedly hopped across the road to another patch. *What's it like*, I wondered, *from the day you're born to know something wants to eat you? Were animals like this in the Garden of Eden? Did they hunt and kill each other there? The Eden children*, I thought. *Lance called us that.*

I shook my head as if I could shake the memories out of it.

"You almost went all the way with Lance," Trevor suddenly said, still looking forward. I had almost forgotten he was sitting there. "What would or could have happened then?" he asked. "Mama says you shouldn't think of it as being punished when she put you in the nursery, even though she was angrier than she can ever remember. You heard her. You must think of it as being protected."

He turned to me. "As all of us are being protected," he said. "She only wants us to stay a family. She always told me that adopted children need that more."

"Do you believe her, still believe all that?"

"Yes," he said.

"Everything? Even that story about her giving her mother the herb to help her?"

There was a little hesitation, but he nodded.

"I don't," I said. "I think everyone believes what makes them happy. Don't forget what she told us years ago. The world is so much more difficult for people who cannot lie. Imagine how much more terrible it would be for her to admit the truth and live with what's in that room. You can't sing lullabies and read nursery rhymes to it then, hoping that will make the truth disappear.

"When you realize that, you'll really be a man," I said.

I rose and walked into the house. For a moment, I simply stood there looking at the living room as if I had entered the house of a stranger. I knew I was crying even though I couldn't feel any tears. Then, as if it was inevitable, which it probably was, I plugged in the vacuum cleaner and began to do as Mama had asked.

I was working mechanically and didn't realize he was standing next to me.

"What?" I asked, turning off the vacuum cleaner.

"Are you going to watch me learn how to drive tomorrow?"

"That's what you're worried about? Why do you want me along?"

He gave me that Trevor shrug. *Not this time*, I thought.

"Why?" I repeated, more intensely.

"I think I'd do better with you there. We've learned so much together."

"Not everything together, not what *really matters* in this house," I said. The pain stung him through his eyes. "Mama made you lie and keep secrets from me. Don't ever forget it. I won't."

I turned my back on him. He walked away, through the kitchen, out the back door, and to the driveway. While I was polishing furniture, I heard him shooting baskets. I thought about Lance for a few moments and then thought maybe he wouldn't have gone back to his girlfriend if Mama and Trevor hadn't found us. Maybe he would still be here. Maybe everything would be different, and I wouldn't yet know about the nursery and what was in it. *Why can't I believe that? Why does it have to be everything Mama wants us to believe? I have a right to lie to myself, just like she does.*

Anger overtook my sorrow. I tossed the polishing cloth and marched upstairs to our bedroom.

I would not sleep there tonight or any other night. If she tried to make me, I would tell Big John exactly what had happened while he was gone. He'd believe me, wouldn't he? *I'm going to sleep in Big John's den and when he comes home and sees me there, he'll know the truth*, I thought. *She won't be able to lie to him then.*

When I opened my drawer to get some of my things, I saw that sheer nightgown. Now I understood why she had given it to me, and the sexy panties. I bundled both up. I'd throw them in the garbage, I thought. Then I took out my pajamas and put them and some panties and socks in an empty pillowcase. I folded what I thought I'd wear tomorrow when I woke and put that in, too. Then I went to the bathroom and collected my toothbrush, my hairbrush, and some toothpaste. I found a wrapped bar of soap and took a towel and a washcloth, putting everything into the bulging pillowcase. Doing all this helped keep my rage in a cage, as Mama would say.

I wished I could forget all her sayings, but they were all I knew, and there did seem to be a time and a place for one of them every day. How was I going to hate her, ever? Now, after all these years and all the love, the wonderful dinners and laughter, the family stories, and the home teaching, it would be like hating a big part of myself. These contradictory feelings tore at my insides. I was crying again as I continued to get my things together.

My arms full, I started out and headed for the stairs. When I reached them, I stopped. Mama was halfway down, moving with her right arm on the banister and her crutch in her left so she could keep her foot in the cast off the steps. She turned and saw me.

"What are you doing?" she asked.

I stood there, silent.

She switched to the banister on the left and took a step back up. "Well?"

"I'm not sleeping with Trevor," I said, as firmly as I could. "I'm going to sleep on Big John's sofa bed."

She took another step and another.

"No, you're not," she said. "You go put all that back."

"I want to be alone for a while, Mama."

"You sleep where you should," she said, and took the next two steps until she was just a step from the top.

I shook my head. I never defied Mama to her face, almost to avoid upsetting Trevor as much as it would her. I cried and moaned but always did what she told me to do. This time, I didn't move.

Her eyes widened. Her rage was out of her cage.

"Get that back into your room," she ordered. "Now!"

I still didn't move.

She raised her crutch and poked the filled pillowcase to push me back, but my resistance was strong and solid. I could almost see the surge of force rebound like a current of electricity and catch her off-balance. The crutch seemed to bounce off the pillowcase and fly up. Her eyes exploded with surprise. I dropped the pillowcase and reached for the crutch, grabbing it, but she had lost her grip, and she fell backward, her legs flying up and turning her over, catching her foot in the cast, which seemed to lift her up, sending her over again, a backward somersault that ended with her head slamming on the floor and her body turning just a little to her left.

The world stopped.

There was no sound, just the beginning of a scream so deep inside me that it took what seemed to be minutes to get it out. It was probably less than a second.

"TREVOR!" I shouted.

I shouted so hard and so long that I thought my vocal cords snapped.

When he finally heard me and came in, I was still grasping my full pillowcase and holding Mama's crutch.

fourteen

He didn't move. The sight of Mama on the floor, blood trickling out of her ear, her body twisted and her eyes closed, froze him. He looked up at me with such a childish expression of helplessness that I started to cry. No matter what our age, when we're confronted with injured or sick parents, we rush back to our childhood, when all could be fixed, all could be saved, simply with a kiss and a comforting smile.

"She lost her balance," I said, and hurried down the steps. He was still frozen as I laid her crutch down and knelt beside her. "Mama?" I turned her to be more comfortably on her back and then gently shook her. "Mama?"

Her eyes were closed. I leaned over and felt her breathing on my cheek.

"Her leg!" Trevor cried, and I looked at her cast. There was a trickle of blood leaking out of the bottom of it. My body trembled as my face flushed with fear. I battled back my panic, knowing I would just sit there crying.

"What should we do?" Trevor asked.

"Call Mr. Longstreet. The number's on the counter. Tell him what happened."

"What happened? What should I say?"

"She fell down the stairs and hit her head. Tell him about the cast bleeding. Go," I ordered, and Trevor hurried to the kitchen phone. I felt for Mama's pulse. The blood wasn't coming out of her ear as quickly, but it wasn't stopping. I patted her arm gently and kept saying, "Mama? Mama?"

There was no response. Her lips didn't even quiver.

"He's coming right over, and he's called for an ambulance," Trevor reported. "How is she?"

"I don't know. She's still unconscious."

I looked up the stairs and saw that my pillowcase was still at the top. The image of Mama poking it and losing her balance once again rushed over me.

"Keep talking to her," I said. "I'm going to get a pillow for her and some cotton and antiseptic for her ear. Come on," I demanded. "We have to do what we can until they come."

Slowly, he knelt beside her and took her hand. I hurried up the stairs, grabbed my pillowcase, and went to the bathroom to get the cotton and antiseptic. Then I tossed the pillowcase into the bedroom and hurried back downstairs.

"Did she wake up?" I asked.

"No. She's really hurt."

I knelt beside her and began to dab her ear. We heard Mr. Longstreet pull up. He hurried in and stood there for a moment absorbing the scene. Then he knelt and searched for Mama's pulse, moving her eyelids gently. He shook his head.

"What?" I asked.

"I took a course in first aid," he said. "One of her pupils is fixed and dilated. Don't worry. A friend of mine is a paramedic and luckily is on duty. They'll be here faster than usual, for sure. She has a steady pulse. Paula?" He held her head very gently. I saw on his face how serious he thought it was. He tried not to look at either of us.

"Did you see her hit her head?" he asked, still staring at her.

"Yes," I said, so weakly that I wasn't sure I had said it. "Trevor was outside," I added, so he wouldn't have to say anything.

Mr. Longstreet gently touched her head and explored with the tips of his fingers.

"Oh, yeah," he said. Whatever he saw and felt frightened him.

"Should we put her on the sofa?" I asked.

"Oh, no, no. We can't move her. Let the paramedics do it. They know how. They'll put her in a neck brace first."

We could hear the siren in the distance. Tears were streaming down Trevor's cheeks. His eyes rolled with fear. He looked like he might faint.

"Sit, Trevor. There's nothing to do until they arrive."

I saw he was afraid to move away from Mama, so I got up and stood by his side, holding his hand.

"What exactly happened?" Mr. Longstreet asked me. For a moment, I couldn't speak.

"She lost her balance going up the stairs. I tried to stop her from falling backward by grabbing the crutch when she raised it in the air, but she lost her grip on it, and then . . . then she flipped over, falling down the stairs, and landed like this, striking her head first."

He nodded and kept calling to her and gently patting her wrist. We heard the ambulance pull up, the siren go off. Moments later, two paramedics came hurrying into the house.

"Took a bad one off the stairs, Peter," Mr. Longstreet said to the taller one. He stood. "She had broken her ankle and navigated about with that crutch."

They knelt beside her, checking her vitals.

"She was going up the stairs with a crutch?" Peter asked.

"She wouldn't stay downstairs," I told him, "in our daddy's den, where we had fixed a bed. She wanted to be in her room."

I felt like an idiot trying to explain everything in a few sentences with gasping words.

They asked us all to step back while they worked on Mama, putting on the neck brace Mr. Longstreet had described. The other, shorter and stouter paramedic went back out and brought in the stretcher for the ambulance. They carefully lifted Mama onto it and then triggered it to make it go higher. A blood-pressure cuff remained attached to her arm, and they put an oxygen mask over her face. As they began to roll her out, Mr. Longstreet shot ahead to get the door open. Trevor and I, holding hands, followed.

We stopped on the porch and watched them navigate Mama down the steps and then into the ambulance. I couldn't tell whose hand was colder, Trevor's or mine. Mr. Longstreet stood by as the stouter paramedic got into the ambulance with Mama. Peter said something to him and rushed around to get into the driver's seat.

Both of us, just as we often had done from our Wexler days until now, shouted the same word, simultaneously.

"MAMA!"

"C'mon," Mr. Longstreet said. "We'll follow the ambulance to the hospital. Get what you need."

"We don't need anything," I said.

Neither of us went to get into the front of his car, but rather we both sat in the rear, and soon we started after the ambulance.

"She'll be all right," Mr. Longstreet said. "All right. She has a strong pulse. They'll get her into treatment instantly. She'll be all right."

It sounded as if he was chanting it, maybe praying for us. Trevor barely moved, much less spoke. We were still holding hands, tightly.

"She's still a young woman, very strong," Mr. Longstreet continued. He was even more afraid of the silence than we were. "She may look fragile, especially now, but I've seen her do some pretty manly work. Always admired her for that whenever I rode by. She'll be fine," he said. "Fine," he added, more in a whisper. At this point, I was sure he was talking himself into it more than he was talking us into it.

We could see the ambulance ahead. Traffic moved out of its way, not that there was much. We were able to stay very close.

"They deal with home accidents daily," Mr. Longstreet said. "You'd be surprised at how many there are. We're all just more careless at home. It's as if we believe the house can protect us."

That's just what Mama would have said, I thought. The house would always protect us, because the family forever lingered in the walls, their voices and laughter planted in them, absorbed by them as if they were all made of sponge. How many times did I see her press her hand to a wall and close her eyes as if she could draw strength from it? Sometimes I'd do it, too, just to see if something would happen. Nothing ever did happen for me, but Mama had promised that someday something would. She promised me that I'd always find comfort and strength in the house. Often, although he never admitted it, I saw Trevor do the same thing, press his hand to a wall and close his eyes, waiting for some message.

Mr. Longstreet reverted simply to telling us where we were on the way and how much longer he estimated the ride. Neither Trevor nor I had any sense of time, anyway. We were both too frightened to care or realize anything but our own fear. Finally, we turned onto the hospital grounds and followed the ambulance to the emergency entrance in the rear.

"Can't park here, but we'll do it for a while, anyway," Mr. Longstreet said, pulling into a spot reserved for doctors.

We all got out and watched them take Mama out of the ambulance and wheel her into the hospital. I had been hoping she'd be awake by now and complaining, telling them to stop fussing over her and take her home, but she was clearly still unconscious.

Mr. Longstreet stopped for a moment. "Oh, we should have called your father before we left," he said. "Do you know how to reach him?"

"His cell-phone number is in the kitchen," I said.

"Oh."

"But . . ." I looked at Trevor. "But it should be on Lance's phone. He showed me how the numbers you called or those from people who called you could be found on the phone."

"Right . . . good. I'll call him," he said. "You guys go in. Tell them who you are."

Trevor looked so lost and frightened. I tugged him to follow me, and we entered the hospital emergency area. Almost instantly, a security man who looked older than Mr. Longstreet approached us.

"You have to enter through the main entrance," he said. "And talk to the receptionist before coming in here."

"The ambulance just took our mother in," I said. I looked past him and saw that the paramedics had wheeled Mama into a room and were working frantically to get her hooked up to something. "That's her!"

"Go to the main desk there," he said, nodding, "and tell them who you are."

After we did, one of the nurses showed us where to sit and wait. She could see how frightened we both were now and gave us each a cranberry juice.

"The doctor will talk to you as soon as they know more," she said. She even squeezed my hand for reassurance.

Minutes later, Mr. Longstreet found us.

"You had a good idea. Lance had the number, and I reached your father. He's calling his partner's sister, Gabrielle, to come over and be with you. I'll hang around, too. No worries. I think they think I'm your mother's father," he added, smiling. "Didn't say I wasn't. That way, they're sure to come to us when they know more to do for your mother. They have a specialist coming in to examine her. You gotta hang in, just the way she would surely for you two."

"Thank you, Mr. Longstreet," I said.

Trevor barely nodded, and then it seemed as if Mr. Longstreet's words finally reached Trevor's brain.

"What kinda specialist?" he asked.

"Oh, I imagine cranial . . . you know . . . for the head injury."

"Is it very bad?" Trevor asked.

Mr. Longstreet shook his head. "We'd better wait for the doctors' opinions. I almost knocked myself out once, hit my head rushing down the basement steps, but . . ."

But it wasn't as bad as Mama's injury, I thought. Trevor was too lost in his own words to hear or care about Mr. Longstreet's injury. I was sure he didn't hear another word he said describing it and how it had happened.

Time seemed to move so slowly that seconds became minutes and minutes became hours. I let go of Trevor's hand, and he sat back with his head lowered. Mr. Longstreet did his best to keep us occupied, describing more of his own injuries over the years and how he had healed. He blamed himself for each and every one of them. Could I blame Mama? He got us more to drink and spoke to one of the nurses but didn't give us any new information, except to say the examination was continuing with a CT scan.

And then Nick's sister arrived. I couldn't remember when last we had seen her. It would have had to have been one of those nights Nick and she came over to play pool or darts and drink beer. Mama wasn't interested in any of it and watched television upstairs. However, she permitted Trevor and me to watch them play until she called down for us to go to bed.

Gabby didn't look as pretty to me then as she did now. It was funny how in the midst of all this, that was what came to my mind. Maybe it was because she looked older and her freckles didn't seem so prominent. Her hair, which I remembered was long, just below her wing bones, was short and in a style I had seen in one of Daddy's magazines, on a woman in an advertisement, layered and to neck level. It made her raspberry-red hair look even brighter. She looked slimmer, too, and that made her seem taller. She was wearing a light blue sweater shirt and a knee-length dark blue skirt. For some reason, I thought she was out of place here. She looked too bright and sexy for a hospital emergency room. I caught the way some nurses, especially the male ones, glanced at her.

She slid in beside me and Trevor like a runner on a baseball team sliding into one of the bases and seized my hand and Trevor's.

"Oh, you poor children. John and Nick called me, and I left work as soon as I could."

"This is Mr. Longstreet, our neighbor," I said, because he was standing right in front of us and looking at her. "He called the ambulance."

"Oh. How do you do?" she said, offering her hand. "Have we heard anything?"

"Not yet, but soon," he said.

"What a horror. Your father wants me to call him as soon as we know something," she told us. "He and Nick are somewhere between Florida and New Orleans. As soon as they reach an airport, John will fly back and get here. Nick can handle their driving," she told Mr. Longstreet, who smiled and nodded but seemed about as interested in that as I was.

"Can I get you two anything?" Gabby asked us.

I realized that Trevor had yet to say a word.

"No, we're fine," I said. I looked at Trevor, who looked down. I put my hand on his shoulder, and then we both looked up as a doctor approached.

Gabby rose quickly to join Mr. Longstreet. Both Trevor and I stood slowly. We were behind them, but we could hear. We grasped the gist of it. The CT scan showed cranial bleeding. This was causing pressure, and the surgeon wanted to go in immediately. There were papers to sign, but they couldn't wait for Daddy's arrival, and no one could reach him on the phone. Mr. Longstreet agreed to do it but paused and asked Gabby if she wanted to sign. She shook her head quickly.

The doctor finally realized we were there. He stepped to the side to talk to us.

"It will be a while before we know anything," he told us. He turned to Mr. Longstreet. "There is a waiting area near surgery on the second floor."

Mr. Longstreet followed him to the nurses' station and then, after listening to what the doctor told them, hurried back.

"You can bring them up to the second floor," Mr. Longstreet told Gabby. "I'll look after whatever has to be done here."

"Oh, sure," she said. "I'll call John, too."

"Right. Hang in there, kids," he told us.

Trevor looked at me with that same helpless look he had at the stairway.

I took his hand, and we followed Gabby out. She put her arms around me and told me to wait while she called Daddy. We watched her go outside of the emergency room main entrance and use her cell phone.

"Is Mama going to be all right?" Trevor asked.

As if she were standing right beside us and had heard him, I could hear Mama talking, hear her telling me that girls matured faster than boys. I did feel older, but maybe that was because I was too drained of emotions to behave like a little girl. I couldn't cry. I felt almost hypnotized. Everything that had happened had drained me of all emotion.

"I don't know," I said. I could have simply said *Yes, of course.* But what I had said was the truth.

This was another example, more evidence to support Mama's statement, "The world is so much more difficult for people who cannot lie."

We watched Gabby reenter. From the expression on her face, I knew it wasn't news that would cheer us.

"From where they are and what connections to fly back are possible, your father won't be here until evening. He might have to wait for a morning flight. It's up to you two to be strong and take care of each other. Of course, I'll stay with you."

"That's what we've always done," I said, holding Trevor tightly, "taken care of each other."

Gabby smiled. "Yes, I remember how proud your mother was of the way you treated each other. Most brothers and sisters this close in age don't get along as well."

"*Is*," I said.

"Pardon?"

"Our mother *is* proud of us, not *was*."

"Oh. Yes, *of course*. I was just referring to when I was at your house last time. Oh, here comes Mr. Longstreet," she said, happy to end the conversation.

"They took her up to surgery. I thought maybe we should take you two to the hospital cafeteria. Get you something to eat. It'll be quite a while."

"I'm not hungry," I said.

Trevor shook his head.

"Well, we have a lot of time to wait. Maybe you'll get hungry or want a drink. This way," he said, with more of a commanding tone. We followed him and Gabby down the long hallway and entered the cafeteria.

"You should eat something," he said, talking more to me.

"Get your brother to eat something. Go on. Check out what's available."

"I'll just have a coffee for now," Gabby said, and headed for the coffee dispenser.

Reluctantly, I led Trevor to where we could read the menu and look at the food available. It seemed so wrong to want to do anything but wait for the doctor. I knew Trevor had the same urgent desire to be as close as we could be to where Mama was. It was silly, of course. What could we do? What difference would it make? But both of us were thinking that she wouldn't leave us if the roles were reversed, not for a second.

Mr. Longstreet stepped up beside us and began complimenting some of the food.

"They have pizza," he said.

I turned to him quickly. Did he ever know about that time Lance had brought the pizza to us? Did Lance tell him more about Mama?

"Even if you just nibble on a piece. Get your drink, too," he said.

I took a tray for both of us and did what he practically ordered us to do, and then we all went to the table where Gabby was sitting and sipping her coffee. She was sending a message to someone on her cell phone. *Maybe she has a boyfriend now*, I thought.

"I'll keep updating John and Nick," she said when we joined her. "Oh, that pizza looks good. Maybe I'll get a piece."

Mr. Longstreet had a bowl of chicken noodle soup and some bread and butter. We ate a little while Gabby got herself what she wanted and returned.

"So you two are still being homeschooled, right?" she asked.

"Yes," I said.

"I heard your mother's gotten you pretty advanced. I should have been a better student and gone on to college instead of going right to work. My generation's always been in a rush. What about you, Mr. Longstreet?"

"I went right to construction and contracting," he said. "My grandsons will make up for it."

Trevor looked at me.

I ate what I could and looked at the clock.

"How long do you think it will be?" I asked.

"Oh, a while," Mr. Longstreet said. "Good doctors and nurses here," he added.

Trevor looked like he was going to get up and run out and then up to the second floor. I reached for his hand under the table. He lowered his head and played with what was left of his pizza.

"So who do you work for?" Mr. Longstreet asked Gabby.

"Margaret Amber. She's with State Farm. I'm glad I at least was smart enough to learn computer skills. Thanks to my brother. He became the head of our household when my father had heart failure."

"And your mother?"

"She was a heavy smoker and drinker."

Mr. Longstreet nodded as if that was enough. Neither Trevor nor I cared to listen to them. We knew about Nick's parents, anyway.

"We should go upstairs," I said, with Mama's firmness.

Mr. Longstreet nodded. "We'll put our trays there," he said, nodding to where the dirty dishes and trays were placed.

When I started to rise, Trevor shot up. We went ahead of them and walked toward the entrance.

"Hold up," Mr. Longstreet said. "We're going to stay together."

I looked at Trevor. Whether he or Gabby stayed with us really didn't matter at all to us now. We had each other.

There were two other people in the surgery waiting room. Mr. Longstreet spoke to them, and we learned they were a couple whose teenage son had been in a very bad car accident. There didn't look to be a half inch of space between them as they comforted each other. The husband spoke to Mr. Longstreet, but his wife looked like talking would shatter her at his feet. The second hand on the wall clock moved with their and our heartbeats. Every time a door opened or there was the sound of footsteps, Trevor's grip on my hand tightened and the couple held their breath.

"When Mama is better, we'll bury this in the Cemetery for Unhappiness," I whispered.

Trevor smiled.

I thought Mr. Longstreet had heard me, because he gave me a quizzical look. Maybe he had just heard the word *cemetery*. Gabby was busy on her cell phone.

"There's a bathroom just outside the waiting room on your right if either of you needs it," Mr. Longstreet said.

I could see that Trevor did, but he was afraid to leave.

"We've got a while yet," Mr. Longstreet said.

"We'll take turns," I told Trevor. "You go first."

He didn't want to look weaker, but I assured him I could wait. He said he'd be quick and hurried out.

"You sure take care of him. You two are pretty close," Mr. Longstreet said. "That's nice. I had an older brother. He lived in Upstate New York. Two sons, both lawyers, one in Pittsburgh now and the other in Atlanta, Georgia. Families don't stay as close to each other like they used to," he said nostalgically. "Haven't seen either one or their families for nearly ten years or so."

"My mother told us that family was all you needed. With family, you'd always be safe."

"I imagine she was right to say it," he said. "Wise woman."

We all held our breath when a doctor came in and looked at the husband and wife. Whatever he said brought a smile and tears to both their faces. They followed him. The woman paused in the doorway and turned to us.

"I hope all goes well for you, too," she said. She was gone before we could thank her.

"Good news is often contagious," Mr. Longstreet said, and patted my hand.

Trevor returned, and I went to the bathroom. Afterward, I stood in front of the mirror and started to cry. If I hadn't been so angry and packed that pillowcase . . .

"Please don't die, Mama," I whispered. "I'm sorry."

I spent some time fixing my face so Trevor wouldn't see how frightened I was. If he saw that I had cried, he could very well start to cry and feel terrible because it made him look like a terrified little boy instead of the man Mama wanted him to be, especially now.

When I returned to the waiting room, I was instantly encouraged and happy. I knew in my heart how long this could be. We were there barely more than two hours, and here the doctor was already talking to Mr. Longstreet and Gabby. It must not be as serious as they had all feared. Trevor hadn't gotten up. He was waiting for me. I smiled and started for him.

But I stopped when Mr. Longstreet and Gabby turned around.

fifteen

Once I saw one of those black crows in our forest lifting off a tree branch and cawing as it flapped its wings over us. Trevor had said it was probably going to swoop down on a smaller, vulnerable bird's nest to steal the eggs or eat whatever food the mother bird dropped in the nest for her babies. I think I was just a little more than seven at the time.

"You're making that up," I had told him. "Just to scare me."

He had shrugged, which meant *Believe it or not. I don't care.*

After we had gone into the house, I had asked Mama about what Trevor had told me. She had paused, looking lost in thought while I had waited hopefully for her to tell me it wasn't so. But instead, she had looked at Trevor approvingly.

"He sees through my eyes sometimes," she had said.

Big John wasn't in the kitchen. He was watching television in his den and didn't hear what Trevor had told me.

"I often think of death as a big black bird. Not fair to the crows, I know, but it's a shape it often takes."

Trevor wasn't gloating over Mama's reaffirmation of what he had said. He wasn't like that. He was never a *There, see?* or *I told you so* person. He simply accepted. Sometimes I couldn't tell if he was pleased to be reassured or not. It annoyed me even more, but Mama liked this about him.

"Trevor will be happier in life than you will, Faith. Or maybe just less unhappy," Mama had said, still looking at him with admiration. "He knows what he can change and what he can't. He won't mourn over lost causes and disappointments. He will grin and bear it when failures or regrets occur, so that he can go on to a better day."

He was that way when we learned that Mama hadn't survived the surgery, that the blood rushing into her head was too fast for the surgeon to overcome. He wasn't frozen and lost as he had been after Mama's fall and during the examination and operation. It was over, and he was suddenly older than I was, listening and nodding at the doctor's explanation of Mama's fatal injury and then Mr. Longstreet saying that he had to be the man of the house for a while and be sure to care for me.

The whole time, I was gasping beside him and holding back a flood of tears. I was hugging myself so tightly that someone would think my body might otherwise fly apart. He stood firmly with that perfect, almost arrogant posture, nodding and reassuring them that he had understood every word. The black bird had come and gone.

He simply had accepted it.

He would be less unhappy.

Of course, I wasn't only mourning Mama's passing; I was mourning how responsible I felt and how guilty I was about it. Anyone who knew what I was thinking and feeling wouldn't be sure which was more devastating to me, Mama's dying or my feeling remorseful.

Afterward, when he took us home, Mr. Longstreet resembled an undertaker taking us to the cemetery. He didn't look at us, and he said barely more than "I'm so sorry."

Gabby had already sent a text to Daddy. She didn't tell us what he had said in response. She told us that she had promised him she would look after us until he came home. He was at the airport in New Orleans and looking into the possible flights. She followed us in her car.

When we arrived at our house, Mr. Longstreet told us he would check with Gabby later to see how we were doing. He'd get whatever we needed. Just let him know. The devastating events made him look older suddenly. He seemed anxious to get back to his own home, probably wishing he had never beckoned for us to come over that day. He had been happy in his own world, and Mama, Big John, and we had been happy in ours.

I thought about that poem by Robert Frost reminding us that "good fences make good neighbors." If we had listened to the lesson and I had not gone over that wall, maybe none of this would have happened.

There was a card stuck in our doorway when we pulled up. After we got out and Mr. Longstreet left to go home, I looked at it first.

"The driving school. They threatened to charge Mama for today's lesson."

"What?" Gabby said. She practically tore the card from my hand. "I'll see about this. Insensitive bastards."

"How would they have known?" I asked, and she thought a moment.

"Well, I'll take care of it, anyway. Don't you two worry about it."

When Trevor, Gabby, and I entered the house, I was immediately struck by the sight of Moses and Becky sitting at the base of the stairway where Mama had lain, looking as though they were waiting with cat patience for her.

"Oh, I forgot about your cats," Gabby said. "How adorable."

"I'll get them their food and water," I said, grateful for something immediate to do. They followed me into the kitchen.

"We've all got to eat something," Gabby declared. "Sadness drains us. It's why there is always food after a funeral."

"This wasn't a funeral," Trevor said.

"Well, it's the same feeling, isn't it?" she responded.

When he shrugged, I almost laughed.

I fed the cats and later let them out. Gabby looked in our pantry and in our refrigerator, probably hoping for something there simply to warm up.

"I'm not the best cook," she said. "I'll warn you ahead of time."

"Faith is a good cook," Trevor said. He looked as proud of me as Mama would.

"Oh, I'm sure. I imagine your mother taught you."

"Yes," I said. "I often made our dinners during Mama's recuperation and even occasionally before that. With her recipes and advice, of course."

Now Gabby looked very helpless, like someone who didn't know what to do would look. What was more of a feeling of being helpless than feeling like there wasn't anything important for you to do, especially now? She appeared so absolutely lost and confused that I almost felt sorrier for her than I did for us. We were the ones who were supposed to look dependent and vulnerable.

"I told your father I wasn't going to leave you until he was back. He wasn't sure about the connections yet, so he might not be here until the morning. Just in case, I should run home and get some things I'll need to stay overnight. Will you two be all right until I get back? It won't take that long."

"Of course," Trevor said.

"Well . . . I think . . ." She looked around. "I'll sleep on the sofa in the living room tonight if it comes to that. I'll bring my own pillow and blanket. I don't want to disturb anything. I mean, you should be in your own bedrooms, and I can't sleep . . . in your parents' room. I never knew that much about this house. I don't think I've ever been upstairs. Is there a guest room?"

"No," I said quickly. "Mama slept in Daddy's den when she was first brought home. I suppose we can open that sofa bed for you, too."

"Oh, we'll see. I'll be back as soon as possible. You're sure you're okay for now?"

"I'll make something for us to eat in the meantime," I said. "Trevor will help."

She smiled but looked like she was going to cry, like someone smiling in the rain.

"You two are so responsible. Your mother brought you up

right, strong and independent. I'd be shattered to little pieces at this point."

Both of us stared at her. Didn't she know we were shattered to little pieces inside ourselves? We continued to stare at her, neither of us moving, neither wanting to say the obvious. Our silence was stabbing her in the heart. She took a deep breath.

"Oh, my, my, what a tragedy. Okay. I'll be right back."

We watched her rush out. As soon as she was gone, I went for the mop and filled a pail with soap and water.

"What are you doing?" Trevor asked. He had sat at the kitchenette table.

"Mama's blood," I said.

He followed me to the base of the stairway where she had lain and watched me wash it away.

"I'll take that," he said, when I started to lift the pail of bloodstained water and the mop.

He grabbed it and started toward the back door.

"Wait," I said. I knew where he was going.

With his other hand, he grasped the shovel outside the door, and then we went to the Cemetery for Unhappiness. I stood beside him as he dug a grave for the water and poured it in.

"Be gone," he said, just the way Mama would. I repeated it under my breath. It would never be gone for me. I would see those bloodstains in my dreams until the day I died.

Trevor filled in the grave, and we headed back to the house with the shovel, mop, and pail. For a moment, we stood in the kitchen. I almost expected Mama to step in from the living room to tell us to wash up.

"I'll make a bolognese with some pasta, okay?"

"Yes."

"Of course, we'll have salad and garlic bread like always when we have pasta."

"Sounds good," he said.

"We should shower and change first," I said. "Mama would tell us to."

He nodded. "Yes, she would."

The shock and the sorrow were making us do mechanically what we always did. Neither of us spoke with much emotion in our voices, either. What we really were doing was avoiding talking about what had happened. He was better at it than I was, just as Mama had predicted he would be, but that stoicism stopped when we both went up the stairs.

I had forgotten that the stuffed pillowcase was on the floor by our bed, where I had tossed it.

"What's that?" he asked.

I picked it up and began to unload it on the bed.

"So?"

"Mama told me I had to sleep here, and I decided I would sleep in Big John's den on the sofa. I was in a rage, a rush, and shoved things I needed into this pillowcase."

We stared at each other a moment. Trevor was always good at filling in the unspoken details.

"So she was going down when you appeared with the pillow-case?"

"Yes."

Don't shrug, I wished. *Do anything but shrug*. I was hoping that he would be angry and start shouting at me, but he did something else.

He nodded slowly, as if I was confirming something he had suspected, and then, without another word, he started to take off his clothes to shower and change into something for dinner.

"It was my fault," I said.

I thought he wasn't going to respond and wouldn't stop picking out what to wear.

But he did.

"No. That's too simple. It's my fault, too, and Mama's, and maybe a little of Big John's. Things happen for reasons we forget or didn't even know."

"Things? Mama *died*," I said. His tolerant, serious, and mature manner was disturbing me. It was even painful. "Are you even listening?"

"I'm going to use Mama and Big John's shower. You use ours." He gathered his clothes and left.

"*Why didn't the house protect her?*" I screamed after him.

He didn't respond. I cried in the shower, because it was easier to hide my tears. After, I put on a light blue dress with a floral print that Mama had bought me months ago. She said the saleslady called it a "smocked dress," but she didn't like the name. "It's just a simple dress," she said, "that you can wear anytime, for anything."

I was sure now that she meant happy and sad occasions, no difference.

She had a thing about clothes. "Too many people buy them to distract people from seeing them, seeing who and what they really are: too fat or too thin, too old or too young."

A little more than a half hour later, I was in the kitchen making dinner, and Trevor was setting the table, when Gabby returned.

"You two are amazing," she said. "I just spoke with your father on my way back. I told him you were doing well. He said he didn't want to call you because he thought you'd cry and be very upset if he did, and he doesn't like your being that way without him. A sweet man. Always thinking about everyone else."

"When is he coming home? Did he get his flight?"

"Yes." She looked at her watch. "He's left. He thought with the drive from the airport and all, close to nine."

"I hope you like bolognese," I told her.

"What? Oh, pasta. Sure. What can I do to help?"

"Can you prepare garlic bread?"

"Huh? I thought it always came done."

"Never mind, Gabby. We will get it all ready. Trevor can do the bread while I do the salad."

He walked in and started to do it. She watched us for a moment and then retreated to the living room. Mr. Longstreet called while we were working on dinner. Trevor spoke to him and told him Daddy was on his way home and would be here tonight. He said we were doing fine and didn't need anything. He thanked him, and then we brought in the salad and the bread and told Gabby that we were starting.

"This bread smells . . . so good," she said, and then looked at us, at the way we were staring at her. I think we were actually frightening her. "I mean, you two doing all this is amazing."

Trevor shrugged. "It's just dinner."

"Yes, but after what you've both been through, after what's happened . . ."

We sat. While we ate, Gabby talked . . . actually, incessantly. It was clear to us that she feared nothing more than silence. Admittedly, it was a good distraction. She told us her life story, how she almost ran off with a boy in high school, but her brother had talked her out of it, and why, after high school, she wanted to get into work.

"I needed to feel independent as soon as I could. I wasn't even looking to get married quickly. Most men my age or a little older were so immature. I dare say you two are more mature than most men ten, fifteen years older than you are. At least, to me.

"Once our parents were gone, my brother Nick became . . . our parents," she said, smiling. "I pretend to be annoyed, but it's nice to have someone caring for you. I imagine Trevor here always will protect you."

"Of course, I will," he said. "Who else would?"

"Well, you still have your daddy," she said. "He's a young, healthy man."

"He'll be hungry," Trevor told me, ignoring her.

I nodded. "I made enough for six. We'll have leftovers. You know he likes leftovers. Mama always had something left over when he came home from a long trip," I told Gabby.

"Oh, I bet. My mother never taught me much about cooking and baking. Nick says that was because I didn't pay attention when she first tried." She laughed. "I'm sure he's right," she continued. "He makes whatever meals we have at home. We order out a lot. Should I do the dishes and let you two go to your rooms?"

"No. We'll do it," I said. "We want to be here when Daddy arrives."

"Oh, sure. I'm sorry. I'm just not thinking right."

"You don't have to stay overnight," Trevor told her. It was his polite way of saying *Just go and leave us*.

"Yes, I know I don't. But I'm not leaving before he steps in that door. He's a big, powerful man, but we don't know how he feels yet."

Neither of us could imagine what she could do for him. Our

silence sent her into the living room, where she watched television with the volume very low while we cleaned up and I put food away for Daddy.

"I hope you don't mind," she said, when we stopped to look in on her. She was sitting in Big John's chair the way Mama might. I couldn't help resenting it. "I'll turn it off," she said, after another look at us.

She rose to do so.

Neither of us spoke.

"We should just talk until John gets here. It's good to talk at times like this." She returned to Big John's chair, but we didn't sit. "I never asked Mr. Longstreet to give me any details. How did this happen?"

"She fell down the stairs," Trevor said sharply. "Details don't matter now."

"No, I guess they don't. Does your mother have close relatives? I never knew more than she lived here with her parents and had no brothers or sisters. Is there an elderly uncle or aunt?"

"Our mother's family was here in this house. She knew only those in this house," I said.

"Oh." I could see she wasn't fully grasping that. Then she smiled. "John is so proud of you two. He often bragged to Nick and me how she was doing a good job teaching you two at home."

"Both of us could easily pass the Commonwealth Secondary School Diploma right now," I said. I didn't know why, but everything I said sounded angry. I was searching for a way to get mad at her, I thought, and then I felt bad about taking out my feelings on someone who was only trying to be helpful.

"I bet." She laughed. "I'm not sure I could pass even though I graduated high school."

Her cell phone rang. She looked at it. "It's John," she said.

"Hi. Okay. Yes. They're doing fine. I'll tell them." She turned to us after she shut the phone. "He's on his way. Maybe ten minutes. His flight came in early."

"I'll get the food out again," I said, and started for the kitchen.

"I'll be right down," Trevor said. I watched him hurry upstairs.

Neither of us wanted to entertain Gabby now. She looked like the smallest comment might get her hysterical. I didn't fault her for it. I couldn't imagine myself trying to comfort Trevor and me until our daddy arrived. For too long, we had depended on no one else but Mama, Daddy, and ourselves. That was always enough. We didn't know how to be needy in front of strangers.

Every sound I made in the kitchen seemed to reverberate through the house. I had no idea what Trevor was doing. It was so quiet. I really didn't have much to do, but I moved about in slow motion, fighting the urge to collapse on the floor and cry and cry.

But my sorrow was quickly washed away by fear. What would Daddy think and do once he understood what had happened on the stairway? How would I explain it? How much would Trevor and I tell him about Lance and what Mama had done to punish me and what she had forced Trevor to do? Would he blame it all on us? Might he not decide to send us back to a foster home? Trevor was almost sixteen, and I was almost fifteen, but he couldn't leave us here by ourselves and continue his truck driving all over the country, could he?

What will happen to us? I had so many reasons to cry, but somehow I held back my tears.

I heard Trevor hurrying down the stairs.

He looked in on me.

"Daddy's home," he said.

He waited for me to be at his side when Daddy entered our house. When he did, he rushed to us and embraced us in his powerful arms, nearly lifting us off the floor and holding us so hard that none of us could breathe. He saw Gabby in the living room doorway crying and slowly released us.

"Thank you," he told her.

"Oh, it was . . . they're so wonderful, John. How they have gone through this, two adults, I swear. Most of the time, they held me together."

"Yes," Big John said. "I imagine so."

"I have what we had for our dinner warmed and ready for you, Daddy."

"Okay," he said. "Let me clean up a bit. Gabby, I don't want to hold you up any more. If you want . . ."

"I'll stay a while longer, John. It's no problem. I was prepared to stay the night."

"Thank you," Daddy said.

He started for the stairway and paused at the bottom, looking at the floor as if he could still see Mama sprawled there. Then he shook his head and hurried up the stairway, pounding each step as if he wanted to take revenge on them.

Trevor and I headed for the kitchen. Gabby stood by watching us get Daddy's dinner and the setup for the table.

"I think you'll be taking care of him more than he will be taking care of you," she said.

Neither of us knew how to respond. We continued to do what we had to as if she wasn't there. Trevor set up Daddy's place, and I brought in the salad. When I heard him descending, I brought in the heated garlic bread.

"Well," he said, appearing in the dining room. "It's good we have somethin' to eat. Thanks, guys."

He took his seat, and Trevor and I joined him.

Gabby surprised us by entering with her things in hand.

"Where you goin'?" Daddy asked her.

"I realized that I should leave you all to . . . to your privacy. Please call me if you need anything, anything at all, John."

"Okay, Gabby. Thanks again."

"My deepest condolences, of course. Good night, children. Actually, *children* doesn't fit at all. Good night, Trevor and Faith. I'll think about you and pray for you."

Daddy rose to escort her to the door. We could barely hear them talking. Trevor and I waited, seated at the dining-room table.

"This looks fine," he said, returning and taking his seat. "They had nothin' but pretzels on the plane."

"What do you want to drink, Daddy? We weren't sure."

"I'll have one of my beers, Faith."

I hurried out to get one and bring it back. He didn't speak until I returned. Then he poured the beer, took a long draft of it, and sat back.

"Tell me everythin'."

He looked first to me. I glanced at Trevor. He was looking down, maybe even trembling with the possibility that I would. Then Daddy said something that gave me the chills.

"The door to the Forbidden Room is unlocked. It was slightly open. Were you in there?"

"Yes, Daddy," I said.

He looked from Trevor to me.

"Why? Did she know you were in there?"

"Oh, yes. Mama made me sleep in there. She was punishing me for being with Lance, Mr. Longstreet's grandson."

"Ah," he said, sitting back, thinking. "So you know about what's in that room. I wanted her to tell you about it a long time ago, but she insisted we not. You weren't ready, she would say, and she made me promise never to speak of it. I don't doubt that secret was more important to her than I was. So you wouldn't have been in there if she didn't want you to know." He thought for a moment. "She must have been ragin' around this place, and that's how she lost her balance on those stairs," he concluded. "I told her to sleep in my den. I warned her it was dangerous to navigate those steps with a crutch in hand, but she was stubborn."

Neither Trevor nor I spoke. He was staring at the table, and then he slapped it so hard both of us jumped.

"Forget about that room. I'm sorry I put up with it for so damn long. I shoulda done more to convince her to . . . to clean it out. I'm goin' to redo it. It'll be a proper bedroom for you, Faith. Finally, you'll both have your own bedrooms as you should've from the start."

I looked at Trevor. I had no doubt he was about to confess the rest, but I didn't see what good it would do now, and apparently, neither did he.

"I'll get you the pasta, Daddy. Bolognese."

"Okay. Then we'll talk about the funeral. I'll be contactin' your grandparents' church. We went there once or twice in the early days. Everythin' was different then. There were more smiles."

He put his big hands over his eyes. They covered most of his face. Both Trevor and I put our hands on his arms simultaneously. We all sat there like that for a while, and then he lifted his hands away and nodded.

"We'll be all right. We'll figure it all out together."

"I'll get your pasta, Daddy," I said again, and went into the kitchen just to stand there alone for a few moments to stop the trembling. Would Trevor tell him the rest of it while I was away from the table?

It didn't look like he had when I returned. While Daddy ate, we told him about Mr. Longstreet's help, the paramedics, and what went on at the hospital. I provided most of the details. Sticking with facts helped me avoid crying.

"I'm sorry I wasn't here for her, for you," Daddy said. "So what about this grandson?"

"Oh, he returned to New York City before all this happened."

"Seems he had a girlfriend," Trevor added. He looked so happy about that.

"Huh," Daddy said. "Oh. Well, we should all get some sleep. The next few days won't be very pleasant. I'll make my peace with your mother my way. It will be strange sleepin' in that bed without her after all these years."

Now I couldn't help but cry. Trevor looked down. I thought it was finally hitting him. Daddy reached out for both our hands and closed his eyes. He was saying a prayer, I was sure. We could feel it moving to us through his fingers. And then he rose. I said I would clean up. Trevor wanted to help, but I told him I'd be fine. I needed to do it all myself. He went up the stairs right behind Daddy, both in the same posture with their heads down.

My real reason for telling him I'd be fine was simply that I needed to be alone. I hadn't been since Mama had fallen back on the stairway. Everything seemed to have happened so fast. It was still not quite real. When I was finished with the kitchen, I turned off the lights and for a while just stood at the bottom of the stairway looking up, imagining myself standing there at the top looking down, that infamous pillowcase clutched under my arm.

Did this really happen?

Was Mama gone?

I went up and to the bathroom to get ready for bed. It was so quiet. The house wasn't even creaking. When I entered the bedroom, I thought Trevor was asleep. For a moment, I waited for him to move or say something, but he didn't. He was turned on his side, half his face buried in his pillow. His right hand was clutching the blanket.

I had started to take off my clothes and change into my nightgown when I heard footsteps in the hallway. Just as I looked out, Daddy turned to descend the stairway. He had something cradled in his arms. I walked out slowly, listening to him go through the kitchen and out the rear door. Practically tiptoeing, I went down and into the kitchen. Where was he? What was he doing? I saw nothing through the window, so I went to the back door and peered out.

I heard the shoveling and stepped out.

Daddy was digging a deep hole in the Cemetery for Unhappiness. I watched how hard and how fast he worked. I thought I heard him mumbling to himself. When he was satisfied with the hole, he knelt and picked up the bundled blanket from the cradle in the Forbidden Room. He dropped it into the grave he had dug and then quickly began filling it in. I turned, slipped back into the house, and hurried up the stairs to our bedroom. Trevor had woken. He was looking up at the ceiling, his hands behind his head.

"Why did you go back down?" he asked.

"Daddy," I said.

"What?"

"He buried Mama's sister."

"In the Cemetery for Unhappiness?"

"Yes."

"Good."

He turned over and closed his eyes. I heard Daddy coming back up the stairs, but I didn't look out or call to him. I finished putting on my nightgown and then slipped under the blanket and lay there looking up at the ceiling, where moonlight threading through trees spun shadows and shapes. I remembered Mama telling me that shadows were a part of the house, because the sun and the moon brought them to life the same way at similar times since our house was built.

When I first heard his sobbing, I thought the sobs were my own. Trevor hadn't shed a tear or cried in front of me since we were told Mama had died in the operating room. I didn't think he was ever going to cry in front of either me or Daddy.

But he was crying now.

I put my hand on his shoulder. Then he turned slowly.

"I'm sorry," he said.

"Why are you sorry, Trevor?"

"If I hadn't told her about your meeting Lance . . ."

"You did what you did because of how you loved her and what she wanted, Trevor."

He put his arm around my waist, lowering his head to my shoulder.

I patted his hair and kissed his forehead. We were both in such pain.

"I don't want to be without you," he said. "That's all I ever meant to say."

I kissed his cheek and tasted his tears. Then I kissed him on the lips, something I had done only with Lance. He lifted his head a little to look at me and then lowered his lips to mine. It was a longer kiss.

I could feel him sliding closer. His hands went to my hips and slowly began lifting my nightgown. I didn't stop him.

We were still doing what Mama wanted.

We would make her family after all.

epilogue

There weren't many people at Mama's funeral. Mostly they were people with whom Big John had business. Mr. Longstreet attended and sat behind us in the church. Gabby sat with us and came with us to the cemetery, as did Mr. Longstreet. Mama was being buried next to her parents. Her grandparents were buried in the row behind them. I saw Great-Aunt Mary Dowd, who had died in the house fire, beside her husband's grave off to the right, but we didn't look for any other relations.

Big John invited Mr. Longstreet to our house afterward. Gabby had taken care of ordering some food. No one else attended. After Mr. Longstreet left, Big John, Gabby, Trevor, and I sat in the living room. He and Gabby had done a great deal of planning between the night he had returned and Mama's funeral. He had been doing a lot of work in the house, and Gabby had helped him with that, too.

Either out of guilt or simply because he didn't want to disturb Mama's soul, he moved the crib that was in the Forbidden Room to the attic and then hung the new pink and white window drapes. Both Trevor and I realized that Big John had told Gabby almost everything about us. She was more than happy to keep anything he had told her secret. Sometime within the week that would follow, I would realize her loyalty to him was only part of what she felt for him.

Big John wanted to discuss our future the day of Mama's funeral, so after Mr. Longstreet left and we were in the living room, he began.

"You two will attend the public school in the fall. Gabby has agreed, even suggested, she'd move in with us. I'm goin' to put all your classroom furniture into the attic, too, and turn it into a comfortable bedroom for her. So I'll be able to continue my business, and you'll be fine. Until Trevor gets his license, Gabby has volunteered to take you to and from school.

"She knows how independent you two are, but she'll still be in charge when I'm not here. Your bedroom's not quite ready. I want to do some more work in the bathroom and repaper those walls, but you can start usin' it tonight, Faith."

Neither Trevor nor I said anything.

He slapped his knees and stood.

"I'll be taking Gabby home now. Nick will be back in another week or so, and we'll get everything organized. In the meantime, Trevor can help me with the new guest room. You guys take out whatever you don't want put up in the attic."

Neither of said anything.

"This is the best solution for us," he said, as if we had said something to oppose the plans.

Despite the church service and the burial, Mama's being gone forever still hadn't taken hold for either Trevor or myself. He didn't have to say it, but we both looked like we were anticipating Mama coming in the front door at any moment and saying, "What do you think you're doing with my house, my family?"

Big John looked frustrated. It was obvious he was hoping we'd be at least satisfied with, if not enthusiastic about, all his solutions.

"Well, that's it," he said. "That's the best we can do."

He looked at Gabby. "Ready?"

"Yes," she said, rising. She looked at us both. She wasn't crying, but her face was as good as covered in tears. She leaned over to kiss each of us and then followed Big John to the front door.

Trevor looked at me. Neither of us had to say it aloud. We had the same thought.

It will all start that way, making the world Big John wanted, but something deep inside tells me that's not the way it will be.

We rose as if we could see Mama beckoning to us from the kitchen and walked to it, through it and to the rear door. The shovel was where it always was at the side of the house, beside the steps. Trevor took it, and we walked out to the Cemetery for Unhappiness.

It was a remarkably beautiful day for a day that had begun with a funeral. In the breeze, we both could feel the touch of autumn. As if they knew how important this was, Moses and Becky came out of the woods and stood close to us.

Trevor began to dig. It wasn't a big hole, but it was big enough.

He paused and took my hand.

"This is the best solution for us to bury our fears and all the pain we've suffered and could suffer now."

"Unlike Adam and Eve, we'll bury our sins, too."

"Yes," Trevor said. "That's the best we can do," he said, mimicking Big John.

"Be gone," I said.

"Be gone," he whispered.

Then he filled in the hole.

Nothing would ever grow on this patch of ground, not even weeds. We, like Mama, would never permit it. No doubt, there would be more to bury.

He took my hand again.

We started back to the house, Moses and Becky trailing behind us.

Mama had joined her family. We both knew that she would be there, in the house tonight, in the walls, whispering.